The Westminster Mystery

*An
Inspector Reynolds
of Scotland Yard
Mystery*

By Elaine Hamilton

Originally published in 1931

The Westminster Mystery

© 2014 Resurrected Press
www.ResurrectedPress.com

Published by Resurrected Press

This classic book was handcrafted by Resurrected Press. Resurrected Press is dedicated to bringing high quality classic books back to the readers who enjoy them. These are not scanned versions of the originals, but, rather, quality checked and edited books meant to be enjoyed!

Please visit ResurrectedPress.com to view our entire catalogue!

ISBN 13: 978-1-937022-84-6

Printed in the United States of America

Resurrected Press Books in A. E. Fielding's *The Chief Inspector Pointer <u>Mystery</u>* Series

RESURRECTED PRESS CLASSIC MYSTERY CATALOGUE

Journeys into Mystery
Travel and Mystery in a More Elegant Time

The Edwardian Detectives
Literary Sleuths of the Edwardian Era

Gems of Mystery
Lost Jewels from a More Elegant Age

Anne Austin
One Drop of Blood
The Black Pigeon
Murder at Bridge

E. C. Bentley
Trent's Last Case: The Woman in Black

Ernest Bramah
Max Carrados Resurrected:
The Detective Stories of Max Carrados

Agatha Christie
The Secret Adversary
The Mysterious Affair at Styles

Octavus Roy Cohen
Midnight

Freeman Wills Croft
The Ponson Case
The Pit Prop Syndicate

Whose Body?

Sir William Magnay
The Hunt Ball Mystery

Mabel and Paul Thorne
The Sheridan Road Mystery

Louis Tracy
The Strange Case of Mortimer Fenley
The Albert Gate Mystery
The Bartlett Mystery
The Postmaster's Daughter
The House of Peril
The Sandling Case: What Would You Have Done?

Charles Edmonds Walk
The Paternoster Ruby

John R. Watson
The Mystery of the Downs
The Hampstead Mystery

Edgar Wallace
The Daffodil Mystery
The Crimson Circle

Carolyn Wells
Vicky Van
The Man Who Fell Through the Earth
In the Onyx Lobby
Raspberry Jam
The Clue
The Room with the Tassels
The Vanishing of Betty Varian
The Mystery Girl
The White Alley
The Curved Blades

Anybody but Anne
The Bride of a Moment
Faulkner's Folly
The Diamond Pin
The Gold Bag
The Mystery of the Sycamore
The Come Back

Raoul Whitfield
Death in a Bowl

And much more!
Visit ResurrectedPress.com
for our complete catalogue

FOREWORD

The Westminster Mystery also published as *Some Unknown Hand* was published in 1930, the first of a series of mysteries featuring Inspector Reynolds of Scotland Yards' C.I.D. that appeared through the 1930's. Little information is available about the author, Elaine Hamilton beyond the list of books she wrote.

The Westminster Mystery is an example of the style that has become known as "Hum Drum" not because the books are lacking in excitement, but because they try to portray the reality of a police investigation. This style arose in the 1930's as a reaction against the more flamboyant style of detective fiction as epitomized by Agatha Christie's Hercule Poirot or Dorothy Sayers' Lord Peter Wimsey. In place of the eccentricities of these amateur detectives, this style revolves around rather somber police detectives who achieve their results by hard work, dogged attention to details and common sense.

The style was popularized by writers such as Freeman Wills Croft and Ngaio Marsh as well as many less well known authors such John Bude and A. E. Fielding who churned out a seemingly never ending stream of mysteries throughout the period. The style continues to have an influence today in the works of more recent authors such as P. D. James and Colin Dexter who still emphasize the routine aspects of police work, though their detectives may have acquired more personality.

The Westminster Mystery begins in a dramatic enough fashion when a popular actress comes home to her London apartment to discover a body in her dining room. Inspector Reynolds of Scotland Yards' C.I.D. is called in to investigate, and promptly discovers that everyone involved in the case seems to be hiding something including the dead man. Much of the rest of the story revolves around Reynolds' efforts to unravel these secrets and place them in context as they relate to the murdered man.

The Westminster Mystery was the first novel by Elaine Hamilton to feature Detective Inspector Reynolds, and as such it does exhibit some of the flaws of a first effort. There is perhaps an over reliance on coincidences and disguises, but the story does move on at a nice pace as one fact after another is revealed to the reader.

Elaine Hamilton is today a nearly forgotten author, but during the 1930's at least nine of her novels were published though they are today hard to find. It is with pleasure the Resurrected Press offers this new edition of *The Westminster Mystery.*

About the Author

Not much is known about Elaine Hamilton other than she wrote a series of mysteries in the 1930's featuring Inspector Reynolds of Scotland Yard. *The Westminster Mystery* published in 1930 was the first of these. Other titles in the series include *Murder in the Fog* (1931), *The Green Death* (1932), *The Chelsea Mystery* (1932), *The Silent Bell* (1933), *Peril at Midnight* (1934), *Tragedy in the Dark* (1935), *The Casino Mystery* (1936) and *Murder Before Tuesday* (1937).

Greg Fowlkes
Editor-In-Chief
Resurrected Press
www.ResurrectedPress.

TABLE OF CONTENTS

I. THE DRAMA OPENS

BENTLEY, P. C, caught a flash of pink and silver, of golden hair above a girl's laughing face as the taxi came round the corner and drew up at the block of flats fifty yards away.

Maybe there were a thousand pink cloaks, but there was only one golden head like that and Bentley felt sure he knew to whom it belonged. Perhaps his luck would be in again to-night.

Last week she had given him a smile as he picked up the key she had dropped. It wasn't every one who had that favor from Laureen, the revue artist London was raving about.

Police Constable Bentley was very young. He jerked his belt down a shade and, measuring his stride nicely, arrived in time to hear her invitation to her companion—a distinguished-looking man in the forties.

"Come up for ten minutes and share my chocolate. My maid always waits up for me with that stodgy beverage."

The constable heard the man's courteous acceptance, and then what he had greatly hoped for happened.

Laureen glanced over her shoulder and smiled.

"Good night, officer."

The policeman saluted, conscious of a blush that he prayed was invisible.

"Good night, miss," he replied and strolled on.

"You are nothing if not a coquette," said the girl's escort.

"Not at all," she retorted. "You never know when you may be glad of his services in these cat-burglar times."

There was no night porter and the hall was empty at that hour, the tenants operating the lift for themselves.

"Which floor?" Laureen's friend asked, his finger on the switch.

"Second," Laureen, her gray eyes speculative, replied mechanically. Her mind was concentrated on the fact that Ivan Lansberg, the mysterious financial power behind so many theatrical productions was actually beside her, going to share her chocolate. She chuckled at the thought. The man of reputed millions, whose nationality every one guessed at and nobody knew; the friend of every well-known celebrity in Europe—and hot chocolate.

Several times they had met at suppers or night clubs. To-night—Sunday, June 30th—at a gay studio party. And for the first time Lansberg seemed to have recognized that she had an existence apart from the stage. Sallow, strong-featured to the point of ugliness, she decided him to be, but a man who could not be overlooked or forgotten in a crowd.

Laureen led the way to her apartment at right angles to the lift, and pressed the bell.

"My maid always waits up for me. Isn't it respectable! But actresses are the only women careful of their reputations nowadays."

"Well, for once yours would seem to be at stake," he answered as the door remained closed. "Have you a key?"

The girl produced it from her handbag and started to fit it in the lock; but before she could turn the key, at the slight pressure of her hand the door yielded—it opened on to a hall dark but for the light in the corridor.

She drew back with a startled exclamation.

"The latch must have been fastened up! How extraordinary! And where on earth is Bertha?"

"Even the most perfect of maids will run out to post a letter at times," Lansberg suggested lightly.

Laureen's expression relaxed at his casual tone.

"Perhaps that's it, but it would have been awkward if I'd forgotten my key. I so rarely carry it. Shall we chance our reputations and go in?"

Lansberg nodded. "Mine went long ago, my child; there's only yours to consider. But remember I was promised some nourishment."

Laureen switched on the light in the little square hall. The man followed her in, released the catch of the lock and closed the door behind him.

She paused with her hand on the knob of the door facing her and sniffed.

"Oof! What a queer smell. Disinfectant or something. I'm a nervous idiot! Bertha has probably been cleaning my gloves with benzine, so that's that."

The man noticed that her lips trembled slightly. He tucked his arm into hers and led her into the drawing-room, switching on the lights as he passed. She dropped on to the couch with a sigh of relief, glancing about uneasily.

"Look here, my girl, what you need is a stiff drink. Have you any whisky?"

"In the dining-room," she pointed to a half-open

door opposite. "Hello, that benzine smell is stronger here," she whispered.

He pulled back the curtains and opened the window.

"Yes, Bertha seems to have been pretty active," he agreed drily. "I'll get you a toddy. Don't move."

As he was crossing the room Laureen called him back.

"No, I hate spirit; it's a last resource. I'm all right now. By the way, perhaps my maid went off her dot. To-night in Dick Spencer's studio I was handed a parcel. Somebody said it had been left for me by my maid! I thought it was a joke and that I'd spoil their trick by not opening it. Well, they crowded round and insisted, so I pulled off the paper and found a pair of black satin shoes! They were mine, too; I recognized the maker's name and the buckles. I left them in the studio—forgot to bring them back with me. Did you ever hear of anything so idiotic as bringing me a pair of slippers I'd never asked for?"

Lansberg drew out his cigarette-case, his eyes narrowed thoughtfully.

"Have a cigarette? Perhaps the girl fancied you might, like Cinderella, drop a slipper at midnight. Where's that promised chocolate? Let's have it while we're waiting for her and her explanation." He shot a quick glance at Laureen. "Or would you like me to look round the flat?"

"We'll do that if Bertha isn't here in a minute." Rising, she fetched a covered tray with a thermos bottle on it from a table in the corner.

"Now this is becoming really interesting, Mr. Lansberg. This thermos is only used if Bertha has gone to bed—a blue moon occurrence! When she is here naturally she heats the stuff in the kitchen. I'm going to see if she's in her room."

Lansberg put out his hand to check her. "Let me—" he began and broke off at her breathed "Hush! Listen!"

In the tense silence they heard something rustle on the carpet, and then the door into the dining-room slammed suddenly.

Laureen gave a nervous jump.

"A piece of paper blown by a sudden gust of wind which also caused the door to slam." Lansberg spoke in slow, reassuring tones to calm the girl.

But her previous nervousness had gone. She picked up the paper fluttering near the window and held it with steady fingers.

She scanned it through quickly in silence, and then turned to the man with a puzzled air.

"Listen! This is a copy made by Bertha of a telephone call she received at eight thirty this evening. Long ago I insisted that she must write down every call that came through, giving the time, in case she forgot a message."

Over her shoulder Lansberg saw that the paper was evidently a sheet torn from a pad intended for recording telephone messages.

Laureen read it aloud slowly:

Miss Laureen wishes you to take her black satin shoes with paste buckles to Mr. Spencer's studio, 4 Clarence Road, Chelsea, at ten o'clock to-night certain. Don't ask for her but leave parcel with the servant. Also Miss Laureen says she may not return to-night and that you are to sleep out as usual and return to flat at noon to-morrow.

Below this was written a note, which Laureen also read:

Miss Gilbert telephoned this message at 8:15.
BERTHA

"The instructions seem clear and definite," Lansberg remarked.

Laureen folded the paper carefully but absent-mindedly and laid it on the tray.

"Exactly, but who sent them?" she said sharply. "I didn't. I don't know any 'Miss Gilbert.'"

The man regarded her in surprise. This was not the gay laughing girl he had met in the studio, nor the overstrung individual of five minutes ago. Alert and wide-eyed she faced him now with no trace of fear.

"Would you mind going through the flat, Mr. Lansberg?" she asked. "This door," indicating the one behind her, "leads to my bedroom. Beyond it is the bathroom with another door into the hall. You'll find on the left a tiny corridor with two rooms—kitchen and my maid's bedroom. Coming back from her room you'll find the dining-room door in front of you and that will lead you through to this room. A kind of circular tour," she added with a short laugh.

Lansberg bowed, responding immediately to her changed decisive attitude.

"You'll stay here or come with me?" he inquired.

She seated herself on the couch again and poured out the steaming chocolate.

"I'll wait here," she decided. "You'll find switches inside each door. Bring an extra cup and saucer from the kitchen. Please close the doors as you go or they may bang and—and startle me again."

The man saw her composedly add sugar to the chocolate in her cup and stir it. With a shrug as if he cast aside all hope of comprehending a woman's moods, he stepped into the bedroom.

The girl turned as the door closed, listened for his footsteps, then rose and went swiftly to the door that led into the dining-room—the room Lansberg would visit last—opened it noiselessly and slipped inside.

A minute or two later a scream rang through the flat—a scream high-pitched and filled with terror.

Lansberg rushed from the hall into the drawing-room and saw Laureen standing there, holding on to the handle of the closed dining-room door as if that support alone kept her from falling.

He caught her by the shoulders.

"What is it?"

Her breath came in shuddering gasps as she clung to his arm.

"I—don't—know—exactly. A man asleep—drunk —dead perhaps. I only looked in from the door-way."

"Dead!" he repeated blankly as he drew her back to the couch. "Why did you go in there?" he demanded. "You sent me to search the place."

"It seemed ages waiting. I felt I had to go. What are we to do?" She was fighting for self-control now.

Lansberg's face was like a mask as he answered quietly.

"Sit still, Laureen. You'll need all your strength later. First I'm going into that room and then I shall ring up the police station—if necessary."

The girl shivered as he opened the dining-room

door and clicked on the light.

He reappeared in a few seconds.

"Dead!" he snapped out. "Chloroform, I fancy. That accounts for the smell. Where's the telephone?"

She indicated a pink crinolined doll on the bureau, heard the man's crisp tones demanding Scotland Yard.

"What is the exact address of this place, Laureen?" he asked while waiting for the number.

"Flat ten, forty-nine Beresford Street, Westminster," she informed him.

"An inspector and police surgeon will come round at once," he told her a moment later, hanging up the receiver.

"And then?" Laureen's voice was calm again.

Lansberg smiled ruefully.

"Well, then I'm afraid the trouble begins—for somebody. A certain amount for you, possibly, as the scene of action is in your flat. The inspector will ask questions, take possession of the place and search it."

"Search it?" she questioned with a frown. "How —how queer."

Lansberg drummed his fingers on the table a moment. Then: "Did you know this man, Laureen?" he asked sharply.

The girl's eyes wavered.

"Of course not," she replied at once. Then, seeing her mistake, hesitatingly added, "I mean—"

The man laid his hand on hers gently.

"Better make up your mind what you mean before the police arrive," he suggested.

II. SCOTLAND YARD AT WORK

LAUREEN stared at the closed dining-room door. Mechanically she took a fresh cigarette from a box on the table. Lansberg lighted it, lighted one for himself. For a second his fingers—the fingers that had lain on hers—were held near his face as the match flickered.

"Go and wash your hands quickly, Laureen, and spray some perfume on your dress." Fear flashed across her face as he added, "I smell chloroform there and so may the inspector."

She obeyed, still with that withdrawn air of mental indecision.

He heard her moving about the bedroom for several minutes, opening drawers, splashing water.

"Laureen," he called. And again . . . after a few moments, "Laureen."

Something in the steady sound of the water made him walk into the hall. The bathroom door was open, the light burning, taps turned full on. He turned them off automatically, stood there frowning. Three shrill blasts on a police whistle came suddenly from outside, then soft light steps on the stairs.

Lansberg's hand was on the hall door when it opened against him and Laureen slipped in, her frock gleaming, gray eyes ablaze, triumphant. She held out a police whistle.

"I ran down to see if that nice policeman would come," she explained breathlessly. "Quick, let's go to the drawing-room window and call him up if he comes along the street."

The man followed her to the open window.

"Equally I might have whistled from here and saved you a journey," he remarked, "if you particularly wanted him."

She leaned her bare arms on the window ledge and thrust back her hair with a tired gesture. "He seemed friendly and," she laughed mirthlessly, "I look like needing a friend."

"How far is the pillar-box from here?" he asked irrelevantly.

"At the end of the street," was her instant reply, "quite a hundred yards away. Look, there he is." She pointed to a helmeted figure hurrying along, scanning every house. "Call him."

Lansberg leaned out. "Here, officer," he shouted. "Second floor, right."

"Please," her voice trembled, "I want to speak to you alone before the others arrive."

She heard Lansberg open the outer door, heard the policeman's "Anything wrong, sir? I hope the lady is all right?"

"Something is very wrong. We have found a man dead in there. I've telephoned Scotland Yard and the inspector will be here any minute. The lady is naturally somewhat distressed. After you've had a look around you might wait in the hall until they come."

"Certainly, sir." Bentley, P. C, removed his helmet with alacrity, as Laureen appeared in the doorway, a less radiant, paler Laureen than had wished him "good night," but no less beautiful.

"Thank you for coming," she said in her soft, clear voice.

In the drawing-room Lansberg took her hands in his.

"Regard me as your friend, my child, not your enemy," he urged.

Her gray eyes were misty, her lips curved in a tremulous smile.

"There may be limits even to what one can impose on friends," she whispered.

"It's you who make those boundaries; not I." She glanced round the room wearily.

"Well, you've had a messy half-hour, Mr. Lansberg. It might have strained an older friendship than ours." She bit her lip.

He tightened his grasp on her hands, as if he would steady her, give her courage.

"Did you know that man, Laureen?"

"Will *they* ask me that?"

"Of course. Why should a stranger be found dead in your flat? But if you know him—well, you are a beautiful and famous actress and it would not be the first time a foolish youth took his life for such a cause." He paused and looked closely at her. "You went close to that man, maybe you even touched him."

Her lips parted.

"What makes you think that?"

"Because as you could not have seen his face from the doorway, you must have gone near him, and, judging from the strong smell of chloroform on your hands, perhaps touched him."

The girl drooped her head and something splashed on his hand.

"Yes," she admitted. "I know him. I—I bent over him to see his face."

"Who is he?"

"A film actor called Delmond. Once I played in a movie with him—years ago," she added hurriedly. The man caught his lower lip between his teeth.

"Is there any reason why you don't want to acknowledge that acquaintance?" he questioned.

For a second she paused. Then:

"Yes," she said desperately. "The usual reason a woman tries to conceal."

Surprise crossed the man's face.

"He was your lover?" he asked incredulously.

"Yes."

Lansberg released her hands, walked to the window and back.

"I see," he said at last, thoughtfully. "Now, about Bertha, your maid. Quick, that's the taxi with the inspector and the doctor, I expect. Do you know who could have sent that extraordinary telephone message?"

"I do not." Her reply was quick and definite. She was evidently concealing nothing there, he felt.

"That phrase about your possibly not returning and the maid to sleep out—what did it mean?"

"That's the curious part," was her answer. "The woman who sent that message knew my arrangements with Bertha intimately. You see, my maid is terrified to sleep here alone, and we have an understanding that any night I may be away I always telephone or send a telegram warning her I shall not come back. On those occasions she goes to some friends."

They heard the bell ring, and a murmur of voices in the hall.

Lansberg bent swiftly to her.

"Leave as much of the talking to me as you can," he warned. "Tell them you once acted in a film with this man and can only suppose—if you're asked—that he might have come here to ask help to get a job. Of the rest, you know nothing. I hope it will be unnecessary to mention your other relationship to the dead man."

The drawing-room door was opened by the policeman and two men entered. They gave a casual glance round the room and the older man of the two spoke to Lansberg.

"You telephoned the Yard, sir, I believe, saying you had found a dead man here just over half an hour ago. I'm Detective Inspector Reynolds. This is Dr. Tempest," he indicated his companion.

Lansberg bowed gravely.

"That is quite correct, Inspector. First of all you'll both want to see the body, I expect."

"Yes, please. Nothing has been touched, of course?"

"Nothing."

Lansberg opened the door into the dining-room and switched on the light, standing aside to allow the inspector and doctor to pass in.

"Miss Laureen is distressed by the tragedy, Inspector," he said in a low voice. "This is her flat. Unless you wish me to remain here while you make your examination I will stay in the next room with her, and tell you all I know when you have finished."

"Certainly," the C. I. D. man agreed. "She will, of course, be able to identify the deceased?"

Lansberg made a dubious gesture.

"That ordeal awaits her, I'm afraid," he said. "I went in alone, and immediately telephoned to

Scotland Yard."

He went toward Laureen, leaving the door between the two rooms open and holding up a warning finger to her to be silent.

Presently both men returned.

"And now, sir," said the inspector, "I shall be glad to hear all you can tell me. First, did you know this man?"

"No," replied Lansberg definitely. "My name is Lansberg," he went on; drawing out a thin case, he laid a card on the table. "That is my address. I escorted this lady back from a studio party we had both attended to-night at—" He turned to the girl: "Have you the slightest idea what time we arrived here?"

She shook her head. "I'm afraid not."

Bentley from the background spoke promptly. "It was exactly one twelve A. M., sir, as you paid off the taxi."

Laureen's mouth twitched faintly at the constable's answer.

"Miss Laureen asked me if I would come up and share her chocolate," Lansberg explained. He glanced at the policeman. "Possibly you heard the lady's remark, officer?"

"I did, sir. She also said her maid always waited up for her," he replied sturdily.

Inspector Reynolds wrote something in his note-book. Then he looked up. "You both walked upstairs to the flat, Mr. Lansberg?"

"No," corrected the latter. "We came up by lift. At the door we rang the bell and as there was no answer Miss Laureen was going to put her key in the lock when the hall door opened at the touch of her fingers. The hall was in darkness. The latch was fastened back."

For the first time Inspector Reynolds looked steadily at Laureen—a seemingly vacant gaze as if his thoughts were elsewhere.

"The lady was alarmed?" he questioned.

"Not exactly alarmed. Puzzled and uneasy, perhaps, because her maid, she said, had never done such a thing before. I suggested the maid might have gone out to post a letter and that we might as well go in and wait for her return. The next thing was a curious odor. That worried her a little until she thought perhaps the maid had been cleaning gloves with benzine." Lansberg paused. "Please tell me if I am being too detailed, Inspector."

"You are giving me exactly the information I need, thank you, Mr. Lansberg. Later on some of these memories may be blurred. To-night they are fresh in your mind. Omit no small point: it may be of the highest importance. By the way, you have frequently been to this flat?" The detective's dull gaze swept over Lansberg's imperturbable face.

"Never until to-night, Inspector. We came straight into this room and as the smell was very strong I opened the window. Miss Laureen looked pale and uneasy and I wanted her to have whisky, but she refused."

The inspector let his eyes drift idly over the pink and silver diamante frock the girl was wearing. He turned again to Lansberg. "And after that, sir?"

Lansberg puckered his brows in an endeavor to recall things consecutively, and then detailed the slipper episode.

"They were hers—she recognized the maker's

name, and ornaments—but she had not told her maid to bring them there," Lansberg concluded.

"You have the slippers here, madam?" the inspector asked.

"No," replied the girl. "I forgot them. They are at Mr. Spencer's studio."

Inspector Reynolds took up his pencil again. "What is his address, please?"

"Mr. Richard Spencer, four Clarence Road, Chelsea," Lansberg interposed. He waited for the address to be written and then handed Bertha's copy of the telephone message to the inspector, who read it frowningly.

Lansberg turned to the doctor.

"May I ask if you know the cause of death yet, Dr. Tempest?"

"Probably chloroform," the medical man replied guardedly. "One cannot be sure until after the autopsy. He has been dead two or three hours— maybe a little longer."

Lansberg nodded his thanks.

"Who is this Miss Gilbert who telephoned?" asked the detective.

The girl shook her head. Her face was set in a stillness foreign to her usual animation, Lansberg noticed, noticed too that the doctor was studying her.

"I have no idea. I know no one of that name. But, as I told Mr. Lansberg, it must have been sent by some one who knows my arrangements very well," she continued evenly. "Bertha will not sleep here alone at night, so, if unexpectedly I decide not to return, I always send her a message and she goes to friends of hers for the night."

"Where do these friends live?" Reynolds asked.

"At Clapham, I think. I have never needed the address as she has a key and always returns next morning."

The inspector tapped his pencil on the book.

"Um! In that case, madam, she may be there tonight and will return here," he referred to the written message, "at noon, following out your presumed instructions."

Laureen raised her hands in a helpless gesture. "I suppose so, since she has faithfully followed out the first part of them."

The inspector stroked his chin pensively a moment. "When you read this message," he said, "you had no idea there had been a tragedy?"

Lansberg caught Laureen's eyes in one steadying glance and then his calm voice answered for her:

"I think we were both certain by that time that something was wrong and she asked me to search the flat. I began here," Lansberg pointed to the bedroom door, "and went through to the bathroom which led from it."

"The lady accompanied you," suggested the inspector idly.

"No, she remained here."

The C. I. D. man turned swiftly to the girl, pointing an accusing finger.

"And while Mr. Lansberg was out of hearing, you went in and looked at the dead man, madam."

III. THE TINSELED TRAIL

THE words formed a statement more than a question, and Lansberg felt a pulse beat hard in his neck as they waited for the girl's reply.

She raised puzzled gray eyes to the inspector's stolid countenance.

"Yes," she admitted readily. "That is true. Though I can't think how you knew."

Inspector Reynolds frowned, slightly nonplussed by her unhesitating answer.

"Why did you not go with Mr. Lansberg, or wait until his return, as arranged?" he said crisply to the girl.

She shrugged her shoulders lightly.

"Impulse made me change my mind, I suppose, Inspector. I suddenly felt I could bear the suspense no longer and must do something. It was my fault Mr. Lansberg did not tell you this."

Reynolds switched round to Lansberg again.

"You found no signs of disorder in the bedroom or bathroom, Mr. Lansberg?"

"No. All appeared to be normal. As I say, nothing has been touched since. I had just reached the hall and was about to visit the maid's room and kitchen when I heard a scream. I hurried into this room and found Miss Laureen standing over there," he pointed to the dining-room door. "She looked so ill that I feared she was going to faint."

He paused and glanced from Inspector Reynolds to the doctor, who had been a silent listener to the cross-examination. Something curiously sympathetic in Dr. Tempest's expression induced Lansberg to address him directly.

"I suppose a sudden shock like that, following a series of unusual happenings at one o'clock in the morning, would unnerve any woman, Doctor?"

"I can assure you, Mr. Lansberg," Dr. Tempest replied, "that most women would have been in hysterics for less. Miss Laureen has shown remarkable composure."

Reynolds detected a note of admiration in the doctor's voice and interrupted with a touch of asperity. This was no time for compliments.

"No need to waste any more of your time, Doctor," he said bluntly. "You've seen all you want to in there, I suppose?"

"Quite!"

Dr. Tempest rose, and bade good night to Lansberg and Laureen. At the door he stopped, and, calling the inspector outside, said something to him in an undertone.

"She looks all right," grumbled the inspector.

"Very well, do as you please, but don't blame me afterwards," Dr. Tempest warned him. "That girl has had a bad shock and is fighting pluckily—too pluckily—to prevent herself from breaking down. She needs rest. Where is she going to sleep tonight?"

Reynolds looked aggrieved. "That's not my funeral. A hotel, I suppose. Wherever she goes I shall have an eye kept on her, of course."

The doctor's lips tightened. "She'd be better with friends or relatives than alone in a hotel in her over-strung condition," he retorted curtly. "Better defer your third degree methods on her or she'll be ill.

Good night."

He glanced round once more at the girl whose eyes rested on his face wistfully as though she would have wished him to stay. "Good night, Miss Laureen," he said again. "Take a couple of aspirin before you go to bed."

"Thank you, Doctor, I will," she answered gratefully.

Dr. Tempest walked to his home with cold rage in his heart. He and the inspector were on excellent terms, but it was not the first time they had crossed swords over Reynolds's ruthless methods.

As the door closed behind the doctor the inspector spoke almost genially.

"I'm going to look through the flat now. You'd better come too, Mr. Lansberg. The constable can stay in this room in case the lady feels nervous."

The two men went into the bedroom and began their search. In the bathroom the C. I. D. man paused and glanced at the window which was open at the top.

"Did you open that, sir?" he asked.

Lansberg shook his head.

"No. I noticed the bedroom window was open too when I came through earlier."

Reynolds peered through a pane of glass, shading his eyes.

"Umph! Fire-escape staircase just outside, too. All nice and handy!" His eyes wandered vaguely round the tiled walls, came back to the wash-basin with its shining taps. He bent down.

"Some one has just used this," he announced. "The soap is wet."

Lansberg felt a grudging admiration for the

man's deductive powers. Evidently he knew his job.

"Yes. Miss Laureen washed her hands here recently, I believe."

Inspector Reynolds seemed to be on the point of asking a question. Then changed his mind and stalked out.

Laureen could hear their footsteps but no sound of conversation reached her ears. Apparently the inspector was saving himself up for her cross-examination, she decided.

She leaned her throbbing head back on the cushions of the chesterfield and closed her eyes. Oh, if only she dare relax! But she knew quite well that any such weakness would mean a flood of tears. Some people could weep with their eyes easily. With Laureen, who cried rarely, it was a crashing down of all control and she knew she would need every ounce of intelligence she possessed presently, when that stony-eyed inspector began his process of dissection.

Police Constable Bentley from his seat just inside the room regarded the lady's white face with consternation. He ventured on a slight cough and, as she looked across at him, he spoke in a voice husky but sympathetic.

"I'm afraid this unpleasant business has upset you, miss. Can I get you anything?"

She regarded his kindly, honest face, reddened slightly now by confusion at the smile she turned on him.

"Thank you, officer, no. One doesn't find a dead man in one's flat every night, you know, or probably one would get used to it and take the matter lightly."

Reynolds at the door, saw the smile and overheard her remark as he was about to enter. He attributed it to flippancy, and registered a decision to ignore Dr. Tempest's advice to go gently with her.

"Tempest's a nervous old maid," he decided. "This girl's as hard as nails; brazenly making eyes at the constable directly my back's turned. I'll put her through it before she has time to make up her story. She knows a deal more than she'll admit."

Aloud he said:

"And now, madam, I'd like you to follow me, please."

He strode firmly across the room and turned on the lights inside the dining-room door.

Lansberg slipped his arm through that of the girl as she rose a little unsteadily. He could feel her body trembling and the fingers that touched his hand were cold as ice. With instinctive kindliness he laid his other hand on hers and gripped it hard just as the inspector swung round with one of his quick gestures.

Reynolds abruptly turned his back again but he had seen the clasped hands, and interpreted it in his own way. His was not a profession that called for sentiment, and personal ambition played a far larger part in his life than devotion to the gentle woman he had married and to whom he had been doggedly faithful ever since.

His voice cut in coldly as Lansberg led the girl toward a big chair which was beside the fireplace, its back toward them.

"Please stand here, madam, *where you stood before.*" There was an ominous note in his voice. "Do you recognize the deceased?"

Laureen moistened her dry lips, gazed fearfully at the sagging figure almost hidden in the depths of

the big chair. The head was flung back, the face—
that of a dark, clean-shaven man about thirty—
turned upward. She shuddered and Lansberg felt
her lean heavily against him.

"Yes," she said with difficulty. "Yes, I knew him
years ago." She swallowed and went on like a child
repeating a lesson. "He was a cinema actor, his name
was Leslie Delmond. We acted in a film together four
years ago. I haven't seen him since and don't know
why he came here. We were not on friendly terms.
Can I go in the other room now and answer the rest
of your questions there?" she finished tremulously.

The inspector turned, bent over the dead man
slightly and indicated something on the dark
waistcoat, something that glistened.

"Half an hour ago," he said sternly, "you were
not afraid to come in here alone and bend over this
man, maybe to look more closely at him." He paused
for deliberate effect before driving home his thrust.
"Even to search his pockets for letters that might be
incriminating. This," his finger pointed accusingly at
the shining speck on the dead man's waistcoat, "this
dropped from the dress you are now wearing. There
are other traces of them right across this room.
Also—" He checked himself as Laureen covered her
face with her hands and gave a choking cry.

Lansberg felt a queer emotion surge in his heart
at that cry of pain, an overwhelming pity for the girl
who had been broken by the skilled questions of this
official. He curbed his anger, realizing the futility of
it, indeed the danger of losing any measure of
control.

He drew the girl's arm more firmly into his and
addressed the inspector with dignity.

"This interview must be continued in the next room, Inspector, otherwise I shall telephone for the lady's doctor to come immediately." There was authority in his voice.

Reynolds was a cautious man. Dr. Tempest's words of warning came back to him. He glanced at the girl anxiously as she stood pale and rigid.

"Certainly, Mr. Lansberg," he agreed hastily. "I can defer questioning the lady further until tomorrow."

Laureen lifted her head proudly.

"No," she said coldly. "I prefer no delay." She spoke to Lansberg, who still held her arm, as they went back to the drawing-room. "It was stupid of me to break down like that. One would think I was already convicted of the crime! I'll have some of that chocolate now; I can drink it cold. Ah, and a cigarette, please."

She extended the box toward Inspector Reynolds as he stood biting his lip, thrown a little out of his stride by this volte-face. "Will you have one, Inspector?"

There was something of challenge in her casual tone, almost a gamin smile on her face as if she tempted him to do his worst with her now.

Reynolds interpreted that glance as one of daring impudence. "Pretending to be hysterical to get my sympathy," he decided, "and when that failed, now thinks she'll try her wiles instead."

Abruptly he declined to smoke.

"I must ring up the Yard at once. Where is your telephone, please?" he demanded.

Laureen pointed.

"Under that frivolous pink thing. I'm sure you

disapprove of it, Inspector, nearly as much as you do of me."

She crinkled her nose and made a moue at his stiff back as he issued curt orders through the instrument.

Then he strode into the hall and instructed Bentley to stay there until the men with the ambulance arrived. He returned presently, and choosing the hardest chair he could find, took out his note-book.

Laureen was curled up on the couch, one white arm above her head, blowing smoke rings nonchalantly. From an easy chair opposite Lansberg watched her with anxious eyes. Her present mood was a dangerous one, he realized, for she was keyed up to heights of bravado that might have serious consequences.

"And now, Inspector, I am at your service," she observed sweetly.

"Have you any idea where the deceased lived, or if he has any relatives?" Reynolds began.

"I have no knowledge whatever," she replied, "either of his movements, his relatives or his address."

"Your name, age and occupation, please."

She flashed an impish glance at Lansberg. "Marjorie Laureen; age—well, shall we say twenty-five? Occupation, when lucky, actress."

"Better say revue artist," supplemented Lansberg. "Miss Laureen is very well known, Inspector. In fact one might say she is famous."

Inspector Reynolds licked his pencil and applied himself to his note-book. Spelling had never been one of his strong points and he was by no means sure how to spell the girl's name or exactly what was the technical difference between an actress and a revue artist.

Just then the bell echoed and in a moment Bentley announced that the police photographer and a sergeant had arrived.

"Show them into the dining-room," snapped Reynolds. "I want photographs of all the finger-prints they can find." He turned to the girl again.

"So this is your flat?"

"Yes, I took over the rest of the lease from the last tenant and bought some of his furniture ten months ago. And after this episode he can buy it back from me at his own price as soon as he likes."

She flicked the ash from her cigarette and faced the inspector brightly, waiting for his next question with a look of pleased interest.

Reynolds gnawed his lip but refused to be drawn.

"Please confine yourself to the facts we are now concerned with, madam," he said in his earlier dull tone. "You live here alone?"

"With my maid."

"Her name, please."

"Bertha Mackie." She pronounced it in the Scottish way, accenting the last syllable, and lowered one eyelid in Lansberg's direction as she watched the inspector struggle three times to write the name.

"How do you spell it?" he rapped at last.

Laureen spelled it, waiting patiently for him to write each letter.

"Thank you. At what time did you leave the flat this evening, madam?"

She reflected for a moment. "I think it was ten or

twelve minutes past seven."

"Wearing that dress?" He waved his hand at her shining frock.

"Yes—with a cloak over it, naturally."

"You walked downstairs?" he asked.

"No, I pressed the automatic 'ascent' button for the lift to come up, and went down in it."

"You did not return to the flat again until you came here with Mr. Lansberg at one twelve a.m.?"

"I did not," Laureen answered, still with that encouraging look on her face.

Inspector Reynolds lifted his eyes and stared at her.

"Then, Miss Laureen," he said with careful emphasis, "if you went down in the lift at seven twelve P. M., did not return to the flat in the interval, and came up in the lift with Mr. Lansberg at one ten A. M., how is it that I saw tiny glass crystals, like those on your frock, on several stairs when I walked up to-night?"

Laureen's lips parted and terror crept into her eyes as instinctively her mind darted back to the thing she wished to conceal.

"Oh, yes, of course," she added breathlessly, "I—I ran down to whistle for the policeman."

IV. SHADOWED

AGAIN the bell echoed through the flat, and low voices sounded in the hall.

Bentley appeared and whispered something to the inspector.

"All right, I'll come," he said irritably, fully conscious that this interruption gained time for Laureen, whereas experience had proved to him that an examination taken at top speed reduced the victim to the desired pulp. "The ambulance men, Mr. Lansberg," he explained.

Lansberg leaned toward the girl as the detective went out.

"Listen, my child, I don't want to pry into your secrets, but you're involving yourself in a bad tangle. Won't you trust me? Why did you really run downstairs?"

Her gray eyes had the tragic look, her lips the forlorn droop of a lost child.

"I'll explain that—later," she whispered. "Thank you for wanting to help me. What had I better do?"

"Well, although I detest the idea, you'll be safer if you tell the inspector how much"—he hesitated—"I mean about you and Delmond."

She seemed curiously relieved.

"Oh, about *him*. Very well, I will. What's that?" She twisted round toward the closed bedroom and listened to stealthy sounds. "Some one is opening my wardrobe," she breathed. "I know the squeak of the hinge."

Lansberg's lips set in a grim line.

"They're having a preliminary canter through your things, probably," he said with disgust. "Of course one might protest, but, as you've managed to get yourself in rather a corner, I think it's wiser to ignore it. Unless—Laureen," he asked anxiously, "there's something in there you don't want them to find."

She smiled faintly. "Nothing, you kind man."

"No recent letters from Delmond?"

"Not a line," she assured him.

His tense expression relaxed.

"Thank Heaven for that. Where will you sleep to-night? Of course you can't stay here. Have you any relatives or friends near? I don't like your being in a hotel alone."

She puckered her brows whimsically.

"My dear man, I look like spending a large part of my life alone if this mess doesn't get cleared up satisfactorily." She made a grimace as another creak came from the room behind. "They're at my little desk where I've piles of love letters: most of them from men I've never seen! What a fool I was to keep them. Indeed, the righteous Reynolds will think I'm an abandoned woman now."

Lansberg clenched his fist, and drew in his breath. "If it would not make things worse for you I'd go in and stop him," he declared. "As it is, I'm helpless. Think where you can sleep to-night."

She was silent for a moment.

"I know," she said with decision. "Top floor in this building. A nice girl and her mother live there: the girl's in the box-office at our theater. The mother's away on a holiday so I know Betty Marden will let me have her room."

The surreptitious creakings in the bedroom ceased, and from the dining-room opposite heavy shuffling sounds came as the ambulance men performed their task.

"Remember, you'll probably be shadowed from this moment onward until the mystery is cleared up, Laureen," Lansberg warned her. "So be careful; to-morrow particularly. And don't antagonize that detective any more to-night."

Suddenly she snatched up her handbag with an exclamation and from it drew out a sheet of thin paper covered with handwriting. She read its contents as if memorizing it, then swiftly struck a match and held it in the flame until the last corner was destroyed, mixing the ashes with the cigarette ends in the ash-tray.

"Light a cigarette," whispered Lansberg, "or he may smell paper has been burnt."

He was holding the match for her as Reynolds entered with his stolid, noiseless tread. The detective's glance traveled round with its usual vague stare, but this time both Lansberg and the girl knew he was missing no detail.

"You left the flat at seven ten p.m. to-night." The C. I. D. man glanced at his watch as he addressed the girl. "Where did you dine?"

"The Regina Grill Room."

"With whom?"

"Two women I knew years ago." She pulled a card out of her bag and tossed it across the table. "You can verify the statement. That is their address. They have only just gone there to live, hence the card to remind me."

The C. I. D. man took the card and carefully slipped it into his note-book.

"You left the Grill Room at what time?"

Laureen frowned.

"Possibly the waiter may know. About eight forty-five."

"And when did you leave those friends?" asked Reynolds as if the matter had lost interest for him.

"They remained in the restaurant when I came away."

"Where did you go then?"

The girl flushed, hesitated and finally spoke in a quick flurry of words.

"I went for a little walk round that neighborhood. It was a lovely night and the restaurant was airless, so I wandered about a bit as it was too early to go to the party. After"—she gave a nervous laugh—"oh yes, after that I took a taxi to Mr. Spencer's studio."

The detective walked across, picked up the pink brocaded wrap on the couch beside her, and scrutinized it minutely. Even its black satin lining did not escape his attention and the pocket cleverly and almost invisibly made. He patted it lightly and laid it down with approval.

"You were wearing this when you were walking?"

"Yes."

"Quite practical, too, in a way, with that black lining," he observed conversationally.

"Yes," amiably agreed Laureen. "It is made to be reversible," and paled instantly at the change in his face.

"Which side were you wearing outward when you wandered about from eight forty-five until you took the taxi to Mr. Spencer's studio?" the C. I. D. man demanded harshly.

Laureen pressed her hand to her cheek. "I—I forget. Oh, the pink side."

"I see." He resumed his seat and pulled at his chin. "So you wish me to believe that you strolled about the West End streets alone to-night from eight forty-five for an hour; hatless, attired in evening dress, covered by a pink evening cloak and wearing thin black slippers."

"Yes," she murmured. Then with a flush of spirit she looked into his face that was expressionless but for the steely eyes. "At least I don't expect you to believe it. I have merely told you what happened."

"I suggest you called somewhere in the interval—at your flat for instance, madam?"

She flung her bag on the table and stood up, erect, proud.

"And may I suggest, Inspector, that three a.m. is the time limit for this interview? I have my work at the theater to-morrow, and Mr. Lansberg can tell you I don't merely show my teeth and smile at the audience. You doubtless will take the precaution of seeing I don't bolt before morning. What time and just where do you wish to renew my acquaintance?"

A vein stood out like a cord on the detective's forehead but he reined in his anger. Overstrung to the breaking-point, was she? Well, later on, he'd see whether Dr. Tempest was right.

"In this room at eleven to-morrow morning, please," he answered. "I want you to be here before your maid returns—if she does."

Laureen bowed coldly. "I shall be here punctually. Do you wish me to appear in this dress, or am I allowed to go to my room now for some more suitable garments?"

Inspector Reynolds swallowed.

"You may, of course, get what you need for the night and during the day. Where do you propose to sleep?" His eyes scanned the fragile frock she wore, making sure its slim outlines left no room for the concealment of important documents.

"Mr. Lansberg can tell you that while I am putting my things together. Is there anything else?"

"Yes," he snapped. "Give me your key to this flat, please."

She pointed to her handbag.

"You may take it for yourself," she remarked contemptuously, and turned her back on him.

Alone with the C. I. D. man Lansberg ventured to placate him.

"Miss Laureen has had a terrific shock and ordeal, Inspector. You must make allowances for her nervous condition and irritation. She feels you are accusing her in some way of concealing something of grave importance. Any girl with her temperament might react in the same way."

The inspector was a little mollified by Lansberg's quiet voice.

"Her answers lack straightforwardness. She runs on smoothly for a while, gets confused suddenly and becomes either frightened or—" he bit back the word "insolent" and substituted "pert." "Where is she going to sleep?"

Lansberg explained what Laureen had thought of doing.

"Very well, sir," Reynolds assented. "She'll be handy if I want her. Tell her to say as little as possible about this affair." He drummed his fingers on his note-book. "I'd like to get at the truth of when she saw Delmond last."

"Ask her," urged Lansberg quickly, remembering his advice to her.

"You know this lady well?" questioned the C. I. D. man.

Lansberg stiffened noticeably, but his reply was courteous.

"Up to this evening she was an acquaintance, a beautiful and witty girl I had admired on the stage. I had met her casually at various parties, but I had never been alone with her until she allowed me to escort her here to-night. After this, however, I hope she will permit me to call her my friend," he said stanchly.

The detective's back was toward the bedroom door and as Lansberg spoke, he looked up and saw her framed in the doorway, gray eyes blurred, her fingers blowing him a mute kiss. And Lansberg was too wise a man to misinterpret that action for other than gratitude.

In a few moments she returned in a black walking-dress and hat. Lansberg took her dressing-case from her hand.

"Tell Inspector Reynolds about Delmond, will you?"

Her eyes flickered, evading the detective's gaze, but she replied in an even voice.

"Leslie Delmond was my lover—while we were at Nice. We quarreled, finally and definitely, and parted there. Do you want to know any more?" she asked wearily.

The inspector metaphorically rubbed his hands. At last he was getting some sense out of her. He could see a speck of daylight. She and Delmond had disagreed, she had become famous and he had wanted to make it up.

"That accounts for a great deal, madam. Why didn't you tell me before?"

"Yes, why didn't I?" echoed the girl tonelessly.

"Nobody likes to rake up such episodes, naturally," continued the detective rather pompously, "but in a case of murder or suicide there must be no concealment. Maybe one need not use that information publicly."

"Good night," said Laureen, as if the publicity or privacy of her statement were all one to her.

"I'll take you up to the top floor and see if you will be all right there before I leave," Lansberg announced.

Inspector Reynolds looked up from writing something.

"By the way, sir, what is your profession? I think I've heard your name."

The man of millions smiled faintly.

"Maybe you have, Inspector. As to my job—well, my interests are varied and a little difficult to enumerate and explain off-hand. Good night. I'll be here at eleven A.M. sharp."

After seeing Laureen admitted to Miss Marden's flat, Lansberg walked slowly downstairs, thinking hard.

On the two bottom flights he noticed at intervals the diamante specks glistening on several steps.

In the empty hall he glanced round, still engrossed in his thoughts. Then, his eyes followed the track of crystals; he gave an exclamation and stared at something fixed to the wall in a recess behind the stairs. Pulling out his handkerchief he flicked aside that damaging trail of shining specks, fervently hoping that Reynolds had not noticed it led to that spot.

Outside the front door stood what was evidently a plain-clothes officer.

"Want a taxi, sir?" the man asked.

"Thanks, no. I think I'll walk," Lansberg replied and strolled up the street.

At the corner he fancied he heard light regular footsteps at some distance behind.

In the next street as he paused to light a cigarette and shot a swift look round, he no longer "fancied"—he knew.

The plain-clothes man was discreetly but surely trailing him, and for the first time that night Lansberg was conscious of lurking fear.

V. THE MAID'S SECRET

INSPECTOR REYNOLDS was telephoning when Lansberg arrived at the flat two or three minutes before eleven next morning.

The detective nodded in response to Lansberg's greeting and continued to rap sharp orders through the instrument.

"You understand: I want the telephone clerk found who was on duty at eight fifteen last night and any information he or she can give on the subject. If he is off duty, get his address and hunt him up. Send round those prints the minute they're ready."

There was suppressed irritation in the inspector's manner. Usually he could sleep solidly no matter what had happened. But in the few hours at his disposal last night he had tossed restlessly, his mind turning over and over the points of the case.

An hour ago he had arrived and searched minutely through Laureen's rooms for any fresh clue. Beyond the silver specks from the girl's frock, and fingerprints which the photographs would presently show, there was nothing. Temporarily baffled, he felt annoyed, disturbed.

The door-bell rang and Laureen walked into the room as the clock struck eleven. Reynolds felt sure she had deliberately waited for the first stroke of the hour.

She gave him a formal bow and extended her hand to Lansberg. He held it a moment while he studied her face, framed in a small black hat with a smooth wave of her golden hair showing at one side.

"Did you sleep?" he asked her.

"Excellently," adding under her breath, "thanks to the aspirin."

Pale and composed, clad in a soft black-silk suit, she appeared totally different from the temperamental creature of the night before. It was as though she had put on a new personality with her change of dress.

"Splendid," said the man, and thought to himself it would take a wider vision than that of Reynolds to see more than Laureen intended he should see that morning. In other circumstances Lansberg might even have enjoyed the rapier thrusts of her wit against the detective's trained deductions, of instinct against reasoning.

Outside the newsboys were shouting the first editions of the Evening News.

"Mysterious death in Westminster, in famous revue artist's flat."

"Do you hear that?" she asked. "Well, they've got a nice day for it!" She shrugged her shoulders and settled herself comfortably on the couch, pushing aside the tray of chocolate and the overflowing ashtray with disgust.

Reynolds was still talking on the telephone, his voice more controlled now.

"Dr. Tempest asked me to say that he hopes you have had some sleep, madam," he announced stiffly as he hung up the receiver.

"Thank you," she replied with equal coldness. "Is there any chance of seeing a newspaper, Mr. Lansberg?"

Lansberg passed her a copy of one just issued.

"I bought it coming along here. Not much more than the bare statement, of course, but I'm afraid they've 'starred' your name pretty prominently."

The inspector interrupted.

"One minute, please, Miss Laureen. Are you married?"

"No," she answered demurely.

"Is Marjorie Laureen your real or stage name?" the detective questioned.

"On the stage and in private life I am known solely as 'Laureen.' I never use the name of Marjorie, which was inflicted upon me when I was too young to protest."

"One name only—I never heard of such a thing," snapped Reynolds.

The girl raised her eyebrows. "Well, you mustn't blame me for that," she flashed back.

"Do you consider the one name legal?"

Laureen's lips twitched. "It seems to have answered that purpose fairly well up to now, considering that I sign all my checks and contracts that way. Shall I consult my lawyer?" she asked with a gentle anxiety that made the tell-tale vein on Reynolds' forehead—sure sign in him of repressed temper—again show clearly.

"Why," he asked, "did you run downstairs to whistle for the policeman? You could have done that from the window."

She smiled sweetly.

"Of course. But in case he was in sight I thought I could have told him what was wrong more quickly."

Her answer had reason but it failed somehow to convince Reynolds entirely.

"And how long did this journey up and down stairs take?" he questioned.

"Not more than three or four minutes. I ran both ways."

"What time did you arrive at Mr. Spencer's studio last night? I want the exact time, please," he rasped, changing the theme.

"One doesn't 'clock in' at a party," she explained patiently. "I can't tell you to half an hour. About ten fifteen, perhaps. Although it might have been later."

"Mr. Spencer will know, of course," he commented, "as you must have spoken to him on arrival."

"You can ask him," she remarked indifferently. "There were crowds of people there. It's a largish flat and every room was packed."

"Had you been there long when the parcel containing your slippers was given you?"

She glanced at Lansberg. "I believe you were there then. Do you remember the time?"

Lansberg reflected.

"About eleven o'clock, I should think, but it's a rough guess."

Inspector Reynolds tapped his pencil on the table impatiently.

Fencing with these "abouts" annoyed him. Of course the girl knew when she arrived there and at what time the parcel was given to her. He could not possibly visualize that Laureen had been surrounded by a delighted circle of friends the moment she came. A gay laughing crowd with no thought of time, whose one idea was to squeeze the last drop of pleasure from any diversion.

"Where did you pick up the taxi in which you

went to the studio?"

Laureen hesitated an instant.

"Regent Street—near Oxford Circus," she replied slowly.

The detective made a note reminding him to trace that vehicle.

She watched his face, knowing he was mentally measuring the distance between that spot and the restaurant at which she had dined.

The telephone bell jarred. Before the girl could move to answer it Reynolds was at the instrument.

They heard his curt monosyllables. Presently he banged down the receiver and walked back to the table. But he did not sit down.

Laureen looked up at him and was startled to see the stern expression on his face.

"I have just ascertained, madam, that you left the restaurant at eight twenty-five P.M. Two waiters agreed as to that point, which has also been confirmed by the ladies with whom you dined."

"How nice for you," Laureen remarked flippantly. "You have quite enough trouble with me without my friends adding to it. I really must try to start a time chart of all I do. So much simpler—"

"Miss Laureen," the inspector checked her, "do you realize that a man was murdered in this flat last night and that you are hampering the course of justice by these"—he choked back the word he longed to use—"idle jests?" he substituted.

And even he was surprised at the result of his rebuke.

"I don't think I had fully realized that, Inspector," she said at once, gently. "I'm sorry."

It was a difficult remark for the C. I. D. man to

grapple. Her swift apology disarmed him.

"Damned clever little actress," he told himself.

But Laureen had meant exactly what she had said. With the warm, impulsive generosity that characterized her, she was honest enough to see the justice of his words, reasonable enough to express immediate regret. She saw now, however, that he doubted her sincerity, and in her pride almost wished she could recall that apology.

Following a ring of the door a sergeant brought in a parcel and left it at the inspector's elbow.

Reynolds sat down heavily, opened the package and engrossed himself in the contents.

"Will you play to-night, Laureen?" asked Lansberg.

"Why not?" she demanded.

"An Irishman's answer!" he smiled. "I only wondered if you would feel fit."

"It's my job," she said casually. "What right have I to let down my manager and fellow artists?"

"To say nothing of the audience. The theater won't have standing room to-night after that publicity." He pointed to the newspaper on the table.

"Notoriety, you mean," she retorted with that delicious little crinkling up of her nose and mouth that expressed so much. A critic had once said of her that she had reduced restraint in gesture to the last point of economy, which was doubtless why every movement of her hands, every change of expression indicated so much.

"I've reserved a box for to-night. Will you have supper with me afterward?" Lansberg asked her.

She nodded.

"Yes, I'd like to. Anybody else coming?"

"I thought of asking Spencer and that Dr. Tempest who was here last night. I'd met Tempest before but we discreetly ignored that fact. Will they please you and would you like any one else? Any women friends?"

She flicked the newspaper with her fingers.

"After those head-lines I'm not likely to have women coveting my society."

"Nonsense," said Lansberg. "We'll arrange that later."

With a mischievous glance toward the detective's bent head she raised her hand to her mouth and whispered:

"Couldn't ask my nice policeman, I suppose?"

"You could not," asserted Lansberg with twitching lips.

"Ah me," she sighed. "Well, I'll console myself with a cigarette. May I smoke, Inspector?" she asked as Lansberg held the match for her to light it.

The C. I. D. man nodded permission and drew a piece of brown paper thoughtfully over what he had been scrutinizing so closely. Then he looked at Lansberg.

Last night the detective had not had much time to study this man. Briefly he had noted that he was well-dressed, had a cultured voice and manner as of one used to command and be obeyed; forty-ish, a fraction over the medium height and firmly built though slim.

Now he noticed the strength of the jaw, the firm mouth and alert eyes with tired lines round them, the thick smoothly brushed black hair parted in the middle, graying at the temples.

But the C. I. D. man studied more particularly

Lansberg's hands. Strong, thin, beautifully shaped hands with fine sunburnt skin.

Hands were the detective's fetish. He often declared there was far more to be learnt from a hand than a face, and he never forgot a man's hands, as many a criminal behind bars knew to his sorrow.

As far as movement went, there was little to be learnt from Lansberg's hands. He had more than the usual English lack of gesture. When he did make a rare movement, however, it had decision and determination in it.

There were a lot of things Inspector Reynolds wanted to know about Lansberg, but that would have to wait until later. He glanced at his watch and set the door leading into the hall ajar.

"Twenty to twelve," he said aloud. "If your maid comes, where is she likely to go first when she arrives, madam?"

"Probably to her bedroom to take off her hat, providing your sergeant in the hall doesn't scare her to flight."

"I've already seen to that. He is in the dining-room and that door into the hall is locked. I'm anxious to know if she has a key or will have to ring. Mr. Lansberg, I should like to have a talk with you alone this afternoon," he added.

"Choose your time and place, Inspector," Lansberg replied calmly.

"Two thirty," the detective paused deliberately for the fraction of a second, "at your apartment."

Whatever effect he hoped to gain by that slight hesitation produced no result in the courteous mask, of Lansberg's face as he assented.

But the inspector's eyes were watching

Lansberg's hands, recording the slight tension in those slim fingers.

Suddenly there was the click of a key being turned in the lock, the hall door opened and closed firmly, and a woman's voice was heard humming some melody.

"She hasn't heard the news," breathed Laureen.

The inspector gave a sharp glance of approval. Yes, this girl had a quick brain right enough.

The humming ceased, giving way to two loud sniffs.

Laureen pointed to her cigarette silently and raised her eyes in mock despair.

"Are you in, miss?" came from the hall.

Laureen glanced at Reynolds for instructions.

"Call her," he whispered.

"Yes: in the drawing-room. Come in here, Bertha."

A woman of about thirty-five entered the doorway.

"I smelt tobacco and guessed—" she began and broke off in startled surprise to see the two men.

"Don't be alarmed, Bertha," said Laureen quietly. "Something rather tragic happened here last night and these gentlemen are inquiring into it." She looked at Reynolds. "I'll leave the matter in your hands now."

The detective let his glance slide over the woman as he told her to sit down.

"I want to ask you a few questions," he began in a soothing way. He was anxious not to frighten this woman too soon.

"My name is Reynolds, Inspector Reynolds. That gentleman you already know, I expect," he waved his hand toward Lansberg.

The maid looked as directed.

"No," she said definitely. "I don't know him."

"You mean you don't know him personally, or that you've never seen him in this flat before?"

"Both," came the brief retort. Bertha had lived long enough with Laureen to admire and imitate her mistress's crisp style of repartee, and was rather pleased at the chance of showing off her powers now. All this back-chat with an inspector, indeed! What did he want with her? Had there been a burglary?

"You swear you never saw this gentleman before?" the inspector asked.

"I didn't say so," replied the maid unexpectedly.

Reynolds sat back and stared at her, then glanced swiftly at Lansberg, whose countenance showed faint surprise.

"Didn't you tell me you'd never seen this gentleman before?" he questioned in astonishment. Bertha folded her hands calmly.

"Certainly not. I told you I didn't know him personally, and had never seen him in this flat. That's all you asked and that's all I answered." She turned to her mistress. "Excuse me, miss, but have I got to reply to all these questions? I've my work to do."

"The work can wait, Bertha," Laureen told her. "You must answer anything Inspector Reynolds wishes to ask you."

"Very well, miss, but please tell me what has happened." She peered round nervously. "Have there been burglars here?"

Laureen gave a tired sigh. "I'm afraid you'll know soon enough, Bertha."

The C. I. D. man had an opportunity to observe and sum up the maid while she was speaking to her mistress. Scottish accent, not bad-looking, he decided; neat, probably honest, loyal, reserved with that extraordinary faculty for surrender that only the reserved possess; obstinate, proud of her mistress—his sharp ear had already detected the unconscious imitation in her crisp replies. Altogether a harder nut to crack than he had imagined. However, he had resources with which to break down most defenses. Servants usually had a healthy fear of the law. He would try a little more force.

"Your full name, please, and correct age," he demanded bruskly.

The maid barely suppressed a snort. "Bertha Ellen Mackie, age thirty-five," flushing a little as she caught her mistress's amused eyes. Well, she didn't *look* more than twenty-eight, so what did it matter if she had given that as her age when she had been engaged.

"You are English?" went on the detective.

"Born in Aberdeen, as my father was."

"When did you become Miss Laureen's maid?"

"Ten months ago when she took this flat."

"You sleep here?"

"I do, unless my mistress is going to be away and then she lets me know and I sleep out." She turned suddenly to Laureen. "You got your slippers in time, miss?"

Laureen repressed a smile.

"Yes, thank you, Bertha."

"I left the telephone message from a Miss Gilbert written down, miss."

"Yes, I saw it, thank you."

"Didn't you think it strange that your mistress should send orders for a pair of slippers when you knew she had gone out wearing a pair?" Reynolds asked in his mildest tones.

"It's not my business to think about my mistress's affairs. She pays me to do the work and carry out her instructions. She pays me well, too," the maid added loyally.

"Pays you well, eh," the inspector ruminated. Then, pointing his finger at the woman suddenly, he rasped, *"Why?"*

"Got her," he exulted to himself as he saw her jump.

"As I said, to do the work and obey orders," she replied in a dogged voice.

"And keep your mouth shut?"

"Nothing of the sort," she retorted indignantly. "Miss Laureen is as open as the day. And I don't believe you've any right to insult me, inspector or no inspector."

Bertha was angry now, which was all to the good for Reynolds. People were off their guard then.

"How many keys are there to this flat?" he asked. The maid hesitated for the first time.

"There were three. The one my mistress has, one I have and a third that was kept in a drawer in the hall table." She looked a little shamefacedly at her mistress. "I'm sorry I never told you, miss, but I must have dropped mine from my bag a week ago. You let me in when I came back next morning and I just took the other key from the drawer and said nothing about it."

"It doesn't matter, Bertha," Laureen assured her gently.

"No idea where you lost it?" pursued the inspector.

"No," she replied promptly. "I probably pulled it out in the street with my handkerchief." She faced her mistress. "I left the chocolate ready, miss, in case you returned after all. I'm glad you had it."

The chocolate! Laureen's eyes met those of Lansberg ruefully for a second. If it had not been for that invitation she might have come up alone last night. She shivered at the thought.

"Yes," she replied. "It was a good thing you made it, Bertha."

"Where and when did you see this gentleman and by what name do you know him?" the inspector demanded of the maid.

"I don't know him by any name," she answered. "I saw him last night half an hour after I'd left Mr. Spencer's studio."

"Where?"

"Getting on a bus near Victoria."

"And what made you notice him—a stranger— particularly?" asked Reynolds blandly.

"I'd seen him twice before in Miss Laureen's theater in a box: she often gives me a pass. Last night I remembered his face and thought in his evening dress he looked more suited to a Rolls-Royce than an omnibus."

Lansberg's eyes twinkled.

"It's quite correct that I took a bus to the studio, Inspector. I couldn't find a taxi. I wasn't aware I had made myself so conspicuous."

The inspector paused to make a note.

"And after you saw this gentleman get on a bus, what did you do?"

Bertha gave the nearest thing to tossing her head that her standard of manners permitted.

"Then I took a walk before going to my friends at Clapham."

"It seems to have been a night for taking exercise," observed the inspector. "Made you a bit late in getting to Clapham, didn't it?"

"My friends never go to bed until midnight. I got there before that."

"What is their name, address and business?"

"Mrs. and Miss Dean, fifteen Garfield Road, Clapham. They own the house and let apartments. She's an Aberdeen woman. I pay for my room," Bertha added shortly.

"Any particular reason why you took a walk? Any friend you wanted to see?" questioned Reynolds casually.

"I thought I might meet a friend, but they didn't turn up."

"H'm. 'They' being a young man, I suppose?"

The maid reddened, showed signs of losing her temper.

"That's no affair of anybody's but my own," she retorted with heat.

The inspector slipped his hand under the brown paper and drew out a photograph. Sometimes a chance shot brought unexpected results.

"Ever seen that man before?" he asked, swiftly putting the print before her.

The maid stared speechlessly, her hands clutching the sides of the chair.

"That man was found dead in the dining-room here last night," the inspector said slowly and ruthlessly.

But even he was startled at the result of his words, for the color drained from the maid's face and with a gasp she slipped fainting to the floor.

VI. THE LETTER

THE inspector's face showed neither elation at the success of his manoeuver nor regret at the collapse of the girl.

"Sergeant," he called, "help me to carry this woman to her room. Don't worry, madam," he said to Laureen, who was bending over Bertha in consternation. "The sergeant's a 'first aid' man. She'll come round presently."

As they conveyed the woman out there came from the street below a piercing cry, followed by a crash. Lansberg darted to the open window and leaned out.

"Oh, what is it now?" Laureen asked anxiously, pressing her hands to her head.

"A girl has been knocked down by a motor-car," he answered.

"Is she hurt?"

"I don't know. The men have lifted her into the car and driven off."

Lansberg spoke casually; Laureen had had enough shocks in the last twelve hours. "Is the maid recovering, Inspector?" he added as the detective reentered the room.

"Yes, she'll be all right soon, sir. My man's looking after her." "In more senses of the word than one," he supplemented inwardly. There was a great deal more he wanted to know about Bertha's acquaintance with the dead man.

"What were her duties here, Miss Laureen?" the inspector went on. "Please tell me her daily routine."

The girl reflected.

"When I wake she brings me my tea, prepares my bath, gets out any clothes I require, tidies my room and makes the bed. Then Mrs. Carter—"

"Mrs. Carter," interjected the C. I. D. man. "Who is she?"

"The wife of the caretaker. They live in the basement and Mrs. Carter works in the different flats, by the hour, as she is required."

Reynolds wrote something hurriedly in his notebook.

"Go on, please," he urged.

"Mrs. Carter comes in and cleans my bedroom and bathroom and I suppose these sitting-rooms and the hall. Bertha dusts them, arranges the flowers and so on, does light washing and mends and looks after my clothes. She was a dressmaker once."

"That occupies all her time?" Reynolds questioned. "What about meals?"

"Bertha does the shopping in the afternoons usually and she and Mrs. Carter prepare the few meals I have here. During the evenings she is always free to go out, but I don't think she avails herself of her freedom very often."

"How do you know?" he demanded.

"When I've telephoned her from the theater I don't think I've ever failed to get an answer. Except perhaps within the last week or two."

"Oh, been going out more in the evenings lately, has she?"

Laureen raised her eyebrows. "I've already told you she was at liberty to do so, Inspector. It is no business of mine what the maid does on her own time," she said distantly.

Reynolds thumped the table in exasperation. "I daresay, madam, but it happens to be very much my business what she did, where and when she went and with whom. That woman knows a great deal about Delmond."

"Impossible." The word shot from the girl forcefully, inadvertently, and the color rose to her pale face as she realized her slip.

The detective's eyes narrowed a little, though his voice was silky and persuasive.

"And what makes you think your maid—after recognizing the dead man's photograph and fainting at the news of his death—could know nothing about him?"

But Laureen had herself in hand this time.

"I was thinking of my own—episode, of course. How could Bertha have known of it?" she fenced coolly.

"I see," the detective replied. "How about this Mrs. Carter? If she works here daily how is it she hasn't turned up this morning?"

"Whenever I'm sleeping out—as Bertha presumed I was last night—my maid calls down the speaking-tube and informs her, and Mrs. Carter doesn't come up next day until Bertha tells her. I believe that is their arrangement."

"Speaking-tube?" Reynolds looked blankly round the room. "I didn't know you had one. Where is it?"

"In the hall, just outside the dining-room door. It's in a dark corner, rather hidden by some coats that hang there. It was installed by the previous tenant, I believe."

The inspector stamped out, annoyed at having overlooked anything.

"Yes, it's there," he announced glumly. "If I blow down the thing, will Mrs. Carter answer?"

"Probably, unless she's working in one of the other flats. In which case her husband will possibly reply and fetch her if you wish."

"I certainly do wish," he said with finality, and again went into the hall.

"What a morning!" sighed Laureen, raising her hands wearily.

"After such a night, too, you poor child," Lansberg softly replied. "And now we're to have more witnesses and more questions."

Panic came to the girl's heart as she remembered a visitor who *might* call. There indeed would be a witness in whom the inspector would revel. Laureen prayed fervently that no one would come.

They listened to Reynolds shouting urgent instructions for Mrs. Carter to be fetched at once.

"You come up too," he demanded through the tube.

In a few moments a thin, anxious woman appeared, wiping her hands nervously on her apron.

"Are you Mrs. Carter?" Reynolds began.

"Yes, sir. My husband will be here in a minute," she said in a frightened voice. "He's just dressing."

"Dressing!" ejaculated the detective. "Isn't the man up yet?"

"He's only been in bed an hour or two, sir. He's a night-watchman."

The C. I. D. man smiled.

"Oh, I see. Sorry to have to disturb him. I'm Inspector Reynolds from Scotland Yard. By the way, have you seen any newspapers at all this morning, Mrs. Carter?"

The woman looked surprised at his question.

"Me, sir? I've no time to read newspapers weekdays. Why, has anything happened?"

"Yes," Reynolds told her briefly. "A man was found dead in here last night." He pointed to the dining-room.

The woman glanced with an awed expression at the door he indicated.

"Well, I don't know anything about it, sir," she assured him.

Reynolds looked at her kindly.

"There's nothing for you to be alarmed about. I only want you to answer my questions truthfully and clearly."

"I'll try, sir," she murmured.

"Very good. Now tell me why you didn't come up here as usual this morning?"

"Miss Laureen's maid called down to me last night that she and her mistress would be away for the night and that she'd let me know when she wanted me this morning." She turned her tired face to Laureen. "I'm sorry if you wanted me earlier, miss, but I've been working in the flats above and when Joe's asleep—my husband, that is—he don't always hear the speaking-tube."

"You've done exactly as my maid told you, Mrs. Carter. She didn't want you sooner," Laureen replied.

"Have you ever seen this gentleman before?" the detective by a gesture drew the woman's attention to Lansberg.

"No, sir. The maid always opens the door to visitors."

Lansberg turned towards Reynolds with amused

eyes.

"You'll soon have evidence enough to force you to believe my statement that I was never in this flat until last night, Inspector," he remarked.

The detective looked uneasy.

"We are obliged to verify everything, sir," he said in conciliating tones, and bent over his note-book.

"Rather an endless chain, but of course you have your own methods," Lansberg returned indifferently as he offered his cigarette case to Laureen.

She took a cigarette, bent forward to light it from the match he held and pointed to the ash-tray, unemptied of last night's stubs and ashes.

"Might we have that unpleasantness removed, Inspector?" she asked, "or are you preserving it as an important exhibit?"

Reynolds raised his torpid eyes to the tray Lansberg was just about to tip into the coal-scuttle. He rose suddenly.

"Allow me," he said with heavy politeness, and taking it from Lansberg's hand he walked into the hall.

Laureen's brows went up in comical surprise. "Well, well," she murmured. "Quite the little gentleman, isn't he?"

But Lansberg's eyes were serious. Burnt paper, even crushed, never achieves the fine powder of cigarette ash, and he was pretty sure Reynolds's action had been neither accidental nor merely courteous.

They heard a knock on the hall door and a moment later the detective returned, followed by a sleepy-eyed man with tumbled sandy hair, and coat collar turned up to hide the fact that he had had no time to put on a collar.

Carter glared around irritably and centered his indignation on his wife as being the only person on whom he dared vent his anger.

"You'd better get along with your work upstairs," he jerked his head sideways toward the door. "Disturbing a respectable man just as he's got to sleep," he grumbled generally, sending a hostile look in Laureen's direction. He didn't hold with play actresses and wasn't at all surprised there was something wrong in her flat. "Wot's all this about?" he demanded of Reynolds aggressively.

The inspector signed to Mrs. Carter, who was obediently making for the door, to sit down.

"Keep a civil tongue in your head, my man," he said peremptorily, "or you may be sorry for it. I'm from Scotland Yard. There was a mysterious death in this flat last night. Answer my questions carefully. What's your name?"

The bluster died out of the man's tone.

"Death?" he repeated with awe. And then seeing the detective's stern face, swallowed and automatically replied, "Albert Joseph Carter."

"How long have you and your wife acted as caretakers of this house?"

"Five years come Michaelmas, sir." He cast another infuriated glance at Laureen. "And never had anything go wrong until now. First time we've ever had an actress for a 'let.' Very genteel people live here who go to work and come back at reasonable hours."

The girl smiled demurely. "I'm sorry my work brings me back at unreasonable hours, Inspector."

"Work!" interposed Carter with a snort.

"Silence!" The detective thundered. "Answer my questions without insults or comment, Carter. You're a night-watchman, I believe. Where?"

"Garland's garage, Oxford Street," came the sullen reply.

"What are your hours there?"

"Nine at night to six in the morning. Sundays included, more's the shame," he added bitterly.

"Joe's 'chapel,' sir, and feels he ought to have his Sundays free," Mrs. Carter interpreted.

"Ah, I understand. Just what duties have you here?"

"A jolly lot of work and five shillings a week rent to pay besides," muttered the man.

Inspector Reynolds fixed him with a steely eye.

"Don't beat about the bush. What do you do each morning when you return? This morning, for instance?"

"Same as every other morning. Opened the front door—"

"Stop a minute." The inspector held up his hand. "Is that door locked at night?"

Carter shook his head.

"Never is now. Tenants were always forgetting their hall door key and ringing me up."

"Ringing *me* up, Joe," put in his wife. "You're not there at night."

"Well, same thing," Joe continued. "So the landlord said the door need only be shut. Often it stays wide open all night."

The C. I. D. man drummed his fingers on the table.

"Right. Continue your list of duties. You open the front door," he prompted.

"Beat the mats, sweep down five blessed flights of stairs—"

"Oh, I always help you with the stairs, Joe," reproached his wife. "We wash them down once a week, sir."

"Go on," encouraged the inspector. "What next after the stairs, Carter?"

"After I've done the stairs," the man went on doggedly, ignoring his wife's interruption, "I sweep and wash the hall and steps, take the milk bottles and newspapers up outside the different flats, and go down to my breakfast and then to bed."

"Nothing more?" queried the detective.

"The post-box, Joe," prompted Mrs. Carter in an awed whisper behind her hand.

"Post-box?" Inspector Reynolds sat up abruptly.

"A new-fangled box for the tenants to put their letters in," Carter replied. "The pillar-box is a good way from here, so the landlord had this box screwed up in the hall and I've got orders to clear it night and morning. One more job for me just because folks are too lazy to post their own letters."

"Where's the box fixed?"

"In a recess, round by the lift and stairs, sir."

The detective stroked his chin, visualizing the staircase and hall, remembering the track of those glittering beads.

"Now think very carefully, Carter. If any one entered by the hall door and came up here by lift or stairs, need they pass near the post-box?"

The man answered promptly.

"Certainly not, sir. The box is behind the stairs. They'd be going out of their way up or down to go near it."

The C. I. D. man looked speculatively at Laureen. If she had been near that box when she rushed downstairs to whistle for a policeman it was obviously to post something.

"It's very handy if it's wet weather, sir," Mrs. Carter put in. "Very few people use it if it's fine."

"As if that mattered," growled her husband. "Full or empty I got to clear it all the same."

"Who keeps the key?" questioned the C. I. D. man.

"I do, sir," Carter answered.

"Many letters there this morning?" Reynolds asked in his dullest tone, sharpening his pencil as though nothing else interested him.

"Four or five."

"None you noticed a bit different in any way?"

Carter aired his grievance again. "I got too much to do when I've been up all night to bother about other people's letters, sir."

"Quite so," agreed Reynolds, regarding his beautifully pointed pencil with pride. "But you're a smart-brained man and it occurred to me you might have seen something unusual this morning that might have helped me. Caught sight of an address for instance."

Carter preened at the compliment.

"I remember one was a bit heavy, sir, and I sort of weighed it in my hand going up the street to the pillar-box thinking somebody might have to pay extra on it."

Inspector Reynolds turned a fond eye on him.

"Now didn't I say you had a smart brain, Carter? I suppose it's too much to hope for that you noticed any part of the address?"

Carter began to enjoy himself. He screwed himself up to violent mental effort. This inspector evidently recognized intelligence when he saw it.

"I remember looking to see whether it had more than a three ha'penny stamp on it."

"Now that was really bright," appreciated the inspector. "Was the handwriting large or small?"

"Very large. Looked as if a child had scribbled it in a hurry. It was addressed to 'Miss Valerie Somebody,' but I can't remember the surname or the address."

Reynolds handed the man an envelope and flashed a casual glance at Laureen's long lashes as she sat absorbed in the newspaper.

"Just scribble down roughly what it looked like for length of the name, how many lines of address, etc. Do you think it was for London?"

"Yes, sir," said the man promptly. "I remember the W.1. The surname was shortish."

"Like Smith?"

The man nodded.

"Well," said Reynolds pleasantly, handing Carter his pencil, "it's wonderful you should have recalled all that. Half the people in this world go along with their eyes shut. Whereas you—" Eloquence seemed to fail him when he dealt with Carter's gift of observation. "Make that envelope look as much like the other as possible. Fill in crosses to get the length of the words approximately."

The man worked laboriously for a while, conscious of the Inspector's admiring regard.

"That's as near as I can get it, sir," he said at last, pushing the envelope across the table. It was inscribed as follows:

Miss Valerie XXXXX,
XXXX XXXXX xxxxxxx
London, W. 1.

The inspector regarded it slowly. "Splendid!" he said. "You've done exactly what I wanted." He pulled a crumpled piece of paper from his pocket and smoothed it out. It bore the address of the flat in one corner and was evidently a letter for some reason unfinished. Reynolds loved a wastepaper basket as a cat loves canaries.

"Was the writing anything like this, Carter?" he asked, indicating the crumpled paper.

"Yes, it was, rather, sir, only written larger."

Reynolds put the papers carefully into his pocket.

"Excellent," he said with a pleased air, and found Laureen's eyes peering at him curiously.

"Is it necessary to waste Mr. Lansberg's morning listening to these trivial questions? He is a busy man with many engagements. To say nothing of mine," she interposed.

"It's not only necessary but imperative, madam," the inspector assured her. "At any moment I may need your or Mr. Lansberg's help, and for your sakes it's wiser for you both to be present to hear the evidence."

"That's all right, Inspector," assented Lansberg. "Of course we must remain. My appointments are unimportant compared with this. Have you as yet learned of the precise cause of death?" he asked in a low voice.

The detective shook his head.

"Can't know that until latish this afternoon, sir."

He turned to Carter. "Well, I think you can go back to bed, Carter, and your wife to her work. You've both given very honest and helpful replies. I'll call either of you again if necessary."

"Thank you, sir." Carter touched his forehead and rose to go. "Come on," he said roughly to his wife.

But a change had come over Mrs. Carter.

Maybe she resented Laureen's slighting remark about "trivial questions," maybe she was envious of the limelight thrown on her husband's performance compared to her own colorless statements.

Suddenly she stood up in front of the inspector.

"Perhaps I ought to mention that I heard men's voices talking loudly here in this flat soon after the maid went last night, sir," she said and folded her hands, placidly waiting for the effect of her words.

VII. THE SPEAKING TUBE

MRS. CARTER created all the interest she expected. Each member of her audience reacted differently.

Laureen leaned forward amusedly, chin cupped in her hand.

Lansberg's face set into graver lines, while Carter glared stonily at his wife for stealing his thunder.

Into the detective's eyes crept the hazy look that drew his victims on to a sense of false security.

"What business had you got listening at the doors of flats at night?" demanded Carter.

His wife gave him a withering look. "I wasn't listening at any doors," she retorted. "If Bertha leaves the stopper out of the speaking-tube is that my fault? She often does, and then if I pass close to the tube in my kitchen I can hear if people are talking near it up here."

"What time was this, Mrs. Carter?" asked the detective gently. "About ten to half past?"

"That's right, sir. I didn't look at the clock but it was about half an hour after the maid went out, and I went to bed at quarter to eleven, so it must have been as you said."

Reynolds made a hurried note.

"Hear anything? Just tell me what happened."

Mrs. Carter put her head on one side meditatively.

"Well, sir, Joe had gone to work and I was having

a quiet read of the Sunday papers when I heard men's voices. Two or three men, I should think."

She paused a minute, then continued. "Yes, I'm sure I heard three different voices altogether. For a minute I was startled. Then I remembered the tube was right beside me and I'd left my stopper out when the maid called me."

"This is all highly important, Mrs. Carter," the detective said. "I only hope you listened," he added, urgently, in case ill-judged reticence might keep her from admitting that fact and all she had heard.

She twisted her apron and colored. "Yes, sir, I did, because after the maid said she and Miss Laureen would be out for the night it seemed queer that men should be up there talking."

"Very queer," agreed Reynolds. "Could you hear what was said?"

Mrs. Carter shook her head. "Not clearly. But I'm sure they were quarreling. They must have been in the hall. First I heard men's voices. Then they faded away, probably the men went into another room."

"And you couldn't distinguish a word they said?" asked Reynolds eagerly.

"No, sir. I only wish I had."

"You didn't think of coming up to see who those men were in Miss Laureen's flat when you knew she and her maid were out? They might have been burglars." The C.I.D. man's tone was curt.

The woman bristled. After all her help, for this detective to turn round on her like that!

"Burglars, indeed!" she said scornfully. "They wouldn't make a row, would they? They'd be as quiet as they could. Actresses do queer things. It was no business of mine if Miss Laureen pretended she'd be away for the night and sent her maid off, and then brought back some men to gamble. That's my belief if you ask me."

Nobody did, and Mrs. Carter added viciously: "She's got a roulette wheel. I asked the maid what it was once and she said it was a Monte Carlo gambling machine."

Laureen bit her lip to hide her amusement. "It's over there, Inspector," she pointed to a low table, "under a pile of magazines. Somebody gave it me ages ago, but it has a bias, so has not been used."

The inspector lifted the books off and scanned the "gambling machine" carefully.

"It's covered with dust and has evidently not been used for months," he observed. "Sergeant," he called to his man in the hall, "go downstairs with Mrs. Carter and sit where she was last night. Blow up the tube when you're ready. I want to test this speaking-tube."

Presently they heard a whistle and the detective spoke in a loud voice some feet away from the pipe.

"You, too, Mr. Lansberg," the detective requested. "Will you please come here and talk to me in an angry manner?"

Lansberg's eyes twinkled as he caught Laureen's muttered "I wish he'd ask me to talk to him in an angry manner. It would come so naturally!"

"Hear anything, Sergeant?" Reynolds asked a few moments later when his man returned from the basement.

"Yes, sir," came the reply. "Just as Mrs. Carter said. I could hear a voice, yours, I think, sir, but couldn't hear a word distinctly."

The inspector heaved a sigh of relief.

"That's one point proved, anyhow, in this case. Most unusual one I've had for a long time. Anybody could have walked in and killed that man. Every door open, no hall porter, nobody about, windows open, fire-escape outside. Everything handy for the murderer to escape."

"Now who were those people who were here talking?" he meditated. Then with one of his swift moves he turned to the girl.

"Have *you* any idea who the men were, Miss Laureen?" he rasped.

"Presumably Delmond was one. Other than that, I certainly do not know. Neither do I know how, why or when they entered my flat," she replied firmly.

"Sergeant, if that maid has recovered from her fainting fit, fetch her in. I want to ask her a question or two."

Declining the help of the sergeant who offered her his arm, Bertha came in a little unsteadily and took the chair indicated by the inspector.

She looked pale, but obstinate and a little defiant as she sat waiting for Reynolds to open fire. "Going to try and brazen it out," he decided to himself.

The detective began gently, willing to give her a chance.

"About these black satin shoes, Bertha. How could the sender of that telephone message know your mistress had such a pair?"

The maid drew a breath of relief. This was going to be easier than she thought. As long as he only wanted to talk about shoes, she didn't mind.

"I couldn't tell, sir, unless she had been seen in them?"

"May I interrupt, Inspector?" ventured Laureen. She was anxious to help the maid all she could. "It has just occurred to me that may have been a chance shot, because, you see, practically every woman possesses a pair of black satin slippers with paste buckles. Why, I'm sure I have two, maybe three pairs." She looked inquiringly at Bertha.

"You have three pairs, miss," confirmed the maid.

"Thank you," Reynolds responded. "You may be right on that point." He stared vaguely across the room.

"Have you been wearing any of those black satin shoes lately, madam?"

Laureen reflected and shook her head helplessly.

"I'm afraid I really can't remember, Inspector." She smiled at the maid. "Can you, Bertha? You've a wonderful memory for what I wear. I used a black brocaded pair last night, I'm sure."

The compliment produced a flow of eloquence from the maid. She started off volubly.

"It comes easy to me, miss, and I've got to remind you or you'd be wearing the same clothes over and over again. You've not used any of those black satin slippers since you wore your black lace dress at Lady Wentworth's dance the end of April."

"Indeed, an excellent memory," murmured Reynolds with a satisfied smile which made Laureen frown.

Bertha ran on unsuspectingly, pleased at the inspector's tribute.

"Then you said one black pair were a little shabby, another pair hurt you a bit," she ticked them off on her fingers, "and the third pair had the lining torn inside."

"Your maid must be a treasure," Reynolds remarked to Laureen, whose face expressed cold disdain as she met his glance. "Did you notice which pair you took to the studio?" he asked the maid in smooth tones. "I'll guess it was the shabby pair, because the one pair hurt and the other pair had a broken lining."

"Of course I noticed which pair, sir. I take great pride in looking after my mistress's things. But you're wrong. I chose the ones that had had the lining repaired."

"So you'd remembered to have that done," admired the inspector. "When was that?"

"Last week, sir. I took them to Hanbury's myself and—" She stopped abruptly and a flood of color swept over her face.

Instantly Reynolds pounced at an obvious point.

"Who was with you," he demanded, "when you went on that errand?"

Lansberg shifted his position as though he wanted to break the tension in the room.

But Reynolds relentlessly repeated his question. *"Who was it?"*

Bertha hesitated, looked piteously at her mistress, and back at Reynolds's stern face, as if hypnotized.

"My friend," she whispered, "Mr. Jackson."

"Jackson!" murmured Laureen in astonishment.

The inspector hushed her with a warning finger.

"You mean the dead man whose photograph I showed you?" he questioned more kindly.

The maid nodded, tears running down her cheeks. "Yes, sir," she sobbed. "It's dreadful to think we had words on Saturday night and the very next night he must have got in here somehow and been killed."

Over her bent head the two men looked at each other in amazement. Poor deluded woman caught in the toils of her own vanity! But Laureen's eyes were wet as she heard the pitiful sobs, though there was something akin to terror in her heart.

"Tell me, Bertha, when and how did you meet Jackson?" the detective asked.

The maid fought back her distress.

"Three weeks ago, sir. I was going out one evening when he stopped and asked me where the nearest tube station was. I told him but he said he was a stranger and would I be so kind as to show him the way." She sighed at the remembrance of her brief romance.

"And then?" suggested Reynolds quietly.

"Well, sir, I'm the last to pick up with any man like that, but he—he was so different. He was so grateful to me for walking along to the tube with him. He told me he was a single man and had no friends in London. He was here on business for a while."

"Did he say what his business was, Bertha?"

"Oh yes, sir, he was very frank. He was a traveler."

"Did he mention the name of his employers?"

Bertha shook her head. "No, sir; he just said he dealt in soft goods."

The inspector's hand went up to hide his mouth quickly.

"I see," he remarked in a stifled voice, ashamed to see that Lansberg and Laureen had controlled

their expression better. "And after that first walk
you naturally met him often by his wish?"

Bertha wrung her hands nervously.

"It sounds dreadfully bold to talk about it, but he
was such a gentleman and so devoted to me. It
seemed like love at first sight for both of us. We used
to go for walks or to the cinema and once we went to
Miss Laureen's theater when she gave me tickets."

The detective drew little patterns on a piece of
paper.

"Must have been during one of those walks that
you lost your key, I suppose," he hinted.

"It was the night we went to a cinema, sir. My
bag fell down. It must have opened and the key
dropped out."

"Mr. Jackson was concerned probably to know
you'd lost it," stated the inspector.

"I never told him, sir. I didn't miss it until next
morning when I got up to the flat, and then as my
mistress was there she let me in. I took the other key
and said nothing about it until this morning."

"Did Jackson often come to this flat to see you?"
the inspector asked.

The maid flushed indignantly.

"Never," she exclaimed emphatically. "That is,
until last Saturday night. I was to meet him outside,
but he said as he was a bit early he thought he'd call
for me. I asked him inside the hall while I put on my
hat, and was annoyed to find him in here when I
came back ready to go out."

"As any honorable maid would in her mistress's
absence," agreed Reynolds. "Is that what began the
quarrel?"

Bertha's face had a tortured expression as she

responded: "Yes, sir. I found him in this room at that bureau opening the drawers and turning over some letters;"

Laureen made an involuntary sound. Reynolds glanced at her speculatively before he again addressed the maid.

"You were angry?"

"I was; very angry. More than I ought to have been perhaps, for Mr. Jackson explained that he often did a bit of society reporting and as Miss Laureen was a very famous revue artist all the world was interested in her."

"This is very interesting, Bertha," commented Reynolds. "What was your answer to that?"

"Well, sir, I understood a bit better, though I was still annoyed. Then he said he'd heard rumors that my mistress was giving a special surprise party here on Sunday night, June 30th, and probably a member of some royal family was coming."

"And you replied?" the detective questioned eagerly.

"That he'd heard entirely wrong as I happened to know my mistress was going to a studio party at Mr. Spencer's and would be there from ten o'clock that night."

"I see." Reynolds tapped his pencil on the table aimlessly. "Did he ask what time she would return?"

"Yes, sir, he did. That made me angry again. I said, 'Some time after midnight, but I always wait up for her, so it's no use your trying to crawl in here and interview her when she's tired.' Then he fired up and said some horrible things about Miss Laureen. We quarreled dreadfully and at last he went away alone and I had a good cry."

"And you never saw him again, Bertha?"

"No, sir. I walked along to Victoria last night and back hoping to meet him as usual and make it up. But he didn't come and now it's too late." Again her self-control gave way and the inspector signaled to Laureen to take the maid to her room.

Lansberg looked at his watch and rose as he saw Reynolds putting his papers together.

"I'll go and get some luncheon, Inspector, and be at my rooms ready for you at two thirty. Wonderful how the pieces are fitting into the puzzle, isn't it?"

"It will be," corrected Reynolds grimly, "when I can force open the fingers that hold on to some of those pieces."

"Inspector," asked Laureen from the doorway, "can my maid pack up some of our clothes and remove them to St. Andrew's Hotel near by? With your permission I propose to take rooms there for Bertha and myself."

"Certainly. Your maid can stay for an hour or so. The sergeant will be here on guard. And you, madam?"

"I must get some luncheon. Then I'll go to the theater and lie down in my dressing-room for an hour or so," she said quickly. She turned to Lansberg. "It will be quieter than the hotel and after last night I need rest or what will my work be like to-night?"

The inspector nodded and led them to the hall door.

"For God's sake be careful, Laureen," warned Lansberg in a swift undertone as they walked downstairs together. "Reynolds will have a man watching every step you take to-day."

She screwed up her face impishly.

"What's the betting that I elude the creature?" she whispered.

But Lansberg's face was serious, his mind on the ordeal before him that afternoon.

VIII. BUTTERFLIES

DOWNSTAIRS the front door was closed.

"Press photographers and reporters outside, sir," explained the officer in plain clothes, who was on guard. "I'll take you and the lady out the back way if you like."

"Thank you," Lansberg replied.

The man unlocked a door behind the staircase that led through a walled-in yard, opened another door and conducted them through a narrow alley into the street behind.

Lansberg put Laureen into a passing taxi, raised his hat and strolled away in the opposite direction.

Upstairs in the flat Reynolds turned back for a last word with Bertha, who was on her knees packing a trunk.

"Do you know any one of the name of Valerie?" he asked.

The maid bent over the garments she was deftly folding. "No, sir," she responded firmly.

"Any of your mistress's friends called by that name?"

"Not that I'm aware of."

Some latent obstinacy in her tone made Reynolds tap her on the shoulder.

"Don't conceal anything," he warned. "You've heard that name recently. Who mentioned it?"

The woman hesitated; then said reluctantly:

"My friend, Mr. Jackson, asked me once if any lady of that name had ever been to the flat. I said no.

"Did 'Jackson' give his reason for asking?"

Bertha thought a minute. "I'm not quite sure, sir, but I believe he said this Valerie—he didn't give her other name—had once known Miss Laureen, acted with her or something, he'd been told. And I said maybe that was before my time as I'd only worked for my mistress for ten months."

"He never mentioned the subject again?"

"Oh, no, sir. It was only asked casually, I think."

"About this Miss Gilbert who rang you up last night with the message. Have you ever heard her voice before or seen her?"

"No, sir. And I'm sure no one of that name has been here. I never admit any one who won't give her name because my mistress is always being bothered by all kinds of people."

"H'm. Anything peculiar about this woman's voice over the telephone? Could you recognize it?"

Bertha tried conscientiously to describe it.

"I *think* I'd know it again, sir, as it was a very clear, rather high voice."

"Thank you," said the inspector. "That's all I need bother you with now. Good morning."

He was walking away when the maid timidly called him back.

"Please, sir," she clasped her hands nervously, her eyes swimming with tears, "do you think I might have a photo of my friend? One like you showed me this morning. I should be so grateful."

"Yes, you shall," he said with rough kindliness, foreign to a man alleged to be without a heart.

With a word to the sergeant on duty, he strode heavily downstairs and thrust aside impatiently the eager newspaper men awaiting him.

By the pillar-box at the corner of the street the inspector stopped and glanced at the tablet indicating the hours of clearance. Afterward he walked the short distance to Scotland Yard, revolving in his mind the facts he had elucidated and the huge gaps remaining to be bridged in this problem.

One or two things had gone very smoothly. The photograph of Leslie Delmond, for instance. Early that morning he'd sent a man out to try all the film agencies for pictures of the dead man, and within an hour one had been obtained. An excellent portrait, too, judging by Bertha Mackie's instant recognition of it.

In his office he ordered coffee and sandwiches and began sifting out reports that had come in on investigations for which he had previously given instructions.

A thin, scholarly-looking man came in. Reynolds gave him a rapid summary of the facts up to date and then asked:

"Found that telephone clerk yet, Jenkins?"

"Not yet. But I'll have news presently."

"That film agency where you picked up the photo of Delmond. Did they know his address?"

"No. Hadn't seen or heard of him for ages. That photo is two or three years old."

The inspector ticked off those items on his list.

"You saw the women Miss Laureen dined with last night. Did they observe anything unusual in her manner?"

Jenkins shook his head.

"Nothing noticeable, they said. But, after a bit of trouble, I got them to admit she'd seemed in a hurry to get away. Kept looking at her watch, they said."

The inspector's mouth tightened.

"She did, eh! Funny she couldn't remember what time she left there when I asked her last night, or rather early this morning. What about the waiters in the restaurant? Nothing fresh there?"

"Only what I told you on the telephone, sir. Two waiters were positive Miss Laureen left at eight twenty-five, and the porter outside said the lady wore a pink cloak and wouldn't have a taxi."

Reynolds stroked his chin.

"That bit agrees with what she said. But, Jenkins, that cloak is lined with black and is reversible. She let that out. And in the pocket was a black scarf or maybe a little black cap. Doesn't take much to cover a woman's head in these days."

Jenkins pondered. "Reversible, eh!"

"Nothing remarkable in a *black* cloak and hat," went on Reynolds, "whereas in a pink cloak, bareheaded, and with her golden hair, she'd have been marked wandering about before going to Spencer's studio."

"I called at Spencer's address," Jenkins added, "and got hold of the caretaker. Richard Spencer is a bachelor and a bit sweet on Laureen, the woman who cleans his flat told me. She says he's got sketches of her all over the place."

The inspector whistled softly.

"So Spencer's keen on this girl, is he?"

Jenkins laughed.

"Dozens like him from all I can hear, sir. I don't wonder. She's as clever as she's good-looking. I went to see her show last week. Lansberg's got money in it, they say."

The detective made a sudden decision.

"Ring up and book me a seat in her theater for tonight. I'll go and see her myself and find out why people rave about her."

"You'll know all right once you've seen her," predicted Jenkins. "Back of the stalls, side seat will be best, I expect. Not too conspicuous. You needn't dress up, you know, sir," he added.

But the inspector had finished with that theme.

"Get copies of this photograph of the dead man sent to all the newspapers and tell them we want information about him," he ordered. "And while you're about it, get an extra copy for me."

"I'll see to that at once," promised Jenkins.

"Also," went on Reynolds, "I must have news about this girl or woman called Valerie."

He briefly outlined all he knew and showed Jenkins the envelope Carter had worked on with the address. "Get them to reproduce that and ask any one who saw or received that letter to call here immediately."

"Pillar-box cleared at seven fifteen A. M.," mused Jenkins. "Letter for W.1. district. H'm. It would get delivered any time after two P.M., I suppose."

"About that," agreed the inspector, looking at his watch. "I must be off to my appointment. I shall be at Lansberg's flat if you want me. It's somewhere near the Adelphi. Look up his number and ring me if the report of the post-mortem comes in."

"Curious that no key of the flat was found on the dead man," observed Jenkins. "No letters either, or papers. The other oddments we found in his pockets are in this box."

"All right. Within twenty-four hours we may get

some light on this Leslie Delmond from his landlady or wherever he lived."

"Do you want me to comb through all the flats in forty-nine Beresford Street and ask the tenants if they posted a letter addressed to some one called Valerie?" asked Jenkins.

The inspector considered the question.

"No," he said at last. "That maid, Bertha Mackie, says the dead man asked her if a girl called Valerie ever came to see her mistress. So it's long odds the letter came from somebody in that flat, and I'd give something to know what was in it."

"You're having Laureen watched?" questioned Jenkins.

"You bet I am," Reynolds assured him emphatically as he jammed on his hat. "Get on with that newspaper business at once."

Inside the spacious hall of Lansberg's apartment the inspector, against his will, felt impressed. His duties often carried him into palatial mansions, but in the silence and dignity of this place there was something quite apart from anything he had seen before.

It occupied the whole of the first floor and the interior had evidently been reconstructed to suit its owner's taste. Doorways had been widened and hung with rich draperies. Thick carpets deadened all sound. Even Reynolds's untrained eye could realize beauty in the two or three exquisite pieces of statuary that gleamed with color filtering through a large stained-glass window.

He tried to shake off the feeling of awed respect that was creeping over him. Firmly he told himself that this type of furnishing wasn't English, and that the olive-hued, sloe-eyed man-servant who had taken in his card, was a dago.

Almost he started as he found the man at his elbow announcing with a strong foreign accent:

"Mr. Lansberg will see you, sir."

"See me, indeed!" murmured the detective to himself. "He certainly will."

Hat in hand, the inspector followed the man through the portiere, across a lofty room decorated in a style neither ornate nor austere, into a library.

From a huge writing table at an angle to the window, Lansberg rose, dismissed the man-servant with a few words in a language unknown to the detective, and bowed with grave courtesy.

"Where would you like to sit, Inspector? With your permission I will stay where I am." His eyes twinkled. "As you see, I face the light nicely here."

And again Reynolds had that uneasy sense of being out of his depths. Was this the man he had badgered and kept at heel with his commands and questions last night and this morning? Also Reynolds felt he would give quite a lot to know what his superior officers in conference that morning had in mind when they urged he must not annoy Mr. Lansberg unduly.

Lansberg opened a carved ebony box and twisted it toward the detective, who had chosen a hard chair with its back to the window.

"Will you smoke?" Lansberg asked. It was almost as if he were trying to put an awkward guest at his ease.

The inspector selected a cigarette with an effort at being casual, striving for equally composed manners.

"Thank you," he said, repressing the "sir" which rose to his lips almost mechanically, and bending forward for the lighted match Lansberg offered.

Leaning back calmly, Lansberg awaited the detective's opening, one hand idly fingering an ivory paper-knife.

On the little finger Reynolds noticed a heavy gold ring engraved with armorial bearings unlike any he had seen before. He wished—

But even a Scotland Yard man has limits, and he had no adequate excuse for asking leave to examine that ring. Anyhow he could hunt up Lansberg's pedigree later.

He pulled himself together with a frown. "I should like your full name, age, occupation, please," he began formally.

Lansberg pushed a card across to him.

"Anticipating those questions, I wrote the answers down for you, Inspector, as my names are lengthy and a little complicated to spell."

The detective glanced up under his eyebrows as he took the card and read it slowly to gain time. That inability of his to spell! Was Lansberg making fun of him?

But there was no hint of anything except well-bred attention in Lansberg's face.

"Like a blooming Sphinx," the detective muttered to himself. "He'll answer my questions but give nothing away voluntarily."

Aloud he said:

"A good way to avoid any mistakes. Now, Mr. Lansberg, before I go back to the events of last evening, will you tell me what your business is?"

Lansberg smiled faintly, flicked one finger

toward the card Reynolds held.

"It is clearly stated there, Inspector. I have many interests that cannot possibly affect this affair; interests," he added icily, "that I am not at liberty to reveal. It will be sufficient for your purposes if I tell you—what you probably already know—that I have considerable money invested in the theatrical world, including the theater in which Miss Laureen acts."

"That I suppose is your hobby," said the detective with a heavy attempt at sarcasm.

"It's quite a good name. Call it that by all means, if you like," Lansberg agreed genially.

"What is your staff here?" the inspector asked.

"This is a service flat. I rarely take any meals here. The only resident servant of my own is the man you saw, who acts as butler and valet."

"Does he speak English?"

Lansberg shook his head.

"About a dozen words. I have a secretary, an English ex-officer, who comes daily," he added, almost as though he wished to change the subject. "Knowing you were coming, I sent him off for the afternoon."

"Why?" asked the C. I. D. man bluntly.

"Only so that we should be undisturbed," was the quiet answer. He wrote something rapidly on a card and passed it to Reynolds.

"There is his name and private address if you care to call on him."

The inspector tucked the address into his pocket-book.

"We'll now deal with your movements last night, Mr. Lansberg. Where did you dine and with whom?"

"At my club and alone. That address too you will

find both on my visiting card and the supplementary card I gave you just now," he added. Reynolds verified the remark, slightly irritated to realize Lansberg was getting the better of him in some vague way.

"I suppose the hall porter or waiters at your club can confirm that statement?"

Lansberg raised his hand indifferently in one of his rare gestures.

"Possibly. That is your affair, Inspector."

Something in that gesture prompted Reynolds to ask another question.

"Are you English?"

"By birth, no. My origin is rather cosmopolitan since my mother was English and my father was from one of the Balkan States. I was born in Paris, and am a nationalized Englishman."

"And subject to English law," commented the inspector inwardly with a grim satisfaction.

"Please outline what you did, Mr. Lansberg," he added aloud, "from the time you left here and went to your club until you reached Mr. Spencer's studio."

Lansberg reflected.

"I left here about seven thirty last night, strolled along to my club, found one or two letters and read them while dinner was being served."

"Many people dining there?" interpolated the detective.

"Very few. On Sunday nights there rarely are many. That is one reason why I like to dine at my club then."

"Do you remember conversing with any particular member?"

"No, or I should remember it. I dined alone,

nodded to one or two men, smoked a cigar and looked at the papers for a while, and then about half past nine I set out for the studio."

"By taxi, or your own car?"

"Neither. It was a fine evening, I had plenty of time, and I walked as far as Victoria, where you have proof from Miss Laureen's maid that I took a bus to Chelsea."

For one wild second the detective felt almost hysterical. Yet another of them who took a walk after dinner! There seemed to have been a passionate wave of pedestrian exercise last night.

But *was* it all as straightforward as it appeared to be? Mentally he measured the distance between Lansberg's club and Victoria.

A glint came to his dull eyes as he worked out that Laureen's flat was midway and could easily have been visited in the time.

"You had no reason to pass through Beresford Street and call at Miss Laureen's flat during that walk?"

"No," he said, "I had no reason for doing so, and it would have been out of my way."

Lansberg's reply was unhesitating, his face composed. But Reynolds's eyes were not on Lansberg's face. Once before he had seen the man's hands tighten as they tightened now on that paper-knife, which he still fingered unconsciously.

The detective had at last got a lead. Those sensitive fingers made him positive Lansberg knew more than he meant to tell. Reynolds's mind plowed through the events of last night as he endeavored to reconstruct the situation if Lansberg had called at that flat before going to the studio.

On the supposition that there might have been a struggle he swiftly tried his old means of lightning attack.

"I should like to see the garments you wore last night, please. Including the shirt," he added.

Lansberg's face expressed nothing more than the ordinary surprise, tinged with good-natured amusement, that any man might exhibit if called upon to produce his wardrobe.

He pressed a bell. "Certainly, if you wish, Inspector."

The man-servant appeared, but before Lansberg could give him any orders Reynolds addressed him.

"Est-ce-que vous parlez franqais?" he demanded rapidly.

"Oui, monsieur," the man replied.

Continuing to speak French fluently but with a harsh accent, Reynolds asked the man:

"You have been many years with your master?"

The man darted a glance at Lansberg before replying, as if asking permission. Lansberg nodded assentingly and the servant answered:

"I and my people we have served for many years with—monsieur"—Reynolds noted he hesitated before the name—"and his family before him," the servant said proudly.

The inspector turned to Lansberg.

"Please tell your man to answer any questions I ask him."

Lansberg did so, speaking in French—a degree of tact and courtesy which the detective appreciated.

"What time did your master leave here last night to go out to dinner?" Reynolds went on.

"At seven thirty or not more than seven thirty-five."

Although the replies were coldly polite, Reynolds felt the servant's disdain of him as a being of common clay who dared to intrude into his master's life.

"At what hour did he return here last night?" questioned the inspector inexorably.

This time the servant's gaze flickered in quick supplication to Lansberg, who calmly interposed:

"My servant—his name is Neron—does not wait up for me with chocolate, Inspector. He was in bed when I returned about three fifteen a.m. after our late interview last night."

But he had spoken in French! Was that to give the man his cue, Reynolds wondered.

"Bring me the evening suit and shirt your master wore last night," he commanded.

The man turned instantly and went out of the room.

"Did you return here before going to Mr. Spencer's party, Mr. Lansberg?"

Before he could reply, the telephone on the desk rang and Lansberg lifted off the receiver.

"Mr. Lansberg speaking." He passed over the instrument. "It's for you, Inspector."

Reynolds took the receiver, and after a curt monosyllable listened attentively for a few minutes.

"All right, I shall be back very shortly," he said, and ended the conversation.

He looked at Lansberg meditatively.

"The result of the post-mortem on Leslie Delmond has just come in. He died from the effects of —in fact was undoubtedly murdered with— chloroform."

"Chloroform!" There was amazement in Lansberg's face. "Is that certain?"

"Our pathologists are fairly reliable," commented the inspector drily. He paused, his eyes narrowed. "Have you any reason to think there should be another cause for this man's death?" he demanded harshly.

"No," Lansberg replied calmly, "none whatever. Only it seemed an unusual weapon. Surely it takes a large—an awkwardly large—quantity of chloroform to murder a man?"

"Somewhere about half a pint, probably," Reynolds impatiently glanced round the room, again baffled by Lansberg's explanation of his surprise. A natural surprise, he agreed. Chloroform was an unusual weapon and a bulky one.

What was that servant doing? Probably examining his master's suit carefully.

The inspector scrutinized the book-lined walls, noticed a huge safe skilfully built into one corner, a case of vividly colored butterflies above it.

Reynolds longed to get a peep into that safe; maybe it could tell him more than its owner would. Just then the servant entered silently and deposited a pile of clothes on a table.

Reynolds rose, looked the garments over mechanically and without interest; picked up the shirt, stared at it abstractedly and laid it down again. He took his hat from the chair beside him.

"Thank you, Mr. Lansberg. Good day."

But as he walked back to Scotland Yard his mind was not on the shirt he had just seen—in one second he knew it was not the same one as that worn last night, although the cuffs had obviously had studs in them. The one Lansberg had worn last night, the detective remembered, had a smear of cigarette ash on it, and a bulge at one side of the front incompatible with Lansberg's immaculate attire.

Reynolds decided to solve that problem later. For the moment his thoughts curiously turned on butterflies.

IX. A HIDING PLACE

LAUREEN had luncheon in a little tea-shop that was nearly empty. From her seat in the window she could catch glimpses of a man who alternately was absorbed in a newspaper or thoughtfully propping up the wall.

She slid back the curtain considerately so that he could more easily see she was there. Her brain was busy on a plan in which she hoped the faithful hound, as she mentally dubbed him, would play no part.

Presently her eyes twinkled. She hurriedly wrote something on a card, folded it over and called the waitress.

"Take this note across to that poor man standing over there," she indicated him to the girl. "He looks as if he's out of work and needs a meal. Give me his bill if he comes in and orders something."

From the window she watched the shadow unfold the visiting card and read the message:

Why not come in and have luncheon? You can see better and will find it less tiring. I shall be here some time yet.

For a second the man hesitated, then he swung round and entered the tea-room. Raising his hat without looking in Laureen's direction, he chose a table as far from hers as possible, but one that gave him an excellent view of the door.

She heard him give his order.

"Anything you have ready and coffee, please."

When the waitress came to her table again Laureen said in an undertone:

"Ask. the gentleman if he will kindly lend me his newspaper for a few minutes, as I'm interested in sport." She slid a shilling into the girl's hand. "Don't forget the last sentence."

Scenting romance, the waitress obediently gave the message and returned with the newspaper, but not before Laureen had seen the man quickly bend his head to hide a smile.

"Really, I'm getting quite fond of that nice little fellow," she told herself as she handed the girl a pound note.

"Take the money for both bills from that without mentioning it to him, or his pride may be hurt," she warned the waitress.

Laureen knew that only a sense of humor would keep her from screaming to-day.

After her ordeal of last night followed by the inspector's examination, her nerves were screwed up almost to snapping point. And there were things she had to do with a cold brain, as well as get through her work in the theater to-night.

The newspaper she had borrowed from the faithful hound was the mid-day sporting edition. Its front page was emblazoned with huge headlines:

WESTMINSTER MYSTERY

Film Actor Found Dead
In Famous Revue
Artist's Flat

So far, apparently, Inspector Reynolds had spared her reputation, she noticed, inasmuch as no reference was made to her statement that the dead man had been her lover. But she had a growing conviction that that was about all Reynolds would spare her before he had finished.

She shrugged her shoulders as she gathered up her change. Well, she could look after herself. She was used to publicity, and what did a little more or less matter to one who had fought and kicked her way by sheer hard work up to the position she now held? Reached there unaided too, disdaining the easier and speedier methods.

From the other end of the tea-shop came sounds of distress from an embarrassed man struggling to get his bill from a loyal and sentimental waitress.

Laureen smothered a giggle, laid the newspaper on her table and walked slowly to her theater.

The stage-door entrance was in an alley at the side of the theater. There, in the doorway, Laureen paused and in clear tones asked Minnis, the door porter, how he was, how his wife was and his garden; this to give the hound time to get within earshot.

Taking her letters, she yawned audibly and remarked, "Well, Minnis, after last night's ghastly affair in my flat I'm going up to my dressing-room to get some sleep and write a few letters. Don't let any reporters get by you, I don't want to be disturbed." She lowered her voice. "The man now in the alley outside is a detective. If he likes to come in and sit in your office where he can watch this door, let him."

Minnis stared. He admired Laureen very much.

"A detective, miss!" he gasped. "But they can't suspect—?"

She shook her finger to and fro.

"Suspect me? Of course not. He's only taking a kindly interest in me to see I come to no harm. If he speaks to you say I hope he enjoyed his lunch. He'll understand."

She pushed open the swing door and walked up the stone staircase leading to the dressing-rooms.

Half-way up she paused to look closely at a small iron door fastened by two heavy bolts. It was the door that led to the theater. Gently she wriggled the bolts and found they slid easily in their sockets. Then contentedly she went on to her dressing-room.

Except when there was a matinee, at this hour of the day—it was twenty past two—she knew the place would be deserted, save for stage-hands.

About an hour later, a neat old lady, with gray hair and bent shoulders, called at a house in Bloomsbury and asked to see one of the lodgers.

The slovenly maid servant stared at the patient figure clad in an old-fashioned brown coat, and then called over her shoulder:

"Missus. Somebody wants Miss Baird."

"If you'll please tell me where her room is, I will go up," interrupted the old lady. "There is no need to disturb your mistress."

But before the maid could reply heavy steps along the passage heralded the landlady.

"I want to see Miss Baird," repeated the caller.

"So do I," sniffed the owner of the house

indignantly. "She went out at six o'clock last night. Said she was going to church, and I haven't seen her since. Church, indeed! This is a respectable house for respectable people," the woman added fiercely.

"Yes, yes, I'm sure it is," murmured the old lady. She seemed taken aback by the landlady's words. "Probably Miss Baird stayed the night with friends and will be back soon," she ventured hopefully.

The landlady, looking at the pathetic, stooping figure, withheld what she longed to say and substituted:

"Will you call again or leave a message?"

"Thank you, thank you," the caller said nervously, "I'm only in town for the day. Tell Miss Baird her old governess left her love."

The landlady watched the shabbily dressed old lady go down the steps, and called out warningly as she passed the railings:

"Mind, that paint's wet. I'll give your message when she conies back."

Once again in Oxford Street the old lady climbed nimbly on a bus, her face, shaded by its out-of-date mushroom hat, worried and abstracted.

"Not been back since six o'clock last night!" she repeated over and over again to herself.

At Piccadilly Circus she got out and threaded her way to a large imposing hotel. Inside the entrance hall she passed through the crowds to the letter bureau. A man was already there asking for his mail and she overheard the conversation.

"Have you a room, sir?" asked the clerk.

"Not yet," was the man's reply.

"Please register for your room first, sir. That is our rule."

The old lady faded away from that department, and going across to the reception clerk asked for a single room.

"Number 420. Ten and sixpence. Sign your name here, please. Luggage?" The clerk ripped off the formula automatically.

The elderly client signed in a thin cramped handwriting without removing her glove.

"My luggage is at the station. Shall I pay in advance?" she offered timidly.

The clerk cast a practised eye down the old figure, saw faded gentility written all over it, said it didn't matter and handed over the ticket giving the number of the room.

Back at the letter bureau again, the old lady produced the ticket and asked if there were any letters.

The clerk glanced through the file.

"Nothing, madam."

The old lady looked so disappointed that he added, "Wait a minute. I've not had time to sort through this last lot yet." His fingers rapidly dealt with a large stack of letters beside him. "What name did you say?"

The old lady repeated it, watching anxiously as the pile grew less.

"Ah, here you are!" He handed her a thickish envelop, glanced at her casually, and went on with his task.

Twenty minutes later an old lady went unobtrusively in at the front entrance of a theater, slid past the big crowd near the box office and pushing open the door leading into the back of the stalls, found herself once more in the dark, empty auditorium. Silently she made her way to the corridor behind the stage box, opened a small iron door in the wall and vanished.

"Joe," called Miss Laureen presently to one of the carpenters, "you might slip out and get me some cigarettes."

Joe looked approvingly at the dainty negligee the lady was wearing. He liked women to wear pretty feminine things.

"Certainly, miss," he said eagerly. All the staff liked doing jobs for Miss Laureen, and not only because she rewarded them liberally. "I'm doing a bit of papering in number four," he added. "The guv'nor thinks he'll turn it into an extra office as it's not wanted as a dressing-room. What'll you have, miss? Turkish or Egyptian?"

"Virginian, and get some for yourself at the same time, Joe."

The cigarette shop was some distance from the theater. Laureen thought she could reckon on eight minutes before Joe returned.

Silently she went along the passage from her room to number four where Joe had been working. Her breath came quickly as her eyes searched the bare room for some hiding place. It had the usual paper-hanger's table, steps and bucket of paste.

Joe had evidently been hanging a strip of wallpaper when she called him. With a gleam of hope she noticed the baseboard had warped out slightly from the wall and that he had stuck the paper over it to hide the opening.

Bending down she gently raised the bottom edge of the paper. The paste was still wet and the paper lifted easily. Yes, there was ample space behind the board.

In a moment she had slipped a thin white packet between the baseboard and the plaster, thrust it down and delicately pressed the edges of the wallpaper over it again, adding a little more paste to make it firm. Even if Joe lifted the paper he could not possibly see the packet behind the woodwork.

She was in her dressing-room lying on her couch, white arms curved above her head, when the man returned.

"Thank you, Joe," she said, holding out her hand for the cigarettes and yawning.

"It's a wonder you're not ill, miss, after all you went through last night," he remarked sympathetically. "'Orrible affair. Shall I tell Minnis to order tea for you?"

She glanced at her watch.

"Quarter past four. Yes, I'd like some."

Minnis appeared with a tray in a few minutes, obtained from a café near the stage-door. He set it down on a table beside her and said in a low voice:

"That fellow down in the passage has been asking me questions." He grinned. "He didn't get much change out of me though, miss."

Laureen poured out a cup of tea and dropped in some sugar.

"I'm sure he didn't, Minnis. But he's a nice little fellow and very attached to me, so I hope you treated him kindly and asked him into your office."

Minnis looked up under his shaggy eyebrows, not quite sure if Miss Laureen was serious.

"No, miss, not exactly, but he's been leaning against my door ever since you came, trying to pump me as to everybody's movements here. I'm getting sick of the sight of him."

"So he's been leaning against your door all the time, has he?" The lady smiled to herself. "Well, well, that's something. Did you say I hoped he'd enjoyed his lunch, Minnis?"

"I did, miss. He got red."

Laureen put down her cup and chuckled.

"He'll be purple before I've finished with him," she predicted. "Wait a minute while I write a letter."

She scribbled a note rapidly, addressed the envelop, fastened it insecurely, and handed it to the porter with fun dancing in her eyes.

"Like to help me in a joke, Minnis?" she questioned.

Minnis nodded, with a grin.

"Rather, miss."

"Good. You can go down and casually mention I'm going to my hotel to get some dinner before the show to-night. Say I told you to post this letter as I've no stamps. You can grumble and say 'She thinks I can run out at all hours and leave this office, to do her fool errands.' Something like that. Being kind-hearted, he'll offer to post it for you—*which is just what I want*. D'you understand?"

"Exactly, miss," beamed the man.

"I shall just give you time to get that off your chest," Laureen added with a smile, "and then I'll come down."

The man retired with the letter and within three minutes Laureen had hurriedly dressed and strolled downstairs singing.

Minnis was in his office alone. As she was passing out he whispered and pointed with his thumb.

"All gone nicely. He's outside waiting for you, and he's got your letter."

Laureen went up the alley slowly, beckoned a taxi and told the man to drive to her hotel, without troubling to see whether the hound was trailing her. She had had a most successful afternoon from her point of view, with only one anxiety.

In the hotel where she had reserved rooms, she found Bertha had unpacked and was sewing placidly. The maid was paler than usual, but did not allude to the morning's proceedings.

"I've ordered the porter to send up the evening newspapers as soon as they arrive," she informed her mistress, who had gone at once to the telephone.

"Is Mr. Spencer there?" Laureen asked when her call was answered. And seemed staggered by the reply.

"You think he's gone to Paris!" she repeated.

Swiftly she demanded particulars of the caretaker at the other end of the wire, and learned that Mr. Spencer had gone out about eleven thirty that morning with a suitcase, saying he didn't know when he'd be back, and that she—the caretaker— was to clean up the studio, which was "in a nice mess after the party," lock it up and keep the keys. No, he had left no address but she had heard him ring up Croydon and ask about aeroplanes to Paris when she was doing the bedroom. There had been two men there since asking about him, and one of them—a detective—had taken away a pair of black satin slippers. "Belonging to you, miss. Was that all right?"

"Yes," assented Laureen. It was all right. But about the only thing that was right, she felt at the moment.

Dick Spencer dashing off to Paris like that? What did it mean? Was it accidental? Had he read the news of the murder in the papers before he left? If so, surely he would have telephoned to her. *Or had he not needed the newspapers to tell him that news?*

Laureen's head whirled as she lay back and tried to face this new difficulty. She might have been cheered could she have heard a little conversation at Scotland Yard.

Her sleuth—Bradley by name—had reported there after he had seen her deposited at her hotel door.

"I want to see Inspector Reynolds," he told Jenkins importantly. "I've got hold of a letter Miss Laureen wanted to have posted."

It was addressed to one of the women Laureen had dined with last night, the inspector noticed as he delicately raised the flap of the envelop.

He read the note and looked at Bradley.

"You may like to read it," he remarked. "That young woman seems to have a sense of humor."

Bradley's face indeed grew purple as he read:

Dearest Eileen,
So sorry you're being drawn into this mess of mine. I'd come round and see you, only I'm no longer alone and fear you don't like dogs. He's a very faithful hound, extremely attached to me, though rather an ugly brute and not over-bright. One of these days when he's had a bath I must bring him along to see you. We lunched together to-day and I found his table manners are not all one would like; I must really teach him not to put

*his feet in the plate. Still, one can't have
everything in this life, and as I say he comes to
heel most obediently.*
Yours,
Laureen

"I suppose it must be posted, sir," said Bradley
disgustedly as he handed it back to his chief with a
brief explanation of this luncheon.

"It certainly must," the inspector replied firmly
as he re-sealed the envelope and put it with other
letters for the post.

"I hoped I'd get something out of her by going
into that tea-shop," Bradley explained.

"It will take a brighter lad than you to get that
young woman to tell you what she doesn't wish you
to know. I'll have to put somebody else on to her. If
she's fooled you in this she'll fool you in something
else. If she has not already done so," he added with
tightened lips.

"She was in her dressing-room resting all the
afternoon," apologized Bradley meekly. "I never left
the stage-door."

"Humph!" grunted the inspector. "Well, cut along
back to her hotel now and to-morrow I'll make fresh
plans."

As the man went out crestfallen Reynolds
remembered his arrangement to go to the theater
that night, and rang for Jenkins.

"Fixed up that seat?" he demanded.

Jenkins nodded.

"Bit of luck to get one, sir. Just what you want,
too. Wall end of stalls, eighth row. No need for you to
doll up."

"You said that before," said Reynolds tersely. "I shall know what to do." Already he was beginning to look forward to a thoroughly enjoyable evening of business combined with pleasure.

"Maybe I'll get a little light there on this murder," he told himself hopefully.

Motive in this affair seemed to pivot round Laureen, and he had an urgent desire to see more of this girl on her native heath, as it were; find out why men circled round, apparently willing to risk their necks for her.

X. THE MISSING LODGER

THE last editions of the evening papers had done full justice to the information meted out to them by Scotland Yard.

Huge head-lines screamed of the Westminster flat mystery. Photographs of the murdered man, Leslie Delmond, appeared with a brief account of his career. Photographs of Laureen with a lengthy and, mostly, inaccurate description of her career followed. There was a reproduction of the address drawn by Carter, "Miss Valerie XXXXX, etc.," together with a request for information concerning that letter. News was also demanded about Valerie and Leslie Delmond.

The Star had featured the letter episode and its chief head-line read:

WHO IS VALERIE?

The earlier editions of the evening papers had caused every reserved seat to be booked in the theater, and an enormous crowd had queued up for the cheaper seats, willing to pay any price if only to stand in order to see the revue actress on whom the limelight of a murder drama was playing fiercely.

From his secluded seat in the stalls Inspector Reynolds felt the peculiar thrill surging through the packed theater. With his opera glasses he carefully scanned the house, dwelling particularly on the boxes.

There was a stir in the audience as a distinguished looking man with hair graying at the temples entered the stage box, followed a moment later by two women and another man whose face was invisible from Reynolds's angle.

The first man was Lansberg. No mistaking that calm dignified face with its dominant, lustrous eyes. He placed the ladies in their seats, and then with a casual glance round the crowded theater, stood talking with the other man who was in the background.

"That's the Countess of Warnham and her niece, Lady Avice Garth," Reynolds heard a woman behind him say. "Who's the distinguished foreign-looking man with them? He looks worlds above this sort of thing."

"That's Lansberg, a millionaire and Heaven knows what besides," her companion replied. "They say Lady Avice is setting her cap at him. She and her family are poor as church mice and heavily in debt."

Both women in the box had a curiously deferential manner toward Lansberg, urging him to take a seat at the front. Presently he yielded with that aloof, calm way the inspector was beginning to know, and as the other man came into view Reynolds recognized him.

It was Dr. Tempest, the pathologist, and Reynolds's keen eyes noticed that Lansberg paid almost more attention to the doctor than to the ladies in his party.

The curtain rose on the opening numbers which were received with keen enthusiasm.

About a quarter of an hour later there was a strange keyed-up lull in the audience, the chorus divided to form an opening in the middle of the stage, limelights centered, and Laureen darted straight down, a radiant being so full of vitality that the chorus seemed as wax dummies.

Instantly there was a wild crash of applause, drowning the orchestra and preventing all stage action for some time. People stood, waved their programs and shouted, "Laureen, Laureen," disregarding cries of "Sit down."

Without hesitation Laureen raised one hand imperiously for silence, then, both arms akimbo, she leaned across the footlights.

"'Ush!" she said sternly.

There was a roar of laughter and then the house settled down.

Reynolds was amazed at the versatility of the girl. She could sing and dance, but his interest was not in those more ordinary talents. It was her character sketches and quick humor that fascinated him. Her extraordinary changes of voice, age, nationality, language, as in turn she was a Cockney flower-girl, an American tourist, a French tragedienne, an elderly English spinster alcoholically lively at a birthday party, an Italian street singer stabbed by her lover.

No wonder she could deceive him in her flat last night, past mistress as she was of every art of mimicry.

Inspector Reynolds's seat was at the end of the row, an aisle only between him and an exit door, over which the attendant had jerked a heavy velvet curtain when the performance began.

Suddenly, just before the interval, his eye caught a tremor of movement behind that curtain, which was almost facing the stage box on the opposite side of the theater. Presently the tips of a man's fingers stealthily drew aside the folds of the velvet, though the man's face was out of sight.

There was nothing abnormal in any one peeping through to get a glimpse of the stage. It might have been the attendant anxious to see how near the interval was, or some one searching for friends in the stalls.

But in a moment the curtain swayed back a little and he caught sight of a man's hand—a hand that lacked a thumb!

An unusual mutilation which sent Reynolds to his feet. For among the fingerprints that had been photographed in Laureen's dining room was the clear impress of a man's hand showing a stump where the thumb should have been. The photograph had been taken from the dining-room table beside the dead man.

The C. I. D. man made a swift dive across the passageway, but tripped over a cloak that was trailing from the seat in front of him.

That slight delay lost him his chance. When he snatched back the curtain there was nobody there.

Pushing open the exit door he found himself in the corridor, equally empty. On the left it ran down behind two boxes and ended in a cul-de-sac; the right side, up which Reynolds hurried, led round to the back of the auditorium.

Two attendants were there and the detective spoke to them.

"Seen a man just go out?"

"No, sir," both replied.

Reynolds's worried expression made one of them add: "Perhaps you'll find him in the bar, sir. Down there to the left."

The detective searched as directed with no result. There were four youngish men in the bar, laughing together, and not one had a mutilated hand.

He retraced his steps to the corridor and found himself behind the stage box which Lansberg occupied with his party. A roar of applause indicated that the first part of the revue was over and the intermission had begun.

For a moment the detective hesitated whether to knock and ask to speak to Lansberg when his attention was caught by a small iron door in the wall at the end of the corridor. He pulled, found it unfastened and opened it far enough to see that it gave on to a stone staircase.

"Come away from that door, sir, please," said an attendant from behind him.

Reynolds closed it carefully and turned round.

"I wanted a little air," he observed in conciliating tones. "Isn't it an exit door?"

"No, sir, the exit door is farther back. That's a private door leading to the dressing-rooms and greenroom."

"I see," the detective said thoughtfully. A door that led from the dressing-rooms to the front of the theater, while the stage-door was in a side alley!

Suddenly the door of the stage box opened and Lansberg and Dr. Tempest came out.

The two men showed amiable surprise at seeing the detective.

"Hello, Inspector," Lansberg greeted, "are you here to see the show or do you want me for anything?"

Reynolds smiled pleasantly.

"Both, sir, if you can spare me a moment."

Dr. Tempest broke in.

"I'll leave you to talk. Come along to the bar when you've finished, Inspector, and have a drink. Good show, isn't it?"

"Excellent, Doctor. Thank you, I'll join you in two minutes if I can."

The detective twisted round swiftly to Lansberg.

"Do you know a man with a missing thumb, Mr. Lansberg?" he asked.

Even in the half light of the corridor he could see Lansberg recoil and his mask-like face stiffen to severe lines.

"A missing thumb!" he repeated aghast.

"Yes, the right hand. It's a noticeable mutilation."

"Where have you seen this man?" Lansberg demanded agitatedly. "Not here?"

Reynolds nodded, perplexed. There was no mistake about Lansberg's grave concern.

"Hiding behind the curtain over the exit door opposite your box ten minutes ago," he explained definitely. "Who is he?"

"That I cannot tell you, Inspector. But if he's lucky he probably will be my executioner," Lansberg observed grimly. "He made two excellent efforts a year or so ago in Paris. This time he may succeed."

The inspector's eyes were watchful as he put his next questions.

"What has this man against you, sir? And what

makes you think he'll make a third attempt on your life? Please answer me clearly. I can't afford to waste a second longer."

"I can only imagine he wishes to steal certain valuable—" He paused and Reynolds fancied changed his word. "—articles that are in my possession. I can think of no other reason. I do not know his name, his business or his nationality. And I think he may again attempt my life because he has so far not succeeded in obtaining what he desired."

"You've not seen him lately?"

"Not for about a year."

Reynolds turned on his heel. "Thank you sir. I must be off at once."

A hurried search of the corridors and foyer proving hopeless, he telephoned for men to be sent to watch all exits and went back to the Yard, bewildered and annoyed at the new tangle.

That Lansberg was concealing much, he was sure. But he was equally sure that Lansberg was acting within his rights and knew the limits of the detective's power to question him.

Well, Reynolds decided, Lansberg must be forced to open his hand. Some damaging clue might yet come to light.

"Jenkins," he called, when he arrived at his office, "I want another look at the photographs of the impression of a man's thumbless right hand."

A moment later he was staring at them—two excellent prints, each showing clearly four fingers, the palm and the stump of the thumb.

"Humph," grunted Reynolds. "Got any news?"

"Yes. Spencer—that Chelsea artist—has gone to Paris. Left no address, his caretaker says."

"I'll start on him to-morrow. Had no time to-day," grunted the inspector. "Anything else?"

"Yes. There's a hotel clerk waiting to see you. He thinks he handed over that Valerie letter this afternoon."

"What!" the detective roared. "Show him in at once."

Reynolds could scarcely wait for the man whom Jenkins ushered in.

"Tell me your story as precisely as you can," he urged.

"Right, sir. I'm one of the clerks in the mail department at the Hotel Imperial," the man began. "I read in the Evening News at seven to-night that you wished immediate information concerning a letter, so directly I was off duty I came along here."

"I've already taken his name and address, sir, to save time," Jenkins interposed.

"This afternoon at three twenty-five or three thirty," the clerk continued, "an elderly lady asked if I had any letters for Miss Valerie Baird."

"Baird!" exclaimed Reynolds with triumph. "Yes, go on."

"She showed me her room ticket, number four twenty, otherwise I should have asked her for it or for her key."

"What's the reason?"

"Hundreds of people began using our letter bureau as a *poste restante*, so the only way we could reserve it for hotel residents was by making that rule."

Reynolds nodded.

"Well," the man continued, "I looked through the file and there was nothing for her. She seemed anxious and disappointed so I told her to wait while I looked through the mail that had just come in. That's how I fixed the time as three twenty-five or three thirty: the mail arrives at three fifteen."

The inspector rubbed his hands contentedly. This was the type of statement he reveled in, clear, matter-of-fact, concise.

"Excellent," he commented. "Take your time, and don't forget any trifling detail."

"I'll do my best, sir," promised the clerk. "The old lady thanked me. She seemed a patient soul of about seventy though I couldn't see much of her face because she had a drooping brim to her hat and a veil."

"How did you guess her age then?" asked the C. I. D. man.

"She had white hair at the sides and some showing at the back of her hat. Also she stooped like an elderly woman and had a thin quavering voice."

"Well, you sorted the letters?" prompted the inspector.

"Yes, sir, and I found one for the name she had given. A thickish white envelope addressed in big writing to Miss Valerie Baird, care of Hotel Imperial, London, W.1. I handed it to her and she thanked me again and went away."

Inspector Reynolds turned over his papers and found the envelope which the caretaker at Laureen's flat had drafted. He wrote out the address he now knew, compared it with the one Carter had reproduced from memory and showed it to Jenkins.

"Carter wasn't far out, you see," he commented. Then turning to the clerk:

"Can you possibly recall what this woman wore?"

"I thought it was a long dark coat, but was not *quite* sure. So I went at once to the reception clerk and he was positive the woman wore a dark brown coat, rather old-fashioned, a black hat and veil. Also he was sure she was round-shouldered or bent with age.

"Why didn't you bring him along?" asked Reynolds.

"He's on duty until midnight, sir, but you can verify this on the telephone. His name is Foster."

"Did you or Foster notice this woman's hands?" Reynolds questioned eagerly.

"I didn't, sir, but Foster is certain she signed the register with her gloves on. I couldn't bring the hotel register away—besides you can always see it there if you wish—but," he produced an envelope from his pocket and laid it on the table, "Foster and I made a tracing of her signature."

Reynolds scrutinized the slip of paper carefully.

"You and Foster are too intelligent for your jobs," he stated with an approving smile. "You ought to be in this line."

"Thank you, sir. But we've got to use our eyes where we are, too. This isn't so wonderful."

"Isn't it?" The detective cast a look at Jenkins. "We should be glad to have all our witnesses as intelligent, eh?"

"We should," Jenkins agreed with emphasis.

"Anything else you can remember?" Reynolds asked the clerk.

The telephone bell rang before the man could answer. Jenkins took up the receiver.

"A woman's just arrived from Bloomsbury: thinks she has some information concerning this

Valerie business," he announced to his chief.

"Tell them to send her up here immediately," the inspector ordered.

"Shall I go, sir?" the hotel clerk asked.

"No, no. I shall be glad to compare what this woman has to say with your story. Possibly she knows nothing at all. And now before she comes, have you thought of any other detail about this Valerie Baird?"

"It's only a trifle, sir, but Foster says he thinks there was a smear of red plaster or paint on the woman's sleeve. I didn't see it."

The door opened before he finished speaking and the inspector looked up to see a rather untidy, out-of-breath woman enter with Jenkins.

She was obviously ill at ease. The inspector tactfully offered her a chair and thanked her for coming, before beginning to question her.

Jenkins, always a master of method and time-saving, placed a slip giving the woman's name and address before his chief. The inspector read it carefully, found the woman more composed and began his work in easy tones.

"Now, Mrs. Hornett, will you tell me what you know of Miss Valerie Baird, please?"

The woman opened her eyes in astonishment.

"Why, that's what I'm here for you to tell me, sir," she said in a puzzled voice, "considering I've not set eyes on her since she went out at six o'clock last night. Told me she was going to *church*!" she added indignantly.

The inspector raised his eyebrows and gave a humorous glance at the hotel clerk and began again patiently. He knew this rambling type only too well.

"How came Miss Baird to be in your house, Mrs. Hornett?"

"Same way as all my other lodgers. I keep an apartment house and she took a room, fourth floor front, twelve days ago. Very little luggage she had, and a week's rent owing come Wednesday. I might have guessed!" She sighed heavily.

"Guessed what?" Reynolds demanded.

"I suppose she had no money and just walked out leaving her few things. And they're not worth much," Mrs. Hornett added with disgust.

"So as the old lady didn't return last night you looked through her luggage to-day," Reynolds remarked blandly.

"Well and what if I did, sir. I've been cheated that way before." Then, remembering his sentence, she added sharply, "But what do you mean about an *old* lady? I'm talking about Miss Baird."

The detective shot a warning glance at the hotel clerk, who had started at the woman's last remark.

"Ah," he said, "that was just a slip of mine. About how old should you say this Miss Baird was, Mrs. Hornett?"

She looked at him a little suspiciously. She hadn't come here at ten o'clock of the night for this detective to make fun of her, she decided.

"I don't know what age *your* Miss Baird was," she said heavily, "but Miss Valerie Baird who took my room and walked out last night to go to church, so she said, was not a day more than twenty-four. If that!"

"Thank you, Mrs. Hornett. That's a great help to me," commended Reynolds graciously. "Please describe her."

"Thin, pale, fair, blue eyes, medium height or a bit shorter, dressed nearly always in navy blue or black and hadn't got much else so far as I could see.

"What did she do for a living?"

"Well, sir, she was very reserved and stand-offish if I ever asked her a few questions," Mrs. Hornett bridled at the memory of being rebuffed by her lodger, "but I saw a lot of drawings of dresses done in ink in her suit—I mean, in her room."

"Did she receive any correspondence?"

"Never saw a letter and I see all that come to the house."

"I'll bet you do," said Reynolds to himself.

"Any visitors?" he asked aloud.

"None till Saturday night—day before yesterday," she added importantly. "Some girl called to see her but Miss Baird was out."

"Did you answer the bell?"

"Certainly not," Mrs. Hornett replied. "I've a servant to do that, but I heard voices and went up immediately."

"What did this girl wear? I'm sure you've a good memory for a lady's clothes, Mrs. Hornett," said Reynolds, hoping flattery would help a little.

"There wasn't much to remember, sir. A small black hat and a black cape. It was about half past nine and nearly dark. I couldn't see her face. She'd had her answer from my servant and was turning to go down the steps as I came."

"Did you notice her hands or feet?" the inspector asked.

"No, I didn't. Well, as I was saying when you interrupted me, there was that girl came Saturday night, and this afternoon some old lady called to see her."

Reynolds's eyes glinted with excitement, but he asked casually:

"Did she give her name?"

Mrs. Hornett shook her head.

"She said she was only in town for the day and I was to give Miss Baird her love and say it was her old governess who had called."

"Did you happen to mention Miss Baird's surprising absence since the night before?"

"Yes, I mentioned it," she replied, "and the old soul seemed quite upset at first. Then she said probably Miss Baird had unexpectedly stayed the night with friends. Do you know where she is, sir?"

"Not at the moment," the inspector admitted. "Can you describe this old lady's appearance?"

"Black hat, mushroom brim, and veil, dark brown coat, out of date. White hair, very stooping shoulders, shaky old person."

A long brown coat! Reynolds reflected to himself.

"Sounds like the same woman, eh?" he said in an undertone to the hotel clerk, who had listened to the conversation with the deepest interest.

"It certainly does, sir," he replied emphatically.

"Well, I think that's all for to-night, Mrs. Hornett, thank you. Directly I have news of Miss Baird I'll let you know. Meanwhile, lock her room up. I shall come along to-morrow and examine it, so don't touch or remove anything," he warned her. "Good night."

She rose, offended at his warning, and smoothed the folds out of her coat.

"Drat that paint," she said softly, rubbing a piece of the cloth.

Reynolds's head shot up, alertly.

"Paint?" he demanded. "Where?"

The woman pointed to her coat where a red mark showed.

"Off my railings. They were only painted this morning, and I came out in such a hurry—"

The inspector signaled to Jenkins to get her away, his mind intent on linking up details rapidly.

"And Foster saw red paint on the coat of the old lady who called for that letter to-day?" he demanded of the hotel clerk.

"Yes, sir."

"Thank you. Good night," said Reynolds absently.

For suddenly he remembered where he had seen a brown coat on an old lady, a coat that had had a red mark on the shoulder.

Laureen had worn it in her impersonation of the inebriated elderly spinster on the stage that night!

XI. THE MYSTERIOUS VOICE

THE next morning, Tuesday, found Inspector Reynolds in his office at nine as usual. Nearly an hour before that, however, he had paid an early call in Bloomsbury, to the surprise of an indignant Mrs. Hornett.

A thorough inspection of her lodger's modest belongings had revealed little except that Valerie Baird had left no clue to her identity there. Not one of her simple garments bore any initial, not even a laundry mark with the inevitable red cotton. There were no letters, no papers. Only a few half-finished pen and ink sketches of frocks, executed with the fineness of an engraving.

These Reynolds took away with him, after again locking the door and instructing Mrs. Hornett to open it for no one but himself or its owner.

"Telephone me at once," he ordered, "if Miss Baird returns, and say nothing to her of my visit."

"What's she been up to?" questioned the landlady curiously after giving the required promise.

"We have no reason to think she has been 'up to' anything, madam," Reynolds replied as he left the house.

At the Yard he learned that Bertha's statements had been verified as to the time of her arrival at Clapham on the Sunday night; that the porters and waiters at Lansberg's club agreed he had arrived, dined and left there at the hours he had said.

"What about those ashes from Miss Laureen's

flat? Had them examined?" he asked Jenkins.

"Yes. Paper undoubtedly had been burnt, but there wasn't a vestige of it left. The cigarette stubs corresponded to the kind Lansberg used, and others that were found in her cigarette-box."

Reynolds frowned. Another dead end, he grunted to himself.

"Show me the contents of Delmond's pockets again, Jenkins."

A little despondently the C. I. D. man turned over the articles which Jenkins spread before him. An ordinary penknife, two stubs of pencils, three Treasury notes and some odd silver, four small keys on a ring, a cheap wrist-watch and a colored silk handkerchief.

There was no pocket-book or letters of any kind; only a plain crumpled half sheet of note-paper such as might have been torn from a letter. Thick pale blue paper of an expensive make.

Reynolds smoothed it and held it up to the light.

"Hand-made," he mused. "Might be possible to trace it."

Jenkins preened himself.

"I've already done so, sir," he remarked nonchalantly.

"Eh!" Reynolds sat forward abruptly. "Where?"

"In Miss Laureen's flat. I found three notes in her bureau, asking her to dinner or luncheon, all written on this paper. Also I found out she often stays the night with this girl—they're great friends. Laureen even leaves some of her clothes there so that she need not bother with a dressing-case each time."

"What's the girl's name and address?" demanded

Reynolds.

"Lady Avice Garth, Warnham House, Curzon Street," the man replied, handing the chief the written address, together with the notes he had found in Laureen's bureau.

Reynolds drummed his fingers on the desk a moment, thinking hard. Then he reached for the telephone book.

"Mayfair five eight X two," Jenkins said quietly.

The inspector smiled.

"Bright lad," he said, as he picked up the instrument and repeated the number.

"Is that Warnham House? Good. I want to speak to Lady Avice Garth, please. I'm Inspector Reynolds of Scotland Yard," he said over the wire. He listened to the reply with a grim expression.

"Did she give any address or reason for this sudden journey?" he asked.

Presently he hung up the receiver and stared blankly at Jenkins.

"Lady Avice has just left for Paris, the butler says. He doesn't know the reason but says her ladyship usually stays at the Continental and only took a dressing-bag, so evidently doesn't mean to stay long."

"That makes two of them who have had a sudden desire for gay Paree," announced Jenkins. "Spencer went yesterday morning, you remember, sir."

The inspector's lips tightened.

"Ring up Croydon and book me a seat by aeroplane as soon as you can. I've a fancy to make a third who'll pay a visit to Paris. With luck I can get there in time to meet her train."

"Do you know her by sight?" Jenkins asked in

surprise.

Reynolds nodded.

"She and her aunt were in Lansberg's box at the theater last night. I'll know her again easily."

"Yes, she lives with her aunt, the Countess of Warnham, and how they keep that establishment going is a mystery. I learned they're in very low water financially."

"Well, among other things, I hope to find out how they manage it," announced the detective firmly. "Get through to Croydon as quick as you can. Come in," he called, hearing a knock on the door.

Dr. Tempest put his head inside.

"Good morning, Inspector. Am I disturbing you?"

Reynolds beamed amiably.

"Not a bit, Doctor. Come in. I'm off to Paris in an hour or two."

The doctor sat down and filled his pipe.

"Indeed," he remarked. "A flying visit?"

"In every sense of the word," the detective responded with a touch of pride in what was to him an adventure.

Dr. Tempest glanced through the window at the cloudless sky.

"You'll have a good trip. I almost envy you. The inquest on Delmond is at ten thirty this morning, I hear. Will you be there?"

The inspector nodded.

"Only formal evidence will be given, and there will be an adjournment, of course. I shan't be needed more than ten minutes. It won't delay you long either."

"Good. By the way, Inspector, you didn't join me for that drink in the theater bar last night."

Reynolds blew out a cloud of smoke and leaned back in his chair with a tired sigh.

"No, I had to rush off directly I'd seen Lansberg. I say, Doctor, what do you know about that man?"

"Lansberg? Much less than you, I'm afraid, Inspector. I've met him twice casually before seeing him in Miss Laureen's flat the night before last."

"I didn't know that. You met there, I thought, as strangers."

Dr. Tempest smiled quizzically. He had a charming easy manner and cultured voice that Reynolds at times tried to imitate.

"It seemed scarcely the moment to remind Mr. Lansberg that he and I had twice been fellow guests at dinner parties and had exchanged a few commonplaces. I was in an official capacity at the flat as a doctor investigating the cause of death."

"You were quite right, Doctor, of course," agreed the detective hastily. Nobody loved the delicacy of etiquette more than he.

"I was even surprised when Lansberg rang me up yesterday," the doctor went on, "inviting me to join his party in the stage box last night and afterward have supper with them. Laureen was there after the show. By gad, that girl's clever!"

"She is," Reynolds avowed with bitter emphasis. "Do you mind telling me if you knew her before or anything about her."

The doctor laughed.

"My dear chap, ask me anything you like. I met her for the first time on Sunday night, June thirtieth, or rather one thirty A.M. Monday, July first, to be precise, in her flat. You were badgering her like the brute you are."

The detective grinned.

"And," continued the doctor, "seeing her over-strung condition, I warned you. As it happens, all is well. She was in marvelous spirits after the theater last night."

"I can believe that," Reynolds thought.

"Oh, I say, Doctor," he asked, "what sort of a girl is Lady Avice Garth? I hear she's a friend of Laureen's."

"They're great friends, I believe," supplemented the doctor. "I was introduced to her and her aunt last night and found them both intelligent and amusing. Lady Avice has a fearless personality, chooses her friends as she pleases and sticks to them."

"I've just heard she's gone abroad this morning," remarked Reynolds. "Did she happen to mention it last night?"

"Gone abroad?" Tempest raised his eyebrows. "Far from saying so last night I overheard her telling Laureen to be sure to come to tea with her this afternoon."

"Is that so?" the inspector observed indifferently, tapping out his pipe. "No fresh details about the post-mortem on Leslie Delmond, I suppose, Doctor?"

The pathologist shook his head, his expression at once grave.

"Nothing since my report, signed by my colleague and myself. Death by chloroform which could not have been self-administered. Delmond's heart was pretty groggy, so it probably took less than half a pint to kill him. An extraordinary murder," he mused. "What do you make of it, Inspector?"

"Rather early yet to answer that," said Reynolds. "It was good of you to come along with me on Sunday night, Doctor. One doesn't often get the services of a distinguished pathologist on such a case," he added pompously.

Dr. Tempest's thin, serious face lighted with amusement at the inspector's deferential remark.

"It's not often we poor post-mortem individuals get the chance of seeing the *mise en scene*. I'm glad I called in here on Sunday night. Good luck to your trip. You're really very likeable when you're not cross-examining, you know," he bantered.

Dr. Tempest's post of assistant pathologist to Scotland Yard often drew him there on business. Frequently he had been present at Inspector Reynolds's examinations of witnesses and nearly always objected to what he considered a lack of humane treatment. But he was not a detective.

Jenkins entered as the doctor went out.

"I've fixed you up, sir. Car will be here at noon. I'll see your bag is put in. You'll get to Paris in plenty of time to meet the boat train."

The inspector nodded his thanks and handed the man a written list of inquiries to be made. Then he urged:

"And particularly I want Lansberg's laundry found and his dress shirts that were sent this week looked at. You understand?"

Jenkins nodded. The inspector picked up the telephone again and gave the number of his home address.

"That you, Agnes? I'm off to France for a day or two. Starting in an hour. . . . Yes, I've all I need here in my bag. . . . You've had a wire from whom? . . . Oh, Bill? . . . When did his boat get in? . . . Well, make him stay over Sunday, then. . . . Oh, I'll be back by

Thursday probably. . . . Good-by, my dear."

He had only just replaced the receiver when the bell tinkled.

"Hello!" he replied. "Who? . . . Of course I've got time," he snapped over the wire. "Send her up immediately."

A constable presently ushered in a nervous-looking girl of about twenty-four or five, who was obviously in a condition bordering on panic.

Inspector Reynolds knew the symptoms quite well. A witness had something to tell that might be dangerous to conceal, yet also realized that the revelation might be prejudicial to her reputation or position.

He glanced at his watch anxiously. These cases often took time to deal with. "Wrigglers" he dubbed them.

"Sit down, please, Miss —" he looked up questioningly.

"Perring. May Perring." She sat down timidly, her eyes lowered.

"You're a telephone operator, I hear," Reynolds began in conversational tones, "employed at the exchange which connects Beresford Street and therefore Miss Laureen's flat." So much he had learned on the telephone a moment before.

The girl swallowed.

"Yes, sir. I was on duty Sunday night from four until ten thirty."

The inspector bent across his desk.

"What are you worried about?" he asked in kindly fashion.

She raised her anxious face and hesitated a moment.

"Because, sir, we have no right to listen to conversations when we connect up, and if I tell you, I may lose my job. And I can't afford to be out of work."

Reynolds smiled reassuringly.

"Miss Perring, if, as I think possible, your information proves valuable to me, I'll promise you shall not lose your job because you were plucky enough to come here and tell the truth. And if your evidence is useless, nobody shall be a penny the wiser. Does that console you?"

The girl sighed with relief.

"Yes, sir, thank you. Sunday evening is usually rather dull in the office and I'm afraid Miss Laureen's telephone calls always interest us—me," she substituted loyally.

Seeing the inspector's bewilderment she added:

"You see, sir, she's such a popular actress and all sorts of interesting people put calls through to her and when there's time I love to hear what is said. We're all crazy about her in the office and she's so clever and witty on the telephone."

"Know the names of any of these callers, Miss Perring?"

"Several, sir. But of course Laureen—everybody calls her that—has dozens of strangers, men, ring her up and oh! how she snaps at them when they invite her out."

"I'm beginning to understand why you want to listen in," the inspector smiled. "What calls went through on Sunday?"

"The maid replied each time," the telephone clerk said. "She said her mistress was out or engaged, to every call."

"That certainly was tiresome," agreed Reynolds. "There was a call at eight thirty P. M., wasn't there?"

The girl referred to a piece of paper. "From a Miss Gilbert in a call box in Piccadilly, ordering some shoes to be taken to a certain address and saying the maid was to sleep out as Laureen would not be back that night."

"Could you recognize that voice again, Miss Perring?"

The girl's eyes opened with astonishment. "Why, of course, sir. We get to know voices like you know faces. This was easily remembered: high and clear and—queer, somehow."

"Ever heard Miss Gilbert's voice since?" the inspector inquired.

"No, sir," replied the telephone girl promptly. "Never since those two calls."

Reynolds looked up quickly.

"*Two* calls?"

"Yes, sir, that's why I came here. Miss Gilbert gave the message from Piccadilly Circus at eight thirty saying the maid was to go out and leave this parcel at ten P.M. at Chelsea where her mistress would be. So it seemed strange that when at nine fifty a Mr. Spencer rang up Laureen's flat this Miss Gilbert's voice should answer, this time, and say her mistress had already started for the studio!"

Inspector Reynolds felt a pulse of excitement race through him.

"You're quite sure it was the same voice that first spoke from Piccadilly and then spoke from Miss Laureen's flat?" he asked eagerly.

"Quite sure," the girl replied. "When I read of the man found dead there I thought it was a woman who had telephoned first to get the maid away and then had gone there to burgle the flat with some man who died suddenly."

"Do you happen to remember why this Mr. Spencer called up Laureen?"

The girl nodded.

"Yes, he wanted to know if he could come and fetch her. He adores her and is always ringing her up.

The detective rose.

"Your evidence is very valuable, Miss Perring," he assured her. "Don't worry about the consequences *this* time. I'll let you know if I need you again. Good morning."

"Two calls in the same voice and one of them from Laureen's flat," he repeated to himself as he hurried off to-the inquest. "And Laureen is a marvelous mimic! She left the restaurant at eight twenty-five P.M. I wonder . . ."

XII. THE MAIMED HAND

MRS. DE GROOT glanced restlessly at her diamond wrist-watch and for the sixth time that afternoon compared it with the ornate clock on the mantelpiece, which at that moment chimed the hour. She counted its strokes eagerly. Five o'clock at last!

"Therese," she called to her maid.

A serious-faced, neatly clad Frenchwoman of about thirty five came from the adjoining bedroom at her mistress's summons.

"Yes, madame."

Mrs. de Groot spoke irritably:

"Lady Avice ought to be here any moment now. This room's insufferably hot. Open the windows or something, and do try to make the place look a little less ghastly. Push those hideous vases in a cupboard."

Mrs. de Groot glared round at the offending red plush and gilt furnishings. Her suite of rooms was in one of the most expensive hotels in Paris, and, she reflected, evidently the only taste its designer had was in his mouth. She flung herself back on the chaise-longue impatiently.

Therese opened a window, started an electric fan and deftly placed bowls of lilies in place of the ugly vases she put away.

"Shall I ring for tea, madame, or will you wait for her ladyship?"

"I'll wait until she comes," Mrs. de Groot

answered.

She pressed her forehead with thick heavily jeweled fingers. "My headache is worse. Give me another aspirin and some eau de Cologne."

Therese obeyed and brushed her mistress's shingled hair that had been rumpled by the cushions on which she had been tossing. She was a faithful maid who knew and liked her mistress and her duties, but she sighed inwardly as she looked down at the squat figure and clumsy features of her lady. Not even the exquisite negligee Mrs. de Groot was wearing, nor all the artifices of cosmetic delicately and skilfully applied, could turn this ugly duckling into a swan.

Mrs. de Groot smiled good-naturedly as the maid dusted a powder-puff lightly across her face.

"That will do, thank you, Therese. I look a hag and feel a wreck to-day, and touching me up won't hide the facts. I'm forty-five and that's too old for these all-night parties. Got back here at five this morning, didn't I?"

"Half past five, madame," corrected the maid.

"Where are the English papers?" demanded her mistress, turning over a pile of journals beside her. "I don't see the Continental Daily Mail either."

Therese made some confused excuse about sending for them and left the room.

The widow of an American "tobacco king," Mrs. de Groot found existence more agreeable in Europe, and passed her life scouring the fashionable "season" resorts in search of gaiety.

It was on the Riviera four years ago, in a Nice hotel, that she had met Lady Avice Garth. At first Mrs. de Groot's love of a title had led her to court the girl's society, but as she grew to know her, the wealthy American found in Avice a true generous heartedness and loved her.

"Another of Avice's weird friends," the girl's circle had said. But Avice had recognized a certain pathos in this lonely rich woman and the two had become warm friends.

There was a quick double knock on the outer door of Mrs. de Groot's suite, and Therese went hurriedly to open it, closing the sitting-room door carefully behind her.

A tall, slim, dark-haired girl entered the little hall and spoke in rapid French to the maid.

"You had the telegram I sent to-you as well as the one to Mrs. de Groot, Therese?" she questioned anxiously.

"Yes, my lady, and I managed to keep the English papers out of sight as you ordered. My mistress was delighted to know you were coming. May I take your wrap?"

The girl slipped her arms from the loose light traveling coat she wore, and stood as one accustomed to such service, while the maid smoothed out a crease from her frock.

She thanked the maid with a gesture.

"Where is Mrs. de Groot?"

"In here, my lady. She had a late night and has a bad headache."

Therese opened the sitting room door and announced with pride, "Lady Avice Garth."

Mrs. de Groot held out her arms.

"Avice, you're an angel to come over and see me in this dreadful heat wave. I was tickled to death to get your wire this morning, my dear."

The girl kissed her warmly, sat down on the couch beside her, regarding her with a serious face.

Something in the girl's grave expression warned the older woman of trouble.

"Is anything wrong?"

Avice nodded; and as if to gain time, took her hat off and smoothed her hair back with her slender ringless hand.

Mrs. de Groot squeezed the girl's arm affectionately.

"Tony?" she questioned. And as Avice did not reply, she went on, "Well, whatever it is, you know you can count on me to the last ditch."

The girl turned to her with troubled eyes.

"Mary, what I'm going to say will hurt you. It's —it's about Leslie Delmond."

The older woman's lips parted in a startled gasp.

"Leslie!" she breathed. "Where is he? I've not seen him since—he left me."

Avice Garth took her friend's hands in hers and held them tightly as if she would impart courage to the woman on whom she was going to inflict suffering by her news.

"Try to be plucky, Mary dear. Leslie Delmond is dead."

The color drained from Mrs. de Groot's face, leaving the patches of rouge standing out.

"Leslie—dead," she repeated blankly.

The girl looked at her pityingly, knowing the worst of the ordeal was to come for this poor foolish woman who had idolized and been discarded by this struggling film artist.

"Yes," Avice continued steadily. "Two nights ago, June thirtieth. It—it was chloroform caused his death, Mary."

The older woman raised her haggard face.

"Suicide?" she whispered.

The girl shook her head.

"He was murdered," she replied slowly.

"Murdered!" Mrs. de Groot closed her eyes and caught her breath in anguish.

Avice Garth waited until that first terrible moment of knowledge had passed, then she went on gently:

"He was found dead in Laureen's flat. She is a great friend of mine. You remember meeting her in Nice. I can't believe Delmond was there by Laureen's invitation," she added loyally. "No details are known yet but I couldn't let you learn it from the newspapers, so this morning I decided to come over to you."

Slow tears forced themselves from under Mary de Groot's eyelids. For a minute she was silent, then she caught Avice to her.

"Thank you, my dear. He was a worthless scoundrel, but—I loved him. He had me in his clutches because I cared so much."

"He had me in his clutches also in another way," the girl said bitterly. "Tony, too."

Suddenly Mrs. de Groot sat erect, horror-stricken.

"Avice," she gasped, "who murdered Leslie? Oh, my God, you can't mean—" She broke off as she saw the tragic fear on the girl's quivering face.

"I don't know what to think," the girl said. "Tony was in London on Sunday. Dick Spencer saw him and told me so: I was at a party in Dick's studio on Sunday. Oh, Mary, I'm terrified!"

The older woman slid her arm round the girl and held her comfortingly.

"My poor darling," she murmured. "And with all your own worry you took this journey to break this ghastly news tenderly to me."

"Not entirely for that," Avice replied honestly. "Dick Spencer told me that Tony was half mad with drink or rage or both, and said he was going back to Paris when he'd done his job! Dick laughed at him and said he looked more fit for an ambulance than a job. He begged Tony to go to the studio with him, but Tony rushed off. And that very night Leslie Delmond was murdered!"

The sight of the girl's suffering helped Mrs. de Groot to recover from her own shock.

"Avice dear, money can do a lot. We can find Tony and get him away. Do you know where he is in Paris?"

"He wrote me a month ago saying he couldn't bear to meet me—yet. I understood. But now I must find him. I think possibly he may be in his old rooms in— What was that?" the girl broke off. "I heard a creaking sound from over there." She pointed to a door behind her friend.

Mary de Groot twisted round to see what it was.

"No, dear, your nerves are on edge. It's probably the waiter bringing our tea."

"Where does that door lead to?" demanded Avice.

"Into the bedroom of the next suite, which is vacant. All the rooms seem to communicate in this hotel. I knew the woman there; she went away this morning."

Lady Avice stood up, not quite satisfied.

"I'm going to look for myself," she announced.

Crossing the room she pushed back the bolt fastening the door and pulled it open swiftly. In front of her—six inches away—was a second door which she tried to open but failed.

Which was just as well for Inspector Reynolds, who had only a moment before bolted it, and now was crouched closely on the other side, listening.

He had reached the Gare du Nord ten minutes before the boat train was due, after a wild half-hour in a Paris taxi—a journey he had found infinitely more of an adventure than his placid flight from Croydon.

At the train his task was made easier by the fact that Lady Avice Garth did not know him, so there was no need for concealment. There was not a large crowd of passengers. The tourist season had scarcely begun and the intense heat Paris was undergoing had kept away many casual visitors.

In a few minutes Inspector Reynolds had picked out the tall graceful figure of the girl he wanted. Her face appeared wan and pale and he thought there was a strained look in her eyes.

He had half expected that Spencer, whom he had never seen, would meet her, thereby allowing him to kill two birds with one stone. But giving her dressing bag to a porter, she had walked at once to a taxi, looking neither to right nor left.

Reynolds managed to brush past her as she was giving the address, and was lucky enough to hear it as he had hoped. On arrival at the hotel he walked into the hall immediately behind his quarry and straight to the bureau, where he heard her ask for Mrs. de Groot's suite.

"Number 54, madame, first floor. The lift is

there." The reception clerk waved a highly manicured hand vaguely and turned to Reynolds as the lady went in the direction indicated.

"I want a quiet room," the detective said. "First floor preferably. Perhaps you have a suite that would suit me."

The clerk referred to his chart.

"We have three suites vacant on the first floor, sir. You shall see them." He touched a bell and to the attendant who appeared said, "Show this gentleman numbers twenty-seven, thirty-eight and fifty-three."

Within a few minutes Reynolds had settled on Number 53, which was next to the suite occupied by Mrs. de Groot.

He locked himself in, and taking off his shoes, crept to the communicating door between the two suites, unbolted it and placed his ear against the panel of the second door in good time to hear virtually the beginning of the conversation, every nerve strained to the effort of missing no word that passed between the two women.

So now he had another hitherto unknown quantity to reckon with in "Tony," whoever he was. Maybe the fiancé, brother or lover of Lady Avice. And "Tony" had been in London mad with rage or drink on Sunday, and both Lady Avice and Spencer were alarmed.

Ah! thought the inspector, so that is why Spencer is in Paris. He has come over to get "Tony," who is probably a close friend, out of danger. No wonder Spencer and Lady Avice had become infected with this sudden fancy to come to France.

Reynolds was devoutly thankful that he had caught the same malady.

If he could only get hold of "Tony's" address! He blocked up one ear and forced the other even tighter against the communicating door in his keen anxiety to hear the address. And that pressure was his undoing. The door gave an ominous creak and Lady Avice stopped abruptly in the middle of the sentence that was most vital—for Inspector Reynolds.

Instantly he darted back and silently closed and bolted his door only a moment before the girl opened the other and tried his.

He held his breath as he crouched there with beating heart. Sick with disappointment he heard her shut the door and go back to her friend.

But they talked in undertones after that, and though he again ventured to open his door and repeat his former performance, the only phrase he heard was Mrs. de Groot insisting on her friend staying the night there.

Apparently Lady Avice agreed for he heard the American woman order Therese to get the bed prepared in the dressing-room.

Inspector Reynolds rubbed his chin. He was in for a dose of tiresome surveillance during which time he dared not leave his room to get food, dared not even smoke there.

Bitterly he regretted his office in Scotland Yard where, at a touch of the bell, he could despatch trained men to do his present detestable job. But generally he preferred to play a lone hand, with Jenkins as assistant. And his work had been such at the Yard that those in authority over him gave him a fairly loose rope.

Just then three things happened in quick succession in Mrs. de Groot's sitting-room—things which cheered the detective considerably.

Lady Avice asked if she could have a bath, which Reynolds thought would place her safely for half an hour.

Mrs. de Groot announced that they would have a light dinner sent up at seven o'clock and go out afterward.

The telephone bell rang and Mrs. de Groot, being called by her maid, answered:

"Yes, this is Mrs. de Groot speaking," the detective heard her say. "Who are you? . . . Well, that's the best news I've heard to-day. We were going to hunt you up after dinner. You'd better come along here at once and dine with us. Seven o'clock. My suite is Number 54 . . . Who do I mean by 'we'? . . . Oh, I forgot you didn't know Avice was here. . . . Lady Avice Garth," she repeated distinctly. "Yes, she's just arrived. Came to tell me the—the news. . . . Have you found him? . . . Oh, dear, well, we can't do anything by telephone. You come right along."

The detective heard her slam down the receiver and could guess she had gone into the bedroom to tell Lady Avice. He got up from his cramped position and stretched himself.

In the corridor, not far from his door and at the other side of the lift, was an alcove with big chairs. He would order some sandwiches to be brought there at once and keep his eye on Mrs. de Groot's suite for the coming visitor. He expected Spencer, but hoped for "Tony."

Settled in a comfortable armchair in a shaded corner of the alcove, his light meal concluded, Inspector Reynolds lighted a cigar, held a newspaper up to screen his face and gave himself up to patient waiting. He was not sorry for this interlude, for his future plan of action demanded careful thought.

There were many things he needed to ask Lady Avice. The half-sheet of her note-paper found in the dead man's pocket and the conversation he had just overheard, proved she had known Leslie Delmond. Probably knew where he had been staying in London.

Should he wait until Mrs. de Groot's guest arrived, then boldly knock at their door and demand an interview? In which case, he feared, they might deny any knowledge of the mysterious "Tony." Or should he to-night follow Mrs. de Groot, Lady Avice and the man—probably Spencer?

He had just decided on this course when the lift gates opened and the attendant conducted a gentleman along the corridor to Number 54.

Reynolds could not see the man's face, but guessed him to be about thirty years of age. The attendant knocked at the door and then went farther along the corridor and around a corner, leaving the lift gates open. Presently Mrs. de Groot's maid opened the door and the visitor entered.

There was nothing to be done for an hour and Reynolds was continuing his mental resume when some sixth sense made him aware he was no longer alone in the corridor.

The lift gates were still wide open but creeping up the stairs was a man in a light dust coat carrying a suitcase. He turned and walked stealthily to Mrs. de Groot's suite, stooped, and putting his hand to his ear, listened at the door.

The detective inadvertently let the newspaper he held crackle as he tried to rise silently.

The man heard it, turned, and in a second divined that he was being watched. He made a sudden dive for the lift, which was nearer him than it was to the detective, slammed the gates and let it glide upward.

Reynolds dashed for the stairs which circled round the lift, watching as he ran to see at which floor the car stopped.

At the sixth floor! He heard the gates open as he raced up two steps at a time. Half-way up the sixth flight he heard the gates crash again, and saw the lift shoot down past him to the ground, leaving him more angry than he had been for years. Fooled at his age, he growled to himself, by the simplest of tricks!

Rapidly he ran down to the crowded hall, asking two or three porters if they had seen a man in a light dust coat go out. A hopeless question, he knew, as he received negative replies from each person.

Furious and baffled, he went back to his post in the alcove, his interest in Mrs. de Groot's two visitors lessened by the incident of the last few minutes.

For as the man in the dust coat had put his hand to his ear Reynolds had seen that it lacked a thumb!

XIII. ESCAPE!

THE girl opened her eyes dazedly, blinked at the sunlight that peeped through cracks of the curtained window, and lapsed into queer dreams again.

Presently she was aware of voices near.

"Is she conscious yet, nurse?" some one was saying.

"No, she hasn't moved," was the answer.

The girl could feel the bedclothes being adjusted round her, but had no wish to see who was doing it. In a few moments her heavy lids lifted again and, with clearer consciousness, she stared at the screens round her bed, realizing that she must be in a hospital. On the far side of the screen she heard a continuous murmur of conversation, probably visitors to the other patients.

Bit by bit she tried to piece things together. She remembered attempting to cross the road hurriedly in front of a car that morning, and had felt a terrible blow. It must be afternoon, now, hours since her accident. Or was it even the next day? If only she could find out!

There was a bandage round her head which throbbed painfully, some plaster on her cheek, and her right shoulder felt stiff and sore. Gently she tried each limb in turn, trying to assess the damage, raised her head from the pillow and laid it back languidly again. No bones were broken, she was sure. Apparently the car had hit her shoulder,

knocking her down, and she had cut her cheek and
been stunned in the fall.

Who had brought her here, she wondered?
Probably the people whose car had caused the
accident. She closed her eyes in case any one should
look in on her and strained every nerve to hear what
was being said to the patient on the other side of the
screen. At all costs she must lie still until she could
find out more and decide what to do. Suppose they
demanded her name and an account of her accident
was made public!

The visitor on the other side of the screen was
evidently reading aloud from a newspaper. Then as a
light firm step sounded on the wooden floor she
heard a whining voice—presumably that of the
patient in the next bed—ask:

"How's that pore young girl, nurse? She's been
moaning a lot."

"Just the same, Mrs. Rookes," replied the crisp
tones of the nurse.

"Found out her name and address yet?" By
diligent listening Mrs. Rookes had overheard the
nurse inform Sister that there was nothing to
indicate who the unconscious girl was. "Her friends
must be anxious about her," Mrs. Rookes added
mournfully.

"They'll know in good time," responded the
nurse. "Don't let me find that your visitors have
brought you in ham sandwiches this time, Mrs.
Rookes, or I shall have to report it," she warned as
she walked on through the ward.

Mrs. Rookes chuckled, supremely conscious of a
greasy packet now reposing snugly under her pillow.

"Crool hard they are here. No feelin' at all," she

remarked to her visitor. "Did you bring me that shawl you promised?"

"Hadn't time to fetch it to-day. I'll bring it in on Sunday," replied her friend.

The girl behind the screens caught at the remark. "Bring it in on Sunday." Hospital visiting days were usually twice a week, she knew, so that probably meant to-day was Wednesday or Thursday. And she had been knocked down on Monday, at least two days ago!

"Go on reading, dearie," said Mrs. Rookes. "Is there any more about that Beresford Street flat murder? That actress knows something about it, I'll bet. Actresses are never up to much good," she sniffed.

"Beresford Street." The name roused some link of memory in the girl. Laureen lived in that street, and was an actress! But of course other actresses might live in the same street, she reflected.

"Well," went on Mrs. Rookes's friend obligingly, picking out the most thrilling bits, "I think this other girl did it. The one who bolted from her lodgings in Bloomsbury on Sunday night and hasn't been back since."

"What was the name of the man she murdered?" asked Mrs. Rookes.

"Leslie Delmond, a film artist. Between you and me," the friend answered, reconstructing the drama, "I believe he was potty on this Laureen and went to her flat to see her. This other girl followed and murdered him. He'd probably cast her off," she added unctuously.

"What do the papers say about her?" demanded Mrs. Rookes, impressed but cautious in passing judgment.

"They're all demanding news of this Valerie Somebody." Her visitor searched down the columns. "Valerie Baird," she announced. "They've found her landlady and they'll scour London until they get this girl."

"The police'll find her all right for sure," Mrs. Rookes said contentedly, as a bell thundered in the corridor. "That's four o'clock. You must go. Don't forget my shawl, and give my love to Nellie. Goodby."

Behind the screen the girl lay trembling, bathed in a cold perspiration. Leslie Delmond murdered in Laureen's flat and all London being searched to find Valerie! Oh, if she could only see that newspaper, learn more about it all. What was she to do, she thought distractedly.

Perhaps even now the police knew where she was and were waiting to pounce directly she came round. She must lie perfectly still, pretend to be semi-conscious, and moan a little as Mrs. Rookes said she had been doing.

Were her clothes here? Stealthily she raised the lid of the locker and was comforted to see them folded inside. How soon would she be strong enough to stand? And how could she steal away from this place where for her lurked that ghastly fear of detection, of arrest, of a possible trial for murder?

Yes, she must escape, plan it cunningly and watch her chance. For the moment she must concentrate all her will-power on getting well enough to slip away, given the opportunity.

Would they give her any food? she asked herself. A hysterical desire came over her for Mrs. Rookes's ham sandwiches, now being slipped into that lady's locker she judged by the crackling of paper. The locker was quite close—she could see the edge of it as she lay—and if only Mrs. Rookes went to sleep before eating the sandwiches Valerie vowed desperately she would have a shot at securing them that night.

She dozed off and awoke to find some liquid, broth she fancied, being administered from a feeding cup.

Allowing her eyes to open half-way for a second she saw a young, fresh-faced nurse beside her, so intent on preventing the broth from being spilled that she did not observe the girl's swift glance. Evidently *she* didn't suspect her patient was fully conscious, Valerie decided, as the nurse covered her carefully and went away leaving the screen open a little at the foot.

Opposite Valerie's bed, which was against the wall on one side, was a pantry, and leading from that apparently was a back staircase, for at intervals through her half-closed eyes she could see nurses coming up or going down.

She determined to sleep now and wake about three in the morning to watch the routine as a guide for the moment when she could get free. She knew she would not physically be able to attempt it tonight. Even at the risk of being found out the next day, she must lie still.

Fortunately most of her luggage was in the cloakroom at Victoria. She had only taken suitcases to her room in Bloomsbury and, not trusting the inquisitive landlady, had never left any letters or papers there.

For a second her heart almost stopped beating as she remembered the cloak-room ticket.

Days ago she had ripped the lining of her handbag, slipped the cloak-room check inside and sewn up the slit carefully for fear of losing it. Had they discovered it in the hospital when they searched her things? Was her handbag in the locker with her clothes?

Well, she dared not look until the middle of the night when she hoped the staff would be considerably diminished and the patients asleep. Definitely she must rest now.

Just as she was becoming drowsy she heard the stealthy crackling of paper from the next bed. Mrs. Rookes getting ready to attack the sandwiches, Valerie thought angrily; and then almost smiled, for the nurse's quick step was heard coming along the ward and Mrs. Rookes with a muttered "Drat the woman" thrust the forbidden food in her locker.

Valerie woke at three o'clock to the sound of faint snoring. One shaded light burned at a table in the middle of the ward, and she could hear the scratching of a pen. Presently a nurse walked quietly down the ward, spoke softly to the writer at the table, and Valerie heard the reply:

"Yes, I'm coming now."

A moment later the night sister passed through the ward with a glance at each bed and went out.

Valerie sat up quickly, her heart beating fast, and opening her locker felt for her handbag. It was not there! Nearly sick with disappointment she twisted round and saw it underneath a towel on the top of the locker. With breathless eagerness she opened it and searched for the cloak-room ticket. To her joy she felt it safely at the side of her bag inside the lining. In the dim light she examined her face and head with her tiny mirror.

There was a huge purple bruise on her forehead and a slight scar at the side. Lifting the plaster a little she discovered a few scratches on one side of her face. She replaced her bag and sliding out of bed, moved the screen an inch or two to get at Mrs. Rookes's sandwiches from which she was thankful the crackling paper had been removed.

Sitting on the edge of her bed a trifle dizzily, she munched the thick sandwiches with a wary eye for the return of the nurse. There was one thing more to be accomplished before she settled down to the long twenty-four hours of pretended unconsciousness which must pass before she dared attempt flight. She *must* see where those stairs led from the pantry. Suppose they terminated at the floor below!

Staggering a little, she opened the screens and crept across the ward on bare feet.

The pantry contained cups and saucers and so on, and in a cupboard she found bread, butter and cake and a large jug of milk. With her mind on the necessity for gaining strength, she drank a large cup of milk and took a piece of cake to eat, if possible, during the long day ahead of her. A clock on the wall showed the hour to be three fifteen; a fact to be remembered in to-morrow's adventure.

Leaning over, she could see the well of the narrow stone staircase which, she decided, certainly went to the ground floor. She could do no more to-night.

Her head was swimming as she reached her bed, and hiding the cake in her locker, she lay down after

winding and setting the little wrist watch in her
handbag and hoping its ticking would not give her
away.

Carefully she timed the length of the night
sister's absence from the ward. Forty minutes! And
no other sound from the corridors outside. With luck
that would be the routine to-morrow night.

The long day passed more quickly than she had
dared hope. She slept through most of it, taking the
broth at intervals and trying to keep herself limp
and apparently helpless while being fed. The doctor's
visit was brief. He was exceptionally busy, she heard
him tell Sister, and seemed content with a report
that the patient was not yet fully conscious.

She awoke at three A.M. feeling much stronger,
and the pain in her head was bearable. Again the
nurse came in, spoke to the night sister, who
surveyed the ward and they went out.

Now for it, thought the girl. As swiftly as her
trembling fingers allowed, she dressed herself, took
off the bandage and plaster, and pulled her black felt
hat well down over her face.

Taking her shoes in her hand, she stole lightly
across the ward to the pantry. There she stopped a
second to select three newspapers from a pile—she
must read about what had happened in Laureen's
flat—folded them tightly and crept noiselessly down
the stone stairs.

Two flights lower she paused, terrified at the
sound of voices from a room near by, the door being
ajar. The night staff having a meal, perhaps.

She fled shakily down two more flights and
found herself in the hospital basement near the
furnaces, which in this summer weather were not

alight, otherwise she knew men would have been there on duty.

Stumbling weakly around, she at last found a door bolted on the inside, which when unfastened led to the foot of the area steps.

It took her some time to reach Charing Cross, as buses were infrequent. With the pretense of waiting for an early train she spent some hours on the platform, where she studied the newspapers, and afterward entered a near-by all-night café. Before nine o'clock she took a bus to Victoria, bought a thin black coat and long black scarf, and went to the cloak-room where she claimed a trunk and suitcase.

"Boat train, ma'am?" the porter questioned. "If so, better hurry up."

She nodded.

In the train, the morning papers beside her, she arranged her gauze scarf over her hat like a widow's veil and felt fairly secure from detection. At last she knew the day: it was Friday, July 5th.

From the suitcase she took her passport, thankful she had left it there and not taken it to her lodgings. Yes, there was nothing for her but flight and long months of terrible loneliness: a hunted creature, hiding until the chase had died down.

It was an ordeal which seemed the only way out of this impasse. For on opening the morning newspaper huge head-lines had met her eye.

WHERE IS
VALERIE?
Scotland Yard Finds
a Fresh Clue

Then followed an excellent description of her height, coloring and the clothes she had last been wearing.

XIV: ALADDIN'S CAVE

INSPECTOR REYNOLDS often laughingly said of Jenkins that he had a woman's eye for detail and the instincts of a burglar. However true that summing up of Jenkins's character was it would have been incomplete without adding his almost slavish adoration of his chief.

The inspector had the broad vision that could fathom motives. Jenkins, having no imaginative qualities, could concentrate intensively on the more trifling links in the chain, plodding through seemingly irrelevant masses of evidence in the hope of extracting one useful point to pass on to his beloved chief.

Directly Reynolds had left for Paris on this Tuesday after the brief opening of the inquest, Jenkins dealt patiently with various commissions and reports, and then gave himself up to an ambitious idea of his own that was rapidly developing into clarity. It was not the first time he had worked out a plan and succeeded in giving the inspector some pleasant surprise.

Jenkins couldn't forget a remark his chief had made about Lansberg.

"I'd give something to have a quiet hour alone in his rooms, Jenkins," he had confessed. "But it just can't be done. I've not enough against him to justify a search-warrant. He's a big man apparently, and not to be disturbed unnecessarily, I'm informed. All the same I'd like to know a lot more about him."

Jenkins's thoughts were interrupted by the telephone bell. Answering, he discovered its summons was from the detective who was trailing Lansberg.

"Lansberg," came the voice, "has just gone off in his Rolls. His secretary's with him. They've got golf-clubs and a black tin case. There was no taxi about so I couldn't follow, and anyhow their car would go too fast."

"Any idea where they are going?" Jenkins demanded.

"Crowborough. That's near Tunbridge Wells. What am I to do?" asked the man.

"Report here now, and pick him up on his return. I can easily phone the golf house later, and find out if he's been there. It's a pity, but you couldn't help it."

Crowborough and golf, Jenkins reflected with satisfaction! Lansberg couldn't get back for some hours.

A little later a young man, wearing horn-rimmed spectacles and carrying a small bag, rang the caretaker's bell in the basement of a block of flats. He pulled at the brim of his hat without raising it and smiled amiably at the buxom woman who opened the door.

"And phwat may ye be wantin'?" she demanded with a brogue that clearly indicated her origin.

"Shure and it's thinkin' we come from the same old counthry," responded the young man with as unmistakable an accent as her own.

"Waterford was me home and yours was not far away by your voice," replied the Irishwoman.

"Tipperary," the young man said with a sigh. "It's nice to hear a friendly voice in these foreign parts. Ah well, I mustn't be after wastin' your time, Mrs.—"

"Milligan," she supplied. "Me husband's Irish too, and a good enough man when he's not in drink. Can I be helpin' you in any way?"

The young man produced a note-book and pencil timidly.

"I'm workin' for a firm who are bringing out a new directory of this district. I've to be gettin' the names and addresses of all the tenants and an awful job it is," he confided, "for if you go to each flat most of the tenants are out, and if you go to the caretakers you get your head snapped off. They're not all like you, Mrs. Milligan."

She beamed at the compliment.

"Ye'll not be gettin' that treatment here. Come inside and I'll show ye the list of tenants in this house and you can copy it off quick. I've just finished me dinner and was makin' a cup of tea. Perhaps ye'll be joinin' me in one?" she invited hospitably as he followed her round a screen into the kitchen and sat down in a wicker chair which she pulled forward.

"I'll keep my hat on, ma'am, if you'll excuse me, as I've a bit of a chill on me," he explained. "And that reminds me," he added, fishing in his bag and producing a bottle, "a friend gave me this to-day for my cold. I think a dose of it would do us both good and be even better than a cup of tea. Help yourself," he laughed.

"Good whisky's the finest medicine in the world," she announced solemnly as she drew the cork and produced glasses. "There's the list of tenants, me boy; you get on and copy 'em out."

The young man wrote with amazing rapidity, passing brief comments occasionally while she sipped at her whisky.

"This Mr. Lansdown?" he asked. "Has he any family?"

"*Lansberg*," corrected the woman. "No, he's a bachelor, very rich; shure he's got all the first floor. Furnished like a palace too."

"Fancy that now," said the young man in an awed tone. "Lots of servants for certain?"

Mrs. Milligan shook her head and set down her empty glass.

"You're wrong. He's only got one really, a valet. A regular heathen and such a queer name he's got—Neron. Me and me husband do all the cleanin' there as Mr. Lansberg nearly always has his meals out. He's after going off in his motor to-day with his secretary to play golf."

The young man gazed at her admiringly as he refilled her tumbler generously.

"Shows how this gentleman must trust you," he murmured.

Mrs. Milligan sniffed complacently and picked up her full glass.

"Well, Milligan and me knows our work. Butler and parlor maid in the best Irish families we was before we came here. But as for trustin'—that heathen servant is always sneakin' round there of a mornin' when we're cleanin' the place."

"Shure and couldn't you do your work when he goes out?" suggested the young man. "Or perhaps he rarely leaves the flat."

Mrs. Milligan withdrew her lips reluctantly from

the tumbler.

"Oh, that Neron goes out every afternoon for hours," she asserted, "but me husband likes to get his work done in the mornin' and go off. He's gone to Brighton for the afternoon. That's why I'm alone. Good thing, too," she giggled nervously, "and me drinkin' all this fine whisky of yours."

"Suppose there was a fire or anything in this Mr. Lansberg's flat and his servant out," her guest said as he again tilted the bottle over her glass.

The Irishwoman's face assumed a pompous air.

"And haven't I got duplicate keys of all the flats in case of em—em," she suppressed a hiccough delicately and finished the word with care, "— emergency."

"I believe you're jokin'," chaffed the young man. But his eyes watched her keenly as she opened a small cupboard where hung rows of keys on hooks with a name over each.

"I'd take ye through the flats to prove it," she remarked indistinctly as she lurched back to her chair, "but I've got a bit of a headache and think I'll have forty winks."

"No, no, I don't want to see the flats, of course, Mrs. Milligan. You drink up and get a bit of rest while you can, and I'll be off to the next house and hope for as good luck as I've had here. Now one nice little drink to ould Ireland before I go and then off you go to bye-byes."

She smiled at him fondly over the rim of her glass.

"Ould Oireland!" she repeated fervently, "Ye might shut the door as you go out. I'm that sleepy!" And she closed her eyes.

The young man regarded her for a second, then opened the door to the area and slammed it, thoughtfully remaining on the inside behind the screen.

Jenkins waited there until Mrs. Milligan's heavy snoring assured him that he could move with safety. Then slipping a pair of cotton gloves on his hands he stole noiselessly across to the key cupboard in his rubber-soled shoes.

Outside the first-floor flat he pressed the bell several times without response. His heart was beating quickly as he inserted the key, entered the spacious entrance hall and stood listening.

Not a sound broke the silence save the ticking of a clock.

He made a hurried preliminary search through the apartment to make certain no one was there before beginning a methodical scrutiny of each room. Painstakingly he opened drawers and cupboards in what was evidently Mr. Lansberg's bedroom and dressing-room, turning over the linen.

In a smaller bedroom—the heathen servant's, he guessed—between the mattresses he found two things that sent a pleased glint to his eyes. He tucked them both into the handbag he carried and returned to the library.

There he made a tour of the room, memorizing every detail, glanced through some letters on the writing table and investigated the drawers and waste-paper basket.

On the desk was a case which he opened and shut swiftly as his fingers touched something soft inside and a faint smell came to his nose. His eyes narrowed speculatively as he saw a case on the wall and some tall rods in a corner. Then he gave his attention to the large old-fashioned safe. Jenkins knew as much about safes as most experts. This one had a combination lock, which his fingers twisted and swung, his ear pressed closely to it, listening for the faint almost indiscernible fall of the tumblers. The perspiration was standing on his forehead when at last the heavy door opened on well-oiled hinges.

The safe was more than four feet high, with shelves and drawers inside. These contained sealed documents which he could not unfasten and dared not take.

The shelves had black velvet coverings draped over some objects which could be seen bulging beneath them. He lifted up the cloths quickly and drew back with a gasp of surprise. The shelves were spread with jewels of an amazing kind.

Breathlessly he gazed upon magnificent tiaras blazing with huge stones, a pile of rings, at least two diamond necklaces, ropes of gleaming pearls and pendants set in strange design.

Was this the Aladdin's cave of a rich connoisseur or had he stumbled upon the hiding place of some super-thief? Half dazed, he regarded the astonishing collection but was afraid to touch them. This job was beyond him.

With a start, he heard a clock chime and decided it was wiser to go. Gently he pushed the door of the safe and strove to close it. Something prevented it from shutting, some unseen spring, perhaps. He struggled hard, feeling all round for the obstruction, but it obstinately resisted his efforts. The sweat was pouring down his face as he decided he must leave it open and get out quickly.

Picking up his bag he was walking toward the library door when there was a faint sound from the hall. Some one was putting a key in the lock!

Scrambling hurriedly behind the velvet curtains that concealed the huge doors, he flattened himself.

If he were seen by Lansberg or his servant, they would have even less mercy upon him than he would get from Inspector Reynolds, he knew.

It was not the first time he had made a burglarious trip and found undeniably useful information. But each time his chief had warned him of the risk he ran, a risk in which, if discovered, he would get no help from Scotland Yard.

Crouched there with every sense alert, he heard the entrance door open and close, and soft steps on the carpet in the hall. In an agony of fear he waited to find out whether they were coming to this room. After a tension that seemed to last hours he cautiously opened the library door an inch and peered into the hall. It was empty!

Gathering his courage he crept out and listened again. To his ears there came a faint grinding sound which at first puzzled him.

Then he recognized it as a coffee-mill. The heathen was evidently preparing coffee, Jenkins thought with relief, as he stepped warily along the hall. With trembling fingers he let himself out and inserting the key outside, closed the entrance door silently.

Mrs. Milligan was still snoring as he replaced the key.

XV. A NIGHT HUNT IN PARIS

MONEY plays a good speaking part in most civilized countries, but perhaps in France it has a louder voice than in many others. Inspector Reynolds remembered this fact with comfort as he felt the thick packet of thousand franc notes in his pocket-book.

For ten minutes, after the man with the missing thumb had eluded him in the hotel lift he gave himself up to bitterness as he sat in the alcove watching the door of Mrs. de Groot's suite.

Then he became galvanized into action, and his face resumed its usual blank mask.

Near his hand was a telephone. Still keeping his eye on the door of Number 54 he picked up the instrument and asked for the hotel manager.

"I want you," he said, "to send up at once to the alcove near my suite, Number 53, your most intelligent porter. Choose carefully. I may need his services for some hours. Don't send a boy; my business is important. I am willing to pay both the hotel and the man well if he can carry out my instructions."

The Gallic voice at the other end had almost a lilt of joy as it replied:

"Of course, monsieur! Immediately!"

Clients like this were indeed rare and refreshing fruit, the hotel manager reflected, as he proceeded to his task of selection.

In two or three minutes an alert young man stood at Reynolds's elbow reporting for action.

The inspector looked him up and down, asked him his name and a few ordinary questions in concise French, and was satisfied with the porter's swift interested replies.

"Good!" commented the inspector, handing him two thousand-franc notes. "Get these cables off at once. Send them yourself, Pierre. Do you understand English?"

The man's face gleamed to a smile as he replied in that language. "I was a clerk in a shipping office in London for three years after the war, sir. But when I got married my wife wanted to live in Paris where she was born."

"Right!" said Reynolds. "Now, after you've despatched the cables, call at a reliable garage and hire a small, high-powered closed car with a driver who knows his job. I don't want a breakdown. See there's plenty of petrol put in," he added, recalling a previous incident when he had lost his quarry through a car running out of fuel at a critical moment.

"I understand, monsieur. Have you dined?"

"Why do you ask that?"

"The manager indicated you may need me for some hours, monsieur. If you've not had dinner I could bring some food in the car, in case we have a long journey or a long wait."

Reynolds clapped his hand on the man's shoulder.

"Splendid!" he said approvingly. "You've not only got a brain, but it works. Bring enough for the chauffeur as well as ourselves, a bottle of wine, cigars and cigarettes." He studied his watch and glanced keenly at a tray which a waiter was carrying to Mrs. de Groot's suite. "I can give you not more than half an hour." He hesitated a second. "I'm from Scotland Yard. A big jewel theft is expected," he added briefly. "I want to follow another car to-night from this hotel to an unknown destination."

"In that case, monsieur, I will select a car as nearly resembling a taxi as possible. It will be less conspicuous. You will wish the driver to remain near the hotel entrance?"

Reynolds assented.

"Choose the best spot, Pierre, and report here to me."

He pored earnestly over a cross-word puzzle in the newspaper as the man vanished on his errands, in case any one from Mrs. de Groot's rooms remarked his presence in the alcove.

But save for the waiters, no one entered or came out of that suite until Pierre returned. Handing the inspector a list of his expenses and a pile of change, he announced that the car was waiting outside.

"I've changed into an ordinary suit, monsieur, lest my hotel uniform be noticed," Pierre remarked eagerly. It was evident the man not only intended to earn his money but was bringing to the task a vivid intelligence which Reynolds felt to be magnetic.

The inspector's mental barometer was rising. An hour before he had felt lonely and baffled. Now, with this bright-eyed young lieutenant beside him, he was keyed up, equal to any situation.

He gave the man a cigarette. Up to a point he must confide in Pierre if he wished to get his best assistance, he knew.

"Sit there and talk to me," he ordered. "And be ready for my signal. I'm tracking two ladies and a gentleman from Suite 54 in the hope that they will lead me to the man I want."

Pierre's dark eyes flashed with pleasure at the inspector's confidence. "I understand perfectly," he replied. "Also I promise to respect monsieur's trust in me. I will be back in one moment." He ran down the stairs and had only just returned to the inspector when there was a click of a door opening behind them and they heard Mrs. de Groot's voice instructing her maid not to wait up.

Reynolds did not dare to raise his head from the newspaper until they were at the lift. Then he ventured a keen glance.

Both ladies wore small hats well over their eyes: Lady Avice, tall and slender in her traveling wrap, Mrs. de Groot short and square-figured in a black coat with the collar turned up. Their companion was standing with his back toward the alcove and Reynolds could not see his face.

The instant the lift vanished Pierre and the inspector tore down the stairs and made for the car outside. As they entered it Mrs. de Groot and her friends came from the hotel and, ignoring the row of taxis, walked up the street.

"Tell the chauffeur to follow slowly," urged Reynolds in an agony of fear lest he miss his trio in the crowded streets. Pierre picked up the speaking-tube and gave swift instructions.

"He understands, monsieur," consoled Pierre as their car crawled slowly along.

At the corner of the street the man with Mrs. de Groot beckoned a passing taxi and gave his orders.

Apparently the driver demurred, for Mrs. de Groot suddenly pressed some money into his hand, which reassured him. The three entered the cab and drove off.

Reynolds's car followed at a discreet distance, dodging in and out of the traffic skilfully.

"I've taken the number of the taxi," Pierre said, "but we shall not lose sight of it."

The inspector leaned forward anxiously watching the taxi in front as it swirled along the streets.

"We're making for Montmartre," remarked Pierre.

"What I would give to know his name!" Reynolds muttered aloud.

"If monsieur means the gentleman in the taxi with the ladies, his name is Deek.'"

The inspector started with astonishment. "Dick!" he interpreted. "How in the world did you learn that, Pierre?"

"I left monsieur a moment, caught the waiter serving the dinner in Number 54, and asked him if he knew the names of Madame de Groot's guests, in case monsieur was interested."

"Monsieur certainly is!" Reynolds avowed. "Well, Pierre, what could he tell you?"

Pierre shook his head sadly. "Very little, monsieur. Only that the tall young lady had just arrived from England, that two cablegrams came this morning, one for Madame de Groot and one for her maid, and that the ladies had both addressed the gentleman during dinner as Deek. The waiter had never seen either Mademoiselle or Monsieur Deek before."

The inspector sighed with relief. "That's

excellent work of yours, Pierre." "Dick" was undoubtedly Richard Spencer, which proved that they were searching for "Tony."

They were now racing through dingy streets in Montmartre. Suddenly the taxi in front stopped outside a small café and Spencer, as the inspector now knew him to be, hurried inside, returning almost immediately.

That performance was repeated at several cafés. Presently the taxi stopped at a dark shuttered house and Spencer getting out, helped the ladies to descend and paid off the cab.

At Pierre's suggestion Reynolds's car had turned up a small street nearly opposite the house. Through the window at the back of the car Reynolds eagerly watched the door, outside which the three were waiting.

"Shall I get out and walk past the house?" asked the Frenchman eagerly. "I may hear something."

Reynolds nodded quickly.

It was fully two minutes before Spencer could get any answer to his repeated ringing, but at length the door opened a little, and the inspector could see he was arguing with some one inside. An argument which Mrs. de Groot again ended by an offering of money.

Then the three entered and the door was closed.

"Well?" inquired the inspector as Pierre returned to the car.

"I think it's a private gambling house. There are many in this quarter. Would you like to see if we can get in, monsieur?"

Reynolds considered the suggestion. Very badly indeed he wanted to go inside that house, but by doing so he might miss his goal. Lady Avice and her friends would recognize he was English if they were in the same room and saw him. And if they were not in the same room, it would be fatally easy for them to slip away with this Tony.

No, he concluded, he would have to remain here on guard.

"It's a pity to lose the chance, but I must stay in the car prepared to follow them," he told the Frenchman. "We'll have something to eat."

Pierre produced his purchases and passing some to the chauffeur, they began their al-fresco meal.

Presently the Frenchman spoke, his eyes flashing as an idea struck him. "Monsieur, may *I* try to go in? I'm French and they would not suspect me."

"Go to it, my lad!" agreed Reynolds.

The Frenchman laughed gaily and sprang out of the car. "If your people come out of the house before I do," he said, "follow them and don't trouble about me. I will see you at the hotel later."

Reynolds watched him stroll along to the house and ring for admittance. There was a little colloquy, and then Pierre vanished inside.

The inspector looked at his watch. A quarter past ten. Settling himself sideways on the seat, he kept guard through the back window of the car.

It was long after midnight when he woke the sleeping chauffeur and told him to turn the car to save time.

The car was scarcely in its new position before Reynolds saw Pierre stagger out from the house. Up the street he rolled and swayed in the opposite direction from the car, while Reynolds sat in a fever of anxiety to know whether he ought to follow him or remain where he was. Suppose Pierre had been drugged or wounded!

Then suddenly he noticed an old woman's head peering out from the door, and guessed the Frenchman's maneuver.

As the woman withdrew, apparently satisfied, and shut the door, Pierre darted into a doorway, stood still a second listening, and then rapidly retraced his steps to the car. He was barely inside, assuring Reynolds all was well with him, when a taxi drove down the street and stopped at the house.

The cab must have been expected for again the door opened, and the two ladies came out and entered it.

"Quick, tell me," Reynolds demanded of Pierre, "have you found out anything?"

"Yes, there's a big gambling room on the first floor, monsieur. A rough crowd. Your people were not there but I had to stay and play and drink."

He laughed reminiscently. "Oh, the good wine I spilled on the floor! As soon as I dared I slipped out of the room and crept upstairs."

"Plucky but risky," commented the inspector, his eye still on the waiting taxi across the road.

"I heard English voices in a back room on the third floor. The man you look for is there, but is either drunk or ill. He seemed to be very excited, shouting he would not go with them. At last he became calmer and I heard Monsieur Deek say he would telephone for a taxi. Then I crept downstairs and pretending to be drunk, came out. Voila!" He spread his hands deprecatingly.

"You're a jewel, my boy!" remarked the inspector warmly. "Hello! They've called their taxi driver inside the house."

The tall slim figure of Lady Avice suddenly stepped out of the taxi. She glanced anxiously up and down the street.

The detective and Pierre ducked their heads, though there was little risk of their being seen in the narrow dark side street.

"Here they come," said Pierre's voice excitedly as the cabman and Spencer appeared supporting the drooping form of a man clad in a long dark coat that came nearly to his heels. Probably borrowed for the occasion, the inspector surmised. The newcomer was helped inside the cab. Spencer pushed two suitcases in with him, afterward climbing beside the driver. Then the cab started up the street.

The inspector's car pursued at a prudent range; the taxi going at an exceptionally moderate pace.

"This is a queer route!" murmured Pierre.

"Queer?" questioned the detective.

"They're zigzagging up one street and back another. Do you think they've seen us following, monsieur?"

The detective frowned. "I sincerely hope not," he replied uneasily.

"Ah, now we're making for somewhere definite," the Frenchman decided as the taxi in front gathered speed.

It stopped in a few minutes at a small corner hotel near the Louvre. The taxi man and Spencer got down and almost lifted out the helpless man in the long dark coat.

Instantly Reynolds slipped out of his car. He strolled casually along, as near as he dared, and concealed himself in a doorway.

He watched the two men assist the sagging form of "Tony" into the dark hall, saw Mrs. de Groot follow them and the driver run back for the suitcases. Lady Avice evidently intended remaining in the taxi, Reynolds decided.

Presently Mrs. de Groot and Spencer returned. But only Spencer got into the cab.

"I'll be back as quickly as possible," Reynolds heard him say. "Don't leave him."

Mrs. de Groot was turning back into the hotel when she called out: "Avice, you know where to find my keys. Don't forget you'll find that packet in the left pocket of my dressing-case. And for mercy's sake, hurry."

Reynolds hurried back to the car. "I'm going into this hotel," he announced decisively. "The others are evidently coming back here. You can push off now, Pierre. I'll see you to-morrow at the hotel. Good night, my boy, and thank you."

"You won't follow the taxi?" questioned Pierre with a worried expression.

"No, no," said Reynolds impatiently. "The main object is here." He flicked his thumb towards the hotel. "Tony" was all he cared about at the moment, and in the man's present helpless condition Spencer and Lady Avice were bound to come back to him.

Of the sleepy night porter in the hall he demanded the number of the room of his friends who had just entered, and also asked if there was another exit to the hotel.

The room of Monsieur "Spencaire" was Number 19, second floor, he was informed. No, there was no other exit.

The detective thanked the man, said he could

find the room by himself, and ran up the narrow circular staircase with a grim joy in his heart.

This "Tony" certainly had some grave thing to conceal, Reynolds reflected, otherwise why this journey from London of Lady Avice and Spencer, the frantic conversation he had overheard in Mrs. de Groot's room and this subsequent wild search in the Paris cafes?

He listened at the door of Number 19, but hearing nothing except indistinct sounds of some one moving about the room, he stood near an angle of the corridor where he could watch the door and stairs at the same time.

Fully half an hour he remained there. At last he heard soft movements on the stairs.

Some one was stealthily creeping up!

Then as an anticlimax Reynolds heard a whispered "Monsieur," and saw—Pierre!

The Frenchman was pale and breathless. "What is it now?" demanded Reynolds hastily.

Pierre raised his hands in despair.

"I thought, monsieur, you would like me to telephone to your hotel to see if those two had arrived and gone to Mrs. de Groot's suite."

"That was very smart of you," agreed the detective. "Well?"

"The clerk on duty is a friend of mine, monsieur. I asked him to make certain himself. He telephones up and Therese, the maid, answered. She said she had not gone to bed and that no one had entered the suite since her mistress with her friends had left it just after eight o'clock."

"Either they hadn't arrived or they had been and gone without the maid's knowledge," commented the detective.

The Frenchman shook his head. "Impossible, monsieur," he urged insistently. "The maid had decided to wait up for Mrs. de Groot, who had had a bad headache all day, in case her mistress needed something. And Therese had bolted the entrance door to the suite." He paused. "Monsieur, the hotel is not five minutes by taxi from here and they have been gone forty minutes!"

Reynolds clapped his hands to his head with an exclamation, and then started to go along the corridor to Number 19.

"Wait, monsieur," implored Pierre. "There is something more, but my friend is nervous that he may get into trouble for telling me. Can you keep his name out of it if I tell you?"

The detective bit his lip and cogitated a moment. "Pierre," he said with decision, "this is more than a suspected robbery. It is a murder case. I *must* know all you can tell me, and I promise no harm can befall your friend."

"Murder!" the Frenchman gasped. "*Eh alors,* monsieur, indeed you must be told. My friend came on duty at seven to-night and has been in charge of the telephone department ever since. At seven thirty-five a gentleman—this Monsieur Deek, of course— from Mrs. de Groot's suite demanded a number and was given it. After he had finished speaking the person he had called up rang the hotel and wished to speak to the manager. The manager, who was busy, instructed my friend to take the message. He did so. It was to ask if Mrs. de Groot of Suite 54 was financially reliable as she, or the gentleman acting for her, had ordered a private aeroplane to be ready to start at any moment after midnight."

"An aeroplane!" repeated Reynolds—amazed. Pierre nodded.

"Yes, monsieur. The call was from the big aerodrome at Le Bourget. The manager returned an answer to the effect that Mrs. de Groot was very wealthy and entirely to be trusted."

The inspector's lips tightened grimly.

"Well, their little joy ride will be a bit delayed, I think. Stay here, Pierre. I'm going to interview this man in Number Nineteen, whether he's ill or drunk or both."

He strode along the corridor and knocked firmly at the door. It was opened at once by Mrs. de Groot, who puckered her brows in surprise as the detective walked past her into the room. He glanced round quickly. There was only one other occupant of the room.

Sitting on the bed, smoking a cigarette, with a long dark coat thrown back from her shoulders, was Lady Avice Garth, regarding him with cold, amused eyes.

XVI. A NEW FEAR

LAUREEN awoke from troubled dreams to the sound of the telephone bell ringing. Sleepily she punched her pillow into a more comfortable position, and, without opening her eyes, felt for the electric bell push suspended over the head of her bed. Her fingers groped lazily about for a moment, encountering at last a strange knob, which roused her to consciousness.

She looked round blankly at the unfamiliar room, and her brow puckered as gradual remembrance came to her that she was in the St. Andrew's Hotel. She thrust away the memory of why she was there. It was too early in the day to let that horrible shadow creep over her, haunting every hour, as it had, since Sunday night. Could this only be Tuesday morning? It seemed an eternity.

Resolutely she raised herself on her elbow and called her maid.

"Bertha! I'm awake. Do you make tea or shall I ring for it?"

From the adjoining room the maid came in, her face a little drawn. "Good morning, miss. Please don't ring. Hotel tea is awful stuff. I brought our electric kettle with me and it's nearly boiling."

Laureen stretched her arms and yawned. "Now isn't that thoughtful of you! Did you sleep, Bertha?"

The maid averted her head and drew back the curtains. "Not very well, miss, thank you. I hope you did. After all you've been through—"

Her mistress extended a warning hand.

"No," she said sternly. "We won't talk about that yet, please. It's bad for both of us. Who rang me up just now?"

"Mr. Lansberg, miss. I said you were asleep. He told me he would be glad if you would telephone him as soon as you awoke." Bertha added with importance: "Two lots of flowers have come this morning—roses and orchids. Mr. Lansberg sent the roses."

"H'm," commented Laureen to herself with a grimace. "Very devoted after all the bother I've let the poor man in for." She clapped her hands. "Tea, letters, newspapers, quick, Bertha! Oh, the letters will be at the flat, though."

"No, miss. Carter brought them round ten minutes ago. It's a quarter past nine. Shall I bring the telephone in? There's a plug by your bed."

Laureen nodded, her mind on her letters. The mail was delivered at seven thirty at the flats. Had that wretched inspector spent an hour looking over her correspondence first?

She glanced swiftly through the little pile Bertha brought in, throwing one envelope aside after another with a sigh of relief. Suppose Valerie had written and Inspector Reynolds had got hold of it! Oh, if only she could talk to somebody, ask advice.

The maid returned with a tray and an armful of red roses which she laid on the bed. The orchids could wait, she surmised.

Laureen picked up the flowers, burying her nose in the cool scented petals for a moment.

"Ring up Mr. Lansberg, please, Bertha," she asked, knowing quite well how the maid adored doing these little intimate things for her.

Bertha obeyed, her heart warm with gratitude. Her mistress was ignoring the fact that this dreadful tragedy might never have happened but for her — Bertha's—fatal weakness for the dead man.

The maid's lips quivered as she demanded the number and silently passed over the receiver.

Laureen laid her hand on the woman's arm, noticed the brimming eyes, and with an impulsive gesture drew her down and kissed her.

"Don't worry," she said gently. "I'm not blaming you in any way."

"It was all my fault, miss," the maid sobbed. "Look at the trouble I've brought on you."

"I hate looking at unpleasant things," replied her mistress with a smile. She pulled the telephone toward her as a voice came over the wire.

"Speaking," she replied. "Good morning, Mr. Lansberg. Thank you for the marvelous roses. I'm embedded in them. Yes indeed, the reporters would say that I live in the lap of luxury could they but see me now, which thank goodness they can't."

"Two of them tried to half an hour ago, miss," whispered Bertha. "I cleared them off," she added grimly.

Laureen repeated Bertha's rejoinder over the telephone delightedly. Her face grew grave as Lansberg told her the inquest on Leslie Delmond was fixed for ten thirty that morning.

"Very well," she answered, "I'll be punctual."

She listened attentively to a request of Lansberg's and reflected a moment before she replied.

"Thank you, yes, I'd love to come. I believe it's

just what I need and there's no matinee to-day. May I telephone Avice and ask her to come? Lady Avice Garth. . . . Thanks so much. Good-by."

She hung up the receiver and announced to her maid:

"The inquest is at ten thirty, Bertha. After it's over I'm going to motor to Crowborough with Mr. Lansberg and his secretary and play a round of golf. In case Inspector Reynolds wants to know where I am, you can explain."

The maid brought her mistress's dressing-gown and held it for her.

"Your bath's ready, miss," she temporized, secretly determined to tell the inspector nothing. What right had he to pry into Laureen's movements?

"Ring up Lady Avice, Bertha, while I have my bath, and ask her if she's disengaged to-day. If so, will she come with Mr. Lansberg and myself to Crowborough for golf. Say we'll call for her about noon. Explain I'm in a hurry because of the inquest."

In a few minutes the maid came to the bathroom with the reply.

"The butler says that Lady Avice left for Paris unexpectedly early this morning, miss," she reported. "He has no idea of her address or when she will return."

"Oh, ho," sang out Laureen. Then to herself she said, "Gone to Paris indeed! Funny she never mentioned it last night! Why, she even asked me to come to tea to-day!"

The inquest was brevity itself. Laureen and Lansberg deposed to finding the man dead in her flat; she identified him and the coroner then adjourned the proceedings.

After luncheon and a foursome on the links at Crowborough they strolled back across the crisp scented turf, under a blue and gold sky that Lansberg felt was reflected in the eyes and hair of the girl beside him. A soft breeze beat lightly against their faces, cooling the heat of the sun.

"A perfect day," sighed Laureen. "If only one need never leave this heavenly spot for the crowds and noise of London!"

Lansberg bent toward her. "If you're so happy here, why go back?" he questioned.

Her eyes gazed wistfully round the panoramic view before them. "I don't know. Ambition, I suppose. Having worked so hard to get where I am, it seems foolish to abandon it all. Also," she waved her hand toward the landscape, "this won't always be like it is to-day, and London is always London, whatever the weather or season."

They were almost at the Club House when the man stopped and put his hand on her shoulder.

"Laureen, forgive me if I spoil to-day by such a subject, but I've grown to know you very well since Sunday night and," he spoke with diffidence, "I find it difficult to believe that Leslie Delmond was ever your lover."

She raised frank gray eyes to his grave face.

"So do I," she said whimsically.

"You mean—?" he asked.

She shrugged her shoulders and the shadow of a smile drifted over her expression. "When one is in a desperate hole, even a soiled ladder is not to be despised to clamber out by. I wish I could explain, *mon ami*, but I can't, and that's all there is to it."

Some acquaintances seized Laureen as they

reached the big veranda, and Lansberg left her.

"I have an—appointment," he said a trifle formally. "May I fetch you in an hour?" He turned to his secretary. "Lyall, please wait here for me and see to Miss Laureen's comfort."

He bowed to her and to her friends with an almost foreign grace, in which there was nothing effeminate. Indeed, Laureen thought, as she watched him stroll off to the car, she had never seen any man with such extraordinary dignity. He was invariably courteous; yet when he spoke, men listened; when he commanded, he was obeyed. He neither strained after effect, nor sought to impress himself on others.

A beautiful revue actress of her attainments could have been a favorite in any circle. But one reason for her success was that hers was not merely a theatrical personality. Her private life was her own, she had long ago decided, and half-way up the ladder she had kicked herself free from those social invitations which most girls in her sphere would have grasped tenaciously. She did not fawn on a duchess to be asked to her ball, nor expect that duchess's husband to fawn on her! Many acquaintances said she was hard and cold; her friends found her warm and generous.

A little tired and listless after her game—she had played well and Lansberg badly for some reason—she leaned back in the low wicker chair and listened idly to the conversation. Her attention turned to Lansberg's secretary, and subconsciously she began to sum him up. Rather characterless, amiable, honest, probably efficient at his job. A man with no particular ambition, was her decision.

"Don't you golf, Captain Lyall?" she asked,

accepting the cigarette and light he offered her. "I thought you were going to play in our foursome to-day."

"Yes, I often play," he replied, "but Mr. Lansberg wanted me to do something else this afternoon."

He lifted a black tin case from the floor beside him and opened it cautiously.

"I went after these," he explained. "Had quite a bit of luck, too. Those are golden Emperors, not very rare, but rather nice specimens which Mr. Lansberg wanted."

He raised the lid of the box and Laureen glanced in carelessly, her thoughts elsewhere. There were about half a dozen large butterflies inside. A curious hobby it seemed to her for a man of Lansberg's type.

Then a faint odor came to her senses. She sniffed it and frowned. Where had she known that smell before? What did it remind her of?

Suddenly she remembered in one horrified flash. She forced herself to ask a question.

"How do you kill them, Captain Lyall?"

He shut the lid and fastened it carefully. "Oh, just a few drops of chloroform on cotton wool," he answered. "They die quickly."

Chloroform! The world seemed to spin round her. Dimly she heard the light babel of conversation near and strove desperately to fight back a terrible fear.

Was it only a minute since she had been so happy, able for a time to forget the tragedy of two nights ago? And now everything had crashed! Stumbling she rose to her feet, murmuring some excuse, and walked round the veranda—almost into Lansberg's arms.

He surveyed her closely. "You look tired, my

child. Get your wrap and let me take you back at once."

"No, no, I'm all right," she protested.

"It has been too long a day for you," he blamed himself reproachfully. "You must rest before the theater to-night. Lyall ought to have looked after you better."

"He—he was very thoughtful. He showed me your butterflies," she jerked out with a nervous laugh. And fled toward the coat room.

XVII. EVASION

FOR the second time that evening in Paris, Inspector Reynolds knew he had been fooled. The next trick, however, might yet be his, since he had cabled instructions to have all channel ports watched for the man with the missing thumb.

The ruse played on him by Lady Avice Garth was of a complicated nature. It would call for much bluffing on his part, and he was afraid, judging from this evening's escapade, that the young lady might beat him at his own game, the cards being certainly in her hands up to now. Well, he would take his lead from her.

But apparently Lady Avice knew the value of silence.

She regarded the inspector slowly from head to foot with as detached and impersonal a look as though he were a piece of furniture not entirely to her taste.

Then, as if he did not exist, she flicked the ash from her cigarette and turned to her friend.

"Yes, in a measure I agree with you, Mary," she remarked casually. "Climate does affect temperament enormously. The Italian becomes indolent and warbles grand opera more or less well, but none of those Latin races can be compared to the Russians for temperament and mentality. Look at the Russian ballet for instance. . . ."

Mrs. de Groot appeared incapable of looking at

anything but her friend. Her heavy jaw had dropped in astonishment as Avice had begun this rambling monologue of nonsense, ignoring the sudden appearance of a man. Who was he? Why had he forced his way in here? How much did he know? Why had Avice played this sudden trick? Why indeed had Avice sent her back to the taxi to call, through the window, that stupid message about her keys?

All these questions flooded through the elder woman's mind as she endeavored to follow her friend's cue.

"Of course they are—" she began valiantly.

But whatever they were was left unrecorded.

Inspector Reynolds stepped forward briskly, and forced himself into the conversation. A tired and irritable man, he had no intention of being defeated at this hour. He addressed the girl who sat curled up on the foot of the bed, one slender arm dangling negligently over the rail.

"Lady Avice Garth?" he began questioningly.

She twisted round a little in his direction as if she had suddenly become aware of his presence, and gave the faintest inclination of her head.

"You have entered this room, unasked by my friend or myself, to see Mr. Spencer, I suppose," she remarked frigidly. "The procedure seems a little unusual."

"Quite a good card, my Lady," said Reynolds to himself in grim admiration, "but I'll trump it."

"That is correct, madam," he replied with deliberation. "What time will Mr. Spencer return from the aerodrome or is he crossing too?"

If the girl flinched inwardly at his questions she showed no outward indication, as she tossed her cigarette end in the grate and stretched her hand toward Mrs. de Groot.

"Give me a cigarette, Mary. Egyptian, please."

Mrs. de Groot eagerly opened her case and passed it to Avice.

The girl selected and lit a cigarette with studied leisure before she replied to the detective. But she roused no sign of annoyance or impatience on his expressionless face. Stolidly he awaited her answer.

"There is no reason why I should discuss Mr. Spencer's movements with you," Lady Avice hedged.

The C. I. D. man almost smiled. Indeed she had played into his hands. He drew a card from his pocket and gave it to her.

"Detective Inspector Reynolds, Criminal Investigation Department, Scotland Yard," the girl read out slowly, with a steadying glance at Mrs. de Groot, who had visibly paled. She twirled the card in her fingers. "What does this mean, Inspector?"

"I am investigating the murder of Leslie Delmond," Reynolds explained patiently, perfectly aware that a lady of her proved intelligence already knew this. Then with a touch of his old manner he rapped out: "When did you last see Delmond, Lady Avice?"

This time it was Mrs. de Groot who caused a delay. With a faint sigh she leaned back in her chair, cheeks blanched to an alarming pallor.

The girl went swiftly to her side, sat on the arm of the chair and pulled the elder woman's head on her shoulder protectingly.

"It's all right, Mary," she murmured. "Inspector Reynolds must ask these questions," she said with a reasonableness that surprised the detective.

Still holding her friend closely she answered the detective with calm frankness.

"I have not seen Leslie Delmond for more than four years, Inspector."

"It might save time," Reynolds suggested, "if you would explain how and why your friendship with the dead man ceased."

Lady Avice drew her fine brows together with a puzzled air. "But he never was my friend," she announced in surprise.

"Acquaintance, if you prefer," conceded Reynolds.

The girl looked a little troubled, then bent toward Mrs. de Groot. "Mary dear, I'm afraid one of us must tell the inspector. Will you do so or do you prefer that I should?"

The elder woman opened her eyes and spoke in a trembling voice. "Leslie Delmond was my friend. I loved him, foolishly, although Lady Avice warned me against him over and over again. She had nothing whatever to do with him in any way."

"Then, Mrs. de Groot—" Both women started slightly as the man spoke the name with emphasis, for it had not been mentioned since he entered. To them it indicated that he knew more than they imagined. "Then, Mrs. de Groot, if Leslie Delmond was never Lady Avice Garth's friend, will you tell me why she wrote him a letter just before he was murdered?"

The girl's face was blank, but the inspector's eyes flickered to her fingers which had suddenly clenched.

"Wrote him a letter?" gasped Mrs. de Groot. There was almost suspicion in the hurt gaze she turned to her friend. "Avice, you never told me—" she began.

The detective metaphorically rubbed his hands with joy.

"Perhaps Lady Avice would explain better herself," he volunteered mildly.

But that was what Lady Avice did not intend to do. "Are you asking a question or stating a fact, Inspector?" she demanded.

Reynolds's eyes hardened.

"Both," he replied. And decided to make a chance shot. That plain crumpled half sheet of note-paper had undoubtedly been torn from a letter she had written. "A part of a letter of yours was found in Leslie Delmond's pocket after he was murdered, Lady Avice."

The girl faced him without a tremor, her voice clear and firm.

"Then in that case you know the contents and do not need me to repeat them," she retorted.

"Undoubtedly your trick, my Lady," he thought, "but I've not finished yet."

"Nevertheless, Lady Avice," he urged doggedly, "I must ask you the reason for that letter."

The girl drew a quick breath of relief. It was quite obvious this detective had not read the letter and was bluffing. "Inspector Reynolds, if you have read the letter you say you found on Leslie Delmond, then you know the reason. If you have not read it, then I cannot at this stage tell you anything about it."

Reynolds frowned slightly. The girl had courage and the restraint of her class, and added to that, a vivid intelligence.

"Are you reserving your statement, Lady Avice, because it involves some one else? The man you call

Tony, for instance?" he chanced.

His question had a different effect on the two women. Mrs. de Groot clutched her friend's hand in quick sympathy. Reynolds heard her whisper, "What are we to do, Avice?"

The girl's fine features set as if they were chiseled in marble and she stared blankly at the C. I. D. man.

There was a silence, broken by footsteps in the corridor outside. At the sound Reynolds slipped immediately behind the door, hoping to overhear at least one unsuspecting sentence from the newcomer.

The door opened suddenly. A young man burst in and announced breathlessly: "Well, of all the surprising adventures. That boy has grit and deserves—" He broke off, alarmed at the startled faces of the two women.

Lady Avice was the first to regain her poise. "Inspector Reynolds of Scotland Yard is waiting to see you, Dick. This is Mr. Spencer, Inspector," she introduced him tranquilly, with an air of leaving the matter to the two men.

Dick Spencer wheeled round. The inspector saw a frank good-humored face, rumpled brown hair, and merry eyes that were gazing at him in bewilderment.

Before the detective could speak the younger man shot a mischievous glance at Mrs. de Groot. "Mary, I'm surprised at you!" he remarked sternly. "What have you been up to now?" He turned to the detective with a friendly smile. "Well, it's a bit late or early for a call, Inspector, but you've had a long journey, so do sit down and let's hear what it's all about."

"The murder of Leslie Delmond in Laureen's

apartment," replied the inspector crisply, taking the chair Spencer pulled forward.

Spencer nodded understandingly.

"Of course, I might have guessed," he replied. "Jolly rough on Laureen," he flushed as he mentioned her name, "having a tragedy like that in her flat. And I suppose, as her pals, we're all more or less suspected until we can prove our innocence, what?"

"More or less," agreed Reynolds, his eyes twinkling a little at his own thoughts.

Spencer grinned. "Well, I'm going to propose we have a useful little drink all round. Mary, you look as if you need one."

He dug up a bottle of whisky, found glasses and prepared the drinks, keeping up a cheery patter all the time that made even Lady Avice smile.

"Here you are, Inspector." Reynolds shook his head. "Well, well, I suppose you know best. Mary, you drink up yours quickly. Your face reminds me of a bad channel crossing."

Somehow this young man with his disarming friendliness was very likeable, Reynolds felt, particularly after the frosty reception he had had from Lady Avice. Of all the many classes the detective had to deal with, he invariably disliked contact with that into which Lady Avice had been born. Their cold poise baffled him.

Therefore he welcomed this more Bohemian temperament of Spencer's. Quickly he summed him up as a wealthy young dilettante, who dabbled in painting, had no great talent or intelligence, was impulsive and amiable, and had tumbled across to Paris like an eager school-boy to help Tony—

evidently a scapegoat pal—at the request of either Laureen or Lady Avice. The detective decided it would not be difficult to find out all this volatile young man knew.

Spencer was perched on the bed near Lady Avice, his long legs swinging to and fro.

"I say, we are making hay of my bye-byes, aren't we?" he remarked ruefully. "Thank goodness I'll be in London to-morrow night in the good old studio. I never can sleep in these stuffy hotel bedrooms." He grimaced. "Maybe I'll not be so lucky as that, though. I say, Inspector, do I sleep on a box-spring mattress or a plank at Pentonville or wherever you propose to dump me?"

Reynolds was thankful he had refused a drink. He was conscious that a long and exhausting day, following previous sleepless nights, was taking the desire for battle out of him. And outside in the corridor Pierre was waiting for instructions.

Spencer glanced at Mrs. de Groot, whose weariness was apparent, lowered an eyelid at the girl beside him, and said: "Look here, Inspector. My friends are pretty well tired. Shall we call it a day and go to our respective stables? I'll give you my parole to meet you when and where you like in the morning."

The detective fought back the haze of drowsiness and reflected. He was entirely at a loss, he knew. There was no reason to believe Spencer had actually committed the murder. "Very well, Mr. Spencer," he agreed. "I have a car outside and can take these ladies to their hotel, where I also am staying. Will you please meet me in Mrs. de Groot's sitting-room in her suite at nine thirty A. M.?"

"I'll be there, Inspector," promised Spencer, as he wished the ladies good night.

Pierre was standing beside the car, now drawn up outside the hotel. Hat in hand, the Frenchman assisted the ladies and murmured a quick offer to Reynolds, who shook his head.

"No, no, my boy. You've done good work. Get off to bed and come to my room in the morning if you can. It's no use cabling every air-port when I don't know what this man they call Tony is like, or the name he's got on his passport. He's beaten me this time."

At the door of Mrs. de Groot's suite the inspector left her and Lady Avice, reminding them he would be there at half past nine. But he did not mention that he was their neighbor in the adjoining suite.

Singing in his bath was not a vice of Inspector Reynolds's, but at nine o'clock next morning he splashed and hummed cheerfully, reveling in the unusual luxury of his private suite. His sleep had refreshed his optimism. After all if Tony had got away, he could be traced through Lady Avice sooner or later.

Reynolds contemplated with satisfaction all that the forthcoming interview might disclose. He looked at his wrist watch as he wrestled with his collar stud: twenty past nine. Nine minutes more in which to plan a course of action. There were four questions he meant to put before he was much older, questions to which Lady Avice could and should give the answers.

Who was Tony?

Where was he now?

Where was he at the time of the murder?

What had Lady Avice written to Delmond?

Replies to those questions would carry him a long way.

There was a soft tapping at his outer door, and wondering who his visitor could be, Reynolds flung it open.

Pierre, now in his hotel uniform again, slipped inside quickly, an uneasy expression on his face.

"Monsieur," he said urgently, "she has gone!"

The C. I. D. man started back with a frown. "Gone! *Who?*"

The Frenchman spread his hands deprecatingly. "The young lady 'Aveese,' monsieur. I came on duty at nine this morning and as soon as I could, went to the telephone bureau to learn if any calls came through from or to Mrs. de Groot's room last night. I had previously asked my friend to get a record of all calls made even when he went off duty."

"Lady Avice Garth!" Reynolds groaned. "Go on, Pierre."

"Less than half an hour after you went to bed last night, or rather early this morning, monsieur, Lady Avice telephoned the aerodrome and asked if the gentleman had arrived for whom Mrs. de Groot had ordered a private aeroplane to be ready after midnight. She was told he was there waiting and would speak to her himself."

A vein stood out on Reynolds's forehead.

The Frenchman went on: "The gentleman came to the telephone, monsieur, but, alas, my friend in the telephone bureau was off duty and the operator who replaced him knew very little English. All he could understand was that the lady said, 'Wait for me.

"'Wait for me!' " repeated the detective bitterly to himself.

"The young lady left the hotel in a taxi a few minutes after that, monsieur. About two fifteen A. M. it must have been. I'm very sorry I did not know earlier."

The inspector held out his hand kindly.

"I can't thank you enough, Pierre. This is a bit of bad luck but we'll get through. I'll see you again before I leave the hotel. I'm going at once to Mrs. de Groot's suite."

Outside in the corridor he met Spencer coming from the lift.

The young man waved his stick and sang out cheerily: "Hello, Inspector. Had a good night?"

Reynolds studied him a moment. Was this young man as innocent as he appeared, or was he a remarkably good actor?

"Thank you, yes," the detective replied calmly. Then with a keen glance: "Are the ladies all right?"

Spencer gave his boyish grin. "I dunno. Lady Avice should be, but my bet is that Mrs. de Groot's still in bed weeping over her black sheep—" He broke off. "I say, I'm talking too much. Let's go in and see 'em."

The maid admitted them to the salon, her face inscrutable. "I will tell madame," she responded to their request for Mrs. de Groot and Lady Avice Garth.

Spencer lighted a cigarette and strolled about the room, the inspector grimly watching him.

In about five minutes Mrs. de Groot entered the room wrapped in a negligee, her face bearing the signs of recent tears. She was trembling obviously as she greeted the two men and sank into an armchair.

"Mrs. de Groot, where is Lady Avice?" the detective demanded of her, though his eyes were on Spencer.

Mrs. de Groot's lips quivered. "I—don't know," she said in a terrified whisper. "I begged her not to go but she is very impulsive. Please don't be angry, Inspector. She didn't do it to annoy you."

Spencer's face showed nothing but blank bewilderment. "What on earth are you talking about, Mary?" he demanded. "Where's Avice?"

Mrs. de Groot gazed up at him piteously.

"Gone!" she said. "Last night she sent me to bed and then came in with her hat and cloak on and kissed me good-by. She left a message for you, Inspector." Mrs. de Groot pressed a hand to her forehead. "I was to tell you she would be at your service to-night or to-morrow at her London address. That's all I know." She raised her hands despairingly.

"Avice gone!" Spencer's jaw dropped. "Well, of all the prize lunatics!"

It was evident the news had been a surprise to him, the detective decided. "Mr. Spencer," he remarked sternly, "I shall be glad if you will tell me exactly who and where 'Tony' is, and why you came to Paris suddenly to get him safely away?"

Spencer's face was still placid and amiable, but there was a determined glint in his eye as he drawled:

"And that, my dear Inspector, is precisely what I *cannot* tell you—anyhow until I've seen Lady Avice. Y'see, some of it I don't know, some of it I don't want to know, and some of it I couldn't tell you because—

er—well, because it's not my business. You can lock me up as hostage or any jolly old thing you like, and that's that."

And that certainly *was* that, as far as opening Spencer's mouth was concerned. After a rather unfruitful conversation with Mrs. de Groot, Reynolds and the young man traveled back to England together that day.

They were nearing London when the detective had a bright idea. In a measure he appreciated and understood this young man's reticence concerning Lady Avice's affairs which appeared to include Tony. Well, Reynolds decided, he could obtain all his information—insist upon getting it too—from her later. Meanwhile there was one question that had nothing to do with her.

"Mr. Spencer, do you remember telephoning to Miss Laureen's flat on Sunday night at nine fifty P.M.?"

"I do," replied that young man promptly, "though I'm hazy as to the exact time."

"Will you tell me all the conversation that took place?"

"Certainly." Spencer thought a moment. "I asked if Miss Laureen had started for my studio yet and the reply was that she was on her way. That was every word so far as I can remember."

"Was it her maid's voice that you heard?" Reynolds asked.

Spencer shot a glance at the detective. "That's the funny part of it," he declared. "I'll swear it wasn't Bertha's voice." He reddened slightly. "You see, I'm absolutely crazy on Laureen and often ring her up, and I know the maid's voice very well. No, it was high and clear, I wondered who the woman was. If it *was* a woman," he added.

"If it *was* a woman!" caught up the inspector sharply. "What do you mean?"

"Well, it might have been a man's falsetto just as easily," explained Spencer with no particular interest. He peered through the carriage window. "Ah, here we are. Good old Charing Cross."

But the detective's mind was echoing "It might have been a man's falsetto." Why hadn't he thought of that before?

XVIII. THE KNIFE

LAUREEN had proved an unusually silent companion on the journey back from Crowborough with Lansberg. From his seat at the wheel he glanced at her several times as she stared ahead with a troubled expression.

He had over-tired her, he feared. After the tension she had endured since Sunday night this journey down and back, the heat on a shadeless golf-links and a strenuous game had all been too much. And to-night she had her work in the theater!

He metaphorically kicked himself for his thoughtlessness as the big car slid silently along.

Suddenly she relaxed, and leaned back with a little gurgle of laughter as she noticed Lansberg's worried face. "Did you think I'd developed motor nerves or had become 'mental'?" she asked.

Lansberg smiled down into her gray eyes with relief. "Neither," he affirmed. "But I do know you are a very tired girl, thanks to my selfishness. I ought not to have asked you to come on this long exhausting trip after—"

Laureen interrupted him. "I shall scream if you say, as my maid does, 'after all you've been through.'"

There was an extraordinary mixture of tenderness and self-reproach in the look he bent upon her. For one second he took one hand from the wheel as though he would touch hers lying on the light rug. Then his face resumed its accustomed stillness and he drove on steadily with tightened lips.

"If only you need not act to-night!" The words seemed forced from him.

"That's my job," she stated simply. "I'm paid well for it too."

"Yes, but on top—" He stopped like a naughty child as her finger went up with a warning gesture.

"Be careful or my scream will outdo your Klaxon." Her mouth had crinkled comically, but there was a soft radiance in her eyes that sent a sudden fire through the man's veins.

"Mr. Lansberg," she began softly.

"One of my several hideous Christian names is Ivan," he suggested with diffidence.

"Ivan," she repeated tentatively. "It's not at all hideous, though, whatever the others may be."

"Then it's yours to use, if you will. What were you going to say when I interrupted you?"

Her fingers twisted a corner of the rug nervously. "You offered to show me your rooms once. If you're not engaged or tired of the sight of me, might I come to tea when we get back, please—Ivan?"

This time his hand dropped over her fingers and held them closely. "You will make me very happy, my child."

She peeped mischievously over her shoulder at the secretary, who was discreetly studying the streets they were now gliding through. "That very correct person will blush presently," she predicted.

But Lansberg was in a dream that made him oblivious of trivialities, as automatically he guided the car through the traffic and a little later pulled up before his house.

Lansberg put his key in the lock and stood aside for Laureen to pass into the impressive entrance hall of his apartment. She looked round wonderingly, appreciating its dignity and beauty, all enhanced now by the sunlight drifting in iridescent coloring through the old stained window.

"This isn't a flat: it's a fairy palace, Ivan," she said softly.

"Sometimes a palace can be only a dungeon when it lacks a princess," he replied as he led her to the large double doors that opened into his library. "I think you may like this room where I work. If you will go in I'll find my servant and order tea."

Laureen drew back the heavy curtains and entered the room. For a moment, coming from the subdued light of the hall, she was dazzled by the glare.

Then she distinguished a dark menacing figure rising from a crouching position, and gave an involuntary cry that brought Lansberg quickly to her.

"What is it?" he asked.

With a shaking hand she pointed. "That man— he—he was kneeling with his forehead bent over to the floor, I think. He startled me."

Lansberg drew her to the couch.

"That's my servant, Neron. At his prayers, I expect."

He addressed the man in a language the girl did not understand. She saw the servant indicate the open door of a huge safe in the corner and caught a glimpse of marvelous flashing gems on the shelves within.

There followed a rapid conversation between the two men—agitated on the servant's part, coldly angry on Lansberg's. Then he ordered the man from the room, and hurriedly examining the contents of the safe, closed and locked it.

Laureen noticed his face was whiter and more set than usual as he sat down beside her.

"I'm so sorry you were alarmed," he said gently. "My servant found the safe open and hasn't yet got over it. Nothing has been touched so I must have left the thing unfastened this morning," he added reassuringly.

Laureen shivered a little as the thought flashed through her mind that Lansberg had not left that safe open, that he knew it and had only said so to avoid exciting her.

She glanced slowly round the lofty room, noticing subconsciously the different things, until she saw a large case of butterflies.

"Do you collect butterflies?" she asked with apparent casualness. "I see a case of them there, and your secretary showed me some he had caught today." She bit on her lip to still the shudder that passed through her.

But there was no trace of embarrassment in Lansberg's frank answer. "I used to have quite a fine collection," he admitted. "Then I became too busy or lost interest. Now I've started again because a young twelve-year-old god-son of mine has begun to collect and I'm sending all I find to him. He wrote asking for a variety—common enough—to be found in Sussex. That's why Lyall went a-hunting for me to-day."

His explanation was so natural that the girl

almost laughed at her previous fears. Absurd to imagine that a man of Lansberg's type and wealth could have any connection with Leslie Delmond or any motive for murdering him.

They had finished tea and were smoking cigarettes when suddenly Lansberg leaned toward her, idly twisting the long string of pearls that dangled from her neck.

"I've often meant to ask you if you had any sisters or brothers, Laureen."

"My father died a few months after I was born," she replied. "He and my mother believed in a small but good family. I'm *it*," she added with a quaint little smile.

"My dear, forgive these questions, but I'm very worried," he said presently. "Did you write a letter to the girl—I thought maybe it was your sister—called Valerie the night we discovered the murder?"

Laureen shook her head, her eyes on his slim fingers nervously toying with her pearls.

"No," she said definitely.

"Then, Laureen, if you wrote no letter, what was in the envelope you dropped into the hall letter box when you ran down to whistle for the policeman?"

There was a curiously speculative look on Laureen's face. Was it merely his keen interest in her that made him ask these questions, or was there some deeper reason?

She drew away from him sharply before he could release his fingers from her necklace. There was a snap and two of the pearls rolled on the ground.

She caught up the broken thing and tucked it into her hand bag, together with one pearl that had fallen beside her on the couch.

"I'm so sorry," Lansberg murmured with vexation.

"It doesn't matter. Only one has dropped. It is there under your desk."

Lansberg knelt to find it. As he stooped, a tiny article fell from one of his pockets and rolled along the ground close to the girl's feet, unnoticed by him. Something in its appearance made her bend down and examine it closely, turning it over in her fingers. Then with an ashen face she silently rolled it along the carpet away from her and rose.

"Please don't trouble any more," she urged. "It will be found to-morrow. I must get back to my hotel now."

Her lips framed the words mechanically. Lansberg stood up, obviously much annoyed at his carelessness.

"Yes, my man will find it, I'm sure. You must let me get the pearls re-strung for you, Laureen. They're valuable."

"An actress's bank," she managed to say lightly.

As they walked across the room his foot touched the small article he had dropped. Deftly he picked it up and slipped it into his pocket. It was only after she had gone that he remembered she had not answered his question.

But in her mind now there was no question whether he knew Delmond. For, with wildly beating heart, in one instant she had recognized that the small thing dropped from Lansberg's pocket was a seal which Leslie Delmond had worn four years ago in Nice.

It was just after eleven o'clock that same night—Tuesday—when Inspector Reynolds's wife and her brother-in-law came out of a cinema house in Highgate. She blinked a little in the jostling crowds.

"There's our tram, Bill, but we shall have to wait for the next. It's full."

"Trams be blowed!" exclaimed her brother-in-law. "When I take a lady out I like to do things properly. Hi, taxi, ahoy!" he shouted vigorously to a passing cab.

Remonstrating gently at his extravagance she allowed Bill to help her into the vehicle. She adored her husband's bluff-mannered brother—a sea captain.

Bill had not been in England for two years, and early this morning he had telegraphed saying he would arrive that afternoon for a short visit.

"Got any idea when Tom will be back, Agnes?" Captain Reynolds asked as their taxi jolted up the hill.

She shook her head. "Not exactly," she sighed. "He telephoned me this morning from the Yard, as I told you, saying he had to go to France at once, and expected he'd be back by Thursday. He said I was to be sure and make you stay over Sunday."

Captain Reynolds lighted his pipe and blew out a heavy cloud of smoke contentedly. He was very fond of his brother and sister-in-law and nothing pleased him better than to potter about their house and garden when he was ashore.

"Of course I'll stay," he said in his bluff tones. "Couldn't go away without a sight of the old chap. I say, Agnes, what's he gone to France about?"

Mrs. Reynolds looked important.

"He's in charge of a big case that happened two nights ago. Some film actor found murdered with chloroform in Laureen's flat. She's that famous revue artist. I shouldn't be surprised if Tom's tracking a clue in Paris."

The taxi pulled up at the gate of the semi-detached house and Captain Reynolds helped his sister-in-law out.

"A beautiful film," she murmured as he unfastened the door, "but very sad. Thank you, Bill, for taking me. I've enjoyed my evening so much."

"Give me Charlie Chaplin and a good laugh for my money. You put on a kettle for some toddy. Do you good after crying your eyes out over that blessed film."

Mrs. Reynolds entered the house, switched on the lights and obediently put water on to boil. Then hastened to remove the traces of tears still remaining after her evening's enjoyment. She had laid supper and the kettle was singing before she realized Bill had not yet come into the house.

"Smoking that horrible old pipe outside because he knows his tobacco makes me cough," she decided.

Opening the front door she called him. "Kettle's boiling, supper's ready, Bill."

There was no answer. Probably he was walking up and down the road in his restless way.

She went to the gate.

"Bill!" she called again. From somewhere near in the garden she heard a faint choking sound.

As she listened, fearful, she heard it once more, saw something dragging itself heavily, slowly along the ground toward her.

A wild scream came to her lips but she

suppressed it. Inspector Reynolds's wife was no coward.

Deliberately she opened the hall door so that the light should fall on this object, whatever it was, and seized a heavy stick from the umbrella-stand.

But the weapon dropped from her hand as the crawling thing drew nearer to the circle of light and she recognized it to be her brother-in-law. Before she could reach him, he rolled on his back and, with a shuddering groan, lay still.

She knelt on the path beside him, slipping her arm beneath his neck to raise his head. Could he have had a heart attack or a seizure?

"Bill," she cried, "it's all right I'm here." And then sank back trembling, for her fingers felt something warm and moist. Protruding from the man's left shoulder was the handle of a knife.

XIX. FINGERPRINTS

INSPECTOR REYNOLDS felt like a horse nearing its stables as he stepped out of the boat train that Wednesday evening with Spencer.

"You'll find me at my studio to-night, Inspector," said the painter, "or I'll come along to the Yard now if you prefer."

"I'll ring you up probably to-morrow morning," replied the detective, out of his abstraction.

He had more important interviews ahead than the one with this young man who had unwittingly thrown a new light on the problem. A falsetto voice might be the solution of that telephone call. If so, whose? Was it Delmond's before he was murdered? Mrs. Carter had overheard men's voices through the speaking tube. Was it one of those men who had spoken on the telephone?

Thrusting aside the newspaper boys calling up their "six-thirty finals" the detective jumped into a taxi and ordered the man to drive to Scotland Yard. He was eager to see Jenkins and hear all his faithful assistant had discovered. Then he would call on Lady Avice Garth and wring from her the truth about Tony.

Reynolds marched into his office with a jaunty air as if a thirty-six hour trip to Paris and back was an ordinary occurrence.

"Well, Jenkins, get my cables? Had any luck anywhere?" he asked.

Jenkins rose, his face somber, hands fidgeting

with a pen. "I'm afraid I've got some rather bad news for you, sir," he began.

The inspector glanced at him with a frown. "Lady Avice Garth not turned up at her house?" he questioned sharply.

Jenkins shook his head. "It's your brother, sir. He was stabbed about eleven thirty last night in the front garden of your house. Mrs. Reynolds found him and telephoned here at once. He's alive but unconscious."

"Bill!" exclaimed Reynolds in amazement. "Why, he hadn't an enemy in the world." Then as a light broke on him, "I suppose somebody was after me and got him instead. We are very much the same build."

He sat down at his desk and rested his head on his hands. At that moment he bitterly regretted his profession.

"Where is he?" the C. I. D. man asked Jenkins dejectedly.

"Highgate Infirmary, private ward, sir. The Yard sent down two specialists and Dr. Tempest was there most of last night with him and twice to-day. Dr. Tempest told me to ring up directly you arrived. Shall I do so?"

The detective nodded, his face drawn with pain. Poor defenseless old Bill, knifed in his own brother's home by some malicious fiend. Reynolds's fist clenched. If he had to scour Europe he'd get that brute and make him suffer for it!

Jenkins passed over the receiver. "Dr. Tempest is waiting, sir."

"That you, Inspector?"

"Yes, I've only just heard the news," Reynolds replied. "Thank you for all you've done, Doctor. Is there any hope?"

At Dr. Tempest's words the strain on the detective's face relaxed.

"You think he has a chance," he repeated eagerly. "Conscious for a few minutes and now sleeping. . . . A clean wound, missed the lungs by half an inch. . . . Do whatever you think best. Don't spare any money so long as you save him. . . . No, I won't try to see him until you say I may. . . . Thank you again, Doctor."

Reynolds turned from the instrument joyfully. "Did you hear that, Jenkins? The doctor says my brother has a chance now."

He put through a call to his home and waited impatiently.

"Yes, Agnes, I've just got back and heard about Bill," he told his wife, and then gave her the gist of his conversation with Dr. Tempest. "Don't worry too much. I'll be with you as soon as I can."

The inspector hung up the receiver and drummed his fingers on the desk. "I'll find out the scoundrel who did this or change my job," he announced sternly.

His assistant looked uneasy. "I suppose it couldn't have been any one connected with this murder case," he suggested.

His chief reflected a moment, running over the principals in his mind. Certainly no woman could have done it. Bill was a remarkably strong man. Lansberg he dismissed at once as being unlikely. Spencer, Tony and the man with the missing thumb were definitely in Paris at the time.

"No," Reynolds replied slowly. "I shouldn't think it probable. Besides, how would they know my house address? There are dozens of Reynoldses in the telephone book, and my official position is not shown there."

Jenkins stared at his chief aghast. Sweeping over him was the dreadful knowledge of a confession he had to make: of over-zealous efforts that possibly had had tragically far-reaching effects. For he remembered that on Lansberg's desk he had seen Inspector Reynolds's private address written on a slip of paper.

The detective regarded Jenkins's haggard face with a puzzled air. What on earth was the matter with the man? It wasn't his brother who had been stabbed!

"Have we got the knife that was used?" Reynolds asked.

Jenkins pulled out a drawer and produced a cardboard box.

"It's in there, sir. The doctor was very careful not to touch the handle."

Lifting the lid, the inspector gazed at the weapon —a blade, curved on one side like a French table-knife, hinged and set in a wooden handle.

"A most unusual type," muttered Reynolds as he pushed the box away with a shiver. "I've never seen anything quite like it. What about fingerprints?"

Jenkins replaced the cover and put the box back in the drawer before he answered.

"Three different sets were found. Overlapping a bit, but distinct and identifiable. Right hand in each case. Two sets have been identified," Jenkins announced.

Reynolds sprang up with excitement. "One set has a thumb missing?" he demanded eagerly. Adding as Jenkins shook his head, "No, of course he was in Paris at the time, but he might have handled the knife previously." Suddenly he observed his assistant's worried manner, noticed the perspiration standing on his forehead.

"What's wrong? Are you ill?"

Jenkins drew a long breath and raised his eyes. "No, sir. I'm in a mess. Yesterday when you went to Paris—I—tried to be clever, thinking I could help you. You warned me before and now I'm afraid I'm responsible for this—this stabbing affair."

"You, responsible!" The detective echoed the words blankly, surveying his assistant with a frown. Was the man demented? Then he added quietly, "Sit down, Jenkins, and tell me what the trouble is."

The man sank to a chair and moistened his lips, eyes resting piteously on his chief's face as if asking at least for understanding.

Inspector Reynolds's countenance was inscrutable as the man poured out the story of how he had gained admission to Lansberg's apartment, the trick he had played on the caretaker to get the key, his search in the apartment, the opening of the safe and the amazing collections of jewels on the shelves.

The detective interrupted him.

"That's queer," he returned. "Bachelors don't usually hoard tiaras and necklaces and rings such as you describe, in a private safe. Unless they're connoisseurs or jewel thieves. Lansberg seems too austere to be the former and too wealthy, I should have thought, for the latter. However, go on with your story, Jenkins. You locked the safe," he prompted, "and got out without any one seeing you, I hope."

The man mopped his brow.

"That's the mischief, sir. I could not close the darned safe, let alone lock it. There was some catch keeping it open and I'd just decided I daren't stay any longer when I heard some one enter the flat."

He described hiding behind the curtain, creeping out while the servant was grinding coffee, and replacing the keys in the basement cupboard.

"How do you know it was the servant? It might have been Mr. Lansberg or the secretary."

Jenkins negatived the suggestion firmly. "No, sir. They drove up with Miss Laureen about four thirty. The secretary carried in the golf-clubs and a tin case and then took the car to the garage. Laureen and Mr. Lansberg entered the flat and she drove off alone in a taxi at five forty. I had our man watching them. They'd been to Crowborough all right: I telephoned the Club House to make that certain."

Inspector Reynolds pushed back his chair and tramped up and down the room, his features set. Jenkins watched him, expecting a torrent of bitter reproach for his unauthorized adventure.

To his surprise, none came. He felt a hand on his shoulder and heard Reynolds's voice say mildly: "Well, you took a big risk."

The younger man fumbled with a parcel a moment and then opening it, exhibited to the astonished inspector a dress shirt and a silk vest.

"I found this under the mattress in the servant's room, sir," he stated. He pointed silently to a gash in the linen at the side of the starched front, and a corresponding slit in the undergarment.

Reynolds's eyes gleamed as he examined both

cuts with a magnifying glass.

"The gash on the vest has not cut quite through the silk, so apparently never reached the flesh," he announced.

Jenkins played his ace bravely although he knew also he condemned himself thereby.

"On the bottom shelf of Mr. Lansberg's safe, sir, was the knife which stabbed your brother," he said slowly.

And then indeed, Inspector Reynolds was aroused as the probabilities unfolded before him. He could picture Lansberg's servant finding the safe open and guessing it was the inspector who had been there searching the flat. The detective's face hardened as he recalled the scarcely veiled antagonism to him in the servant's eye when he was ordered to bring his master's clothes. His devotion to Lansberg was obvious. Why else had he hidden that shirt and vest under his own mattress?

When the servant discovered that these had been taken it was easy to link up their disappearance with the detective's previous visit, easier still to imagine that fanatical creature bent on revenge, seizing the weapon in the safe and watching outside Reynolds's house in the dark.

Then another vital point occurred to the detective.

How had that knife come to be in Lansberg's safe? From whom had *he* taken it and when?

Aloud he demanded swiftly, "Whose fingerprints were on the handle of that knife?"

"Those of Lansberg were there. Also those of Delmond, the murdered man."

"Lansberg!" shouted the detective. "How can you

be sure they're his?"

"We got some from the cigarette-box left in Laureen's flat," Jenkins replied, "and fresh ones to-day from the driving wheel of Lansberg's car."

Reynolds thumped his clenched fist on his desk.

"D'you see what all this means, Jenkins? That knife must have belonged to Delmond, and he evidently struck at Lansberg the night he was murdered, as this slashed shirt proves. So Lansberg was in Laureen's flat, after all. He must have seized the knife after he or his accomplices had chloroformed Delmond, and locked it up in his safe. Butterflies!" commented the detective grimly. "In this case a butterfly with golden hair and a pretty face! He'll have a job to explain away this evidence, I fancy."

"You would like the fingerprints of Lansberg's servant, sir?" asked Jenkins.

"Like?" snorted the inspector. "I mean to have them. They're an indispensable link in the chain."

Then his animation flickered a little. Was not all this merely circumstantial, a trifle too simple and easy? Why should a man of Lansberg's position commit murder and risk its consequences? Certainly not to obtain Laureen, who, if Reynolds could read character, disliked the dead man and liked Lansberg.

Also, in that case, where did Tony and Spencer, Lady Avice and Mrs. de Groot fit in? What about Valerie Baird and the packet of letters? And who was the man with the missing thumb who had undoubtedly been in Laureen's flat, as his fingerprints on the table proved?

No, Reynolds decided, he wasn't out of the woods

yet, even if there was a glimmer of daylight.

"What about those cabled orders I sent to watch the ports?" he asked suddenly.

Jenkins's face clouded. "No luck, sir," he reported. "No man minus a thumb was seen anywhere."

His chief, however, showed no signs of disappointment.

"H'm, well, I didn't expect any. It was a forlorn hope, but worth trying. Ring up Lady Avice Garth, Warnham House, and if she has arrived say I want to speak to her."

Jenkins gave the number and presently passed over the receiver.

"Inspector Reynolds of Scotland Yard speaking. . . . Left a message. Well, repeat it exactly, please." He put his hand over the mouthpiece and turned to Jenkins hurriedly. "Take down this conversation," he whispered. "Lady Avice Garth arrived at four o'clock and said she would call at Scotland Yard at eleven to-morrow, Thursday morning, and see Inspector Reynolds," he repeated. "Was her ladyship alone when she arrived? . . . She was? . . . Where has she gone now? Her ladyship did not say."

He banged down the receiver angrily.

"If I go off my head with this confounded case, Jenkins, it will be through the tangle of women mixed up in it. They've tied the men's tongues nicely. Chivalry, I suppose, would be their fancy name for it. Concealment of facts hindering the course of justice, that's what I call it."

The inspector was thoroughly irritated by this postponement of the interview with Lady Avice. Jenkins wisely tried to change the subject.

"No news of this Valerie Baird has come in yet, sir. Funny how she seems to have vanished."

"There are a lot of funny things in this case," agreed the inspector gloomily. "Come in," he called as a knock sounded on the door.

"A man to see you, sir," announced a constable. "Says he thinks Delmond was his lodger."

"Show him up at once," ordered Reynolds.

A short narrow-chested man with furtive darting eyes entered and sat down at the inspector's invitation.

"What makes you think the murdered man was your lodger?" demanded Reynolds bluntly. He had already sized up his visitor and knew the best way of tackling him.

"I recognized the photo in the paper and thought it might be the same man who'd had a room in my private hotel up to last Sunday."

The inspector gazed at him with steely eyes.

"This is Wednesday evening," he commented. "The photographs were printed in Tuesday's morning papers. It took you two days to decide whether you recognized it or not, eh?"

The man shuffled uneasily in his chair. "A murder case isn't nice to be mixed up in when you've got your business to consider," he whined.

"And where is this hotel of yours?"

"Near Euston station," replied the man, adding the address reluctantly. "Besides, I never knew he was called Delmond. Mr. Leslie Jackson he said was his name. The room's locked—he has the key."

"I shall be there to see it to-morrow," promised the inspector. "How long had he lodged at your house?"

"Going on for a month. Always paid well too and gave no trouble," replied the man sullenly. "Out all day. So as I didn't know anything against him, I thought I'd wait and see if he came back."

"Although by the photograph you knew he'd been murdered!" commented the detective. "Had he any visitors or letters?"

"No letters ever came for him. But once I found a torn envelope and addressed to L. Delmond, Poste Restante, Charing Cross, so his mail went there in that name probably. As to his visitors, I mind my own affairs so long as my rent is paid and my lodgers behave themselves."

"Answer my question," said the inspector sharply. "Did you ever see any visitors?"

"Well, once I believe a lady went up to his room, but I'm not sure. Might have been to see somebody else. I don't pry into other folk's affairs."

"A slim young lady, fair or dark?" suggested the inspector.

"Neither," affirmed the man. "I'm not certain which room she went to but I know what the lady was like. She was elderly, with gray hair and wore handsome clothes. A real lady, too."

"You're sure she was elderly?" questioned the inspector. "It might have been a young woman disguised."

"Well, it wasn't," said the man definitely. "What's more, I know who the old lady is," he added with a touch of triumph at scoring over the detective. "I've seen her since then."

"Where?"

"I was in the pit of Laureen's theater on Monday night and a lot of swells were in the stage box. I recognized the old party who'd been to my hotel a few days before and I asked the program girl who she was. That's how I know."

The detective bit back his impatience.

"And the program girl knew her name?" he asked mildly.

"Yes. The Countess of Warnham, and with her in the box was her niece, Lady Something Garth."

XX. THE THIRD KEY

"THE Countess of Warnham!" echoed the detective after Delmond's landlord had gone. "Do you hear that, Jenkins? Another woman to deal with. Will you tell me what was Delmond's attraction that all these females hung round him?"

Jenkins shrugged his shoulders.

"From the photographs he seemed a good-looking fellow," he conceded. "And of course a film actor, successful or no, always has a certain glamour."

"Glamour!" Reynolds sniffed disdainfully.

"Surely a woman of the Countess of Warnham's age and social standing—she must be over seventy—was not dazzled. What about that American woman, Mrs. de Groot? She's an astute bird in the early forties. Yet she fell for him."

"Has he some hold on them, do you think, sir?" Jenkins suggested.

"It's an idea, but Mrs. de Groot's feeling for Leslie Delmond was sincere. There is no doubt she really loved him. And I tell you, Jenkins, her grief was pitiful when she knew he was dead. Love! Why she was almost jealous of her friend Lady Avice when it came out that Lady Avice had written Delmond recently!"

The inspector had outlined the whole history of his Paris trip to his assistant. He often did this kind of thing: it arranged the pattern of events in his own mind and often drew valuable suggestions from Jenkins.

Jenkins pondered.

"It seems to me you did fine work in Paris, sir. You've definitely established the fact that this man with the missing thumb knows Mrs. de Groot and Lady Avice. You've discovered the *liaison* between Mrs. de Groot and Delmond, and that Tony is mixed up with them all. Shall I look up Lady Avice's pedigree?" he inquired.

"Look up any darned thing you can about her and her family," he said bitterly. "All *I* know is that they're nearly broke and Lady Avice's father, the Earl of Brentshire, is a dissolute old gambler who lives chiefly by his wits on the Riviera."

Presently Jenkins looked up from the big red book he was poring over.

"Lady Avice has three brothers," he announced, "and one of the younger brother's names is *Anthony*. They've got about five apiece!"

"Aha!" the inspector ejaculated. "Tony is short for Anthony." He picked up the telephone receiver and gave a number.

After a short conversation he hung it up with a look of satisfaction.

"Lady Avice's eldest brother is in India with his regiment. Both the younger ones are abroad and have not been seen for years. One was in the diplomatic service but resigned. The other dabbled in art a bit and then is supposed to have gone into a bank in Paris. That's our precious Tony, I'll lay any odds."

He glanced at his watch.

"Well, I'm through for to-night. If Highgate Infirmary says there's any change in my brother's condition call me at my home. Good night."

The street was deserted as a man came round a corner. Only a few seconds before he had seen the policeman on duty stalk slowly ahead flashing his lantern at each doorway conscientiously.

The man walked along with rapid steps until he reached the building he sought. Still no one in sight. He gave one furtive glance up and down, then vanished inside, his rubber-shod feet making no sound on the stairs.

Outside the door of a flat he paused, listened carefully and gave one light touch to the bell. His heart beat a little faster as he heard that faint summons tinkle distantly inside. A minute, perhaps two, he waited, but no one came.

One glance he bent toward the empty staircase before inserting a key in the lock. Quickly he entered, closed the door and again stood listening in the darkness. Save for the distant faint roar of traffic, there was absolute silence.

He crept through the flat to be sure it was unoccupied. Then satisfied he was alone, he began his work.

At first he searched with method and deliberation, going through drawers and cupboards patiently. But as time passed and still he was unsuccessful, beads of perspiration stood on his brow. He tore frantically at carpets, cut open the cushions and chair coverings with a knife taken from the kitchen, muttering to himself in a frenzy of rage. Pictures he ripped from their frames and flung down, as if lost to all fear of being discovered.

One room was locked, but he forced it easily with his shoulder. Inside was a large leather arm-chair before which he knelt, slashing the arms and seat wildly and inserting his hand amongst the padding. At one side of the seat the springs had sagged a little, leaving a gap between it and the arm.

With a gleam of hope on his white face he pushed his hand down, feeling carefully. But the thing he sought was not there.

Holding his head, he staggered out into the hall, reeling as if drunk, and regardless now of being seen or heard, shut the door behind him and went downstairs.

Walking blindly he came at last to the Embankment and sank on a seat shivering, although the night was warm and dry. Mechanically he moved along if a policeman came in sight, slinking back again when he had passed.

Haggard, the man's frenzy calmed to despair with the dawn, he crossed the nearest bridge and ambled off to his room in one of the murky streets on the south side of the Thames.

Early on Thursday morning Inspector Reynolds telephoned the hospital and learned that Bill had passed a fair night. A little comforted he set out for Euston to inspect the murdered man's room.

"Tell me," he said to the hotel proprietor who had called on him the evening before, "where were you when the Countess of Warnham called that day?"

"I was coming downstairs as she was going up."

"She might have been going to visit some one on the first or second floor perhaps," hinted the C. I. D. man.

The landlord looked at him skeptically. "Then what was she doing half-way up the third flight, where I met her?" he objected.

Reynolds nodded meditatively.

"Who else lives on the third and upper floors?" he demanded.

"A man and his wife, who are always out at business all day, have the next room to Mr. Leslie Jackson's or Delmond's. The only other room on that floor has been vacant for weeks. On the top floor live four shop assistants who have been here for three years."

"So you know quite well that this lady must have been going to call on Delmond as the other lodgers were out."

"I don't know for certain. I only guess," said the man sulkily.

The inspector raised an admonishing finger. "Look here, my man," he warned sharply, "if you do not answer my questions clearly and civilly I shall force your hand in a way you won't like. Go upstairs and show me the room."

"The door's fastened, sir. Mr. Jackson—I mean Delmond—always locked it when he went out."

"We'll try this. It was found in Delmond's pocket."

On the landing of the third floor the man paused and indicated a door.

"That was his room, sir," he said politely. "I can show you the other two on this floor as well if you like."

He opened the other two doors. One room was obviously unoccupied, and the other was as obviously in use but the tenants were out.

"The man and his wife I told you of," he explained. "They've got a little lock-up tobacco shop in the Euston Road."

The landlord was now as anxious to please the inspector as before he had been insolently secretive.

Reynolds inserted the key that had been found on the dead man and went into a good-sized room. He looked round eagerly, receptive always to atmosphere. The furniture told him nothing, but the articles on dressing-table and mantelpiece clearly showed the type of man Delmond had been.

There was a bottle of perfume and also a spray, a box of face-powder, nail polishing pad, brilliantine highly scented on the toilet table, together with two ornate silver-backed hair brushes. A pile of old paper-covered novels and out-of-date film journals were lying on a chair.

The mantelpiece held several photographs of film stars, all dated two to four years ago. There were also half a dozen pictures of the dead man in various attitudes and costumes, probably from the films he had played in.

The wardrobe and chest of drawers showed Delmond's taste in clothes to have been florid.

Reynolds searched the pockets deftly, finding nothing more interesting than old bus tickets.

"Where is his luggage?" the detective asked the landlord.

The man lifted the bed valance and dragged out two suitcases. One was unfastened and empty. The other the detective opened with one of Delmond's keys which he had brought with him.

Inside the suitcase was a small locked compartment. This too Reynolds unfastened with another key and quickly closed again when he saw it contained papers.

"I shall take this with me," he told the man. "The room will be locked again and no one must enter without my permission."

"Very well, sir," agreed the landlord, as they went downstairs to the hall.

"Do you remember which day that elderly lady called on Delmond?" asked the detective.

"Yes, I do," the man replied promptly. "Last Friday afternoon about three o'clock. That was June twenty-eighth, two days before Mr. Delmond was murdered."

"Why should you recollect that so clearly?" the inspector questioned suspiciously.

"Because it had rained heavily all the night before and that morning the lodgers who sleep on the top floor said the roof was leaking. I was too busy to go up and see about it until after I'd had my dinner. Then I remembered and went up."

"Quite so. But that might have happened any night or day." Reynolds was anxious to test the accuracy of this man's statements.

"No, sir, it was Friday, I'm positive, for when I saw the ceiling so wet, I was vexed, knowing Saturday was a half-day and I'd not get any work done on the roof until Monday."

"Have you a telephone here?" the inspector asked.

The man pointed to an alcove behind the hall door.

"Did you ever hear Delmond telephone to any one?"

The landlord shook his head.

"He never called any one up so far as I know, but once or twice I fetched him to the telephone. Each time it was a lady speaking—a haughty kind of voice—a youngish lady, I think."

"Can you remember when those calls were made?"

The man thought a minute.

"Within the last few days that Delmond was here I'm sure, as before that I scarcely saw him except when he paid his bill!" He puckered his forehead in an effort to recall something.

"Ah, now I've got it, sir. One call was last Thursday or Friday. It was a lady speaking. The second call—in the same voice, I fancy—was last Sunday about half past one when I was having my dinner in there." He indicated the room next the telephone.

The detective's eyes gleamed.

"Go on!" he urged.

"I ran up and called Mr. Delmond. He came down at once but I couldn't hear what was said except I think he replied, 'Oh, you've nothing to add to your letter, eh? We'll see about that.' He pushed open my door and thanked me and said, 'Your dinner smells good.' I laughed and replied, 'You'd better have some with me.' His answer was that he'd only just got up and had to go out on business. I never saw him again," the man added, "but I think he went out soon after."

"H'm. A telephone call in a lady's voice about Thursday. The Countess of Garth at three thirty on Friday to see him, and another telephone call about one thirty on Sunday, June thirtieth in the same voice," checked up the inspector.

"That's right, sir," agreed the man.

"Who answers the telephone when you're out?"

The landlord smiled. "Nobody: it just rings. My wife's deaf as a post and the old charwoman doesn't understand it."

In his office, Reynolds opened the compartment in the suitcase and scrutinized the contents carefully.

He found several letters signed "Mary" couched in terms of deepest affection, some indicating that money had been sent with them—without doubt from Mrs. de Groot. A few insignificant trinkets, such as links and tie pins. Three pictures of Laureen, cut out of current magazines, on one of which the address of her flat was penciled. A few other notes and bills.

Three pawn-tickets in his haul pleased Reynolds most of all and he decided to have these investigated at once.

Of passport, bank or check book, or addressed envelops there was no trace. To the detective it suggested that the dead man had much to conceal, and trusted nobody.

Also, Delmond might have been near the end of his resources, as his total cash appeared to be the money found in his pockets.

Again the detective's mind went back to the scene in Laureen's flat when he had questioned Carter the caretaker, about the letter to Valerie which he had posted.

What did that letter contain and where was it now? Could Laureen, or Lansberg, acting either separately or in collusion, have taken papers from the dead man's pocket, and fearing a personal search, posted them in the hall box?

And then at the bottom of the case, tucked inside

the tattered manuscript of a scenario, he found a snapshot. Holding it under a magnifying-glass he peered at it intently, knowing that here was another tiny link.

He was still staring at it when Jenkins came in and handed him a note. It bore the address of the hotel Laureen had moved to. He read:

Dear Sir,
I thank you most sincerely for the photograph you so kindly sent me of Mr. Jackson. In spite of all people may say against him, I shall always think of him the same.
Yours respectfully,
Bertha E. Mackie.

Poor Bertha, he reflected, duped but tenaciously faithful to the memory of this man who had used her merely as a tool. And he thought of that other woman, Mary de Groot, whom Delmond had treated in the same heartless fashion.

Jenkins recalled him from his reverie. "Miss Laureen would like to speak to you on the telephone, sir."

"Good morning, Inspector," Reynolds heard her across the wire cheerfully. "I hate hotels, and couldn't possibly return to that flat even if you allowed me to do so. Have I your permission to remove my own furniture and possessions to another flat which I have been offered? Of course you can leave the dining-room as it is. I never want to see any of that furniture again."

After a moment's reflection the inspector gave the required permission, adding, "Let me know when you wish to get your things."

"I must," came the quick retort, "since you have the keys."

"By the way, Miss Laureen, I meant to ask you before, have you any family living?"

Over the wire he heard a gurgle of laughter. "Inspector Reynolds, I'm surprised at you. I told you I was as yet unmarried."

The detective thanked his stars that television was not yet universal as he suppressed a smile.

"I referred to parents and possible brothers and sisters," he said.

"That's funny," she replied. "You're the second person in two days who has shown interest in my family-tree. I will give you the same reply I gave to— the other person. Which was to the effect that my father and mother believed in a small but good family and I'm *it*. My father died when I was a baby," she added.

"Thank you," replied Reynolds. "May I ask for the name of the other person interested in your family history?"

"Certainly," she answered casually. "It was Mr. Lansberg. Good morning, Inspector. Thank you for permission to get my belongings."

So Lansberg asked Laureen that question, Reynolds mused, as he hung up the receiver. Which meant that the man knew little of Laureen's past, or wished to verify the knowledge he had.

He turned to Jenkins. "Any one likely to be in Laureen's flat if I ring up?"

"Yes, sir. The photographers have gone round again to see if they can pick up any more fingerprints. They must be there now."

"Well, ring 'em up. I want them to get everything they can before Miss Laureen has her furniture removed. The dining-room of course must not be touched, until after the inquest."

Jenkins gave the number and waited for a reply. Presently he turned to his chief with a startled expression.

"Our men have just arrived, sir, and say they are certain the flat has been burgled. Everything is in disorder; drawers turned upside down, clothes all over the floor, carpets torn up and even chairs and cushions slashed open."

Reynolds snatched the receiver from him and asked a dozen swift questions. "Was the lock of the flat broken or the door open when you arrived?" he demanded.

"No," was the reply. "The lock is in perfect order and the door was fastened properly."

"The third key!" the detective snapped. "The person who entered that flat last night had the missing key and got it from Delmond—alive or dead."

The clock chimed the hour and reminded him that his interview with Lady Avice Garth was due. His bet was that she would not keep her appointment.

"A lady to see you, sir," said a constable at the door.

"Show her in," ordered Reynolds. So she *had* come after all.

But he was astounded to hear the constable announce:

"The Countess of Warnham."

XXI. REVELATIONS

INSPECTOR REYNOLDS felt a tremor of excitement pass through him as he rose deferentially to greet the elderly lady who entered. It was not a rare thing for him to come into contact with titled people, but it was certainly the first time a countess, and one of an old and distinguished family, had sought an interview with him.

Or, better still, obeyed a summons by proxy in place of her niece. A subtle distinction with an infinite difference, decided Reynolds, knowing perfectly well that he was at heart a thorough snob.

A little uneasily he sought in his memory for the correct mode of address.

"Will your ladyship be seated?" he invited, drawing forward a chair to face the light.

The old woman surveyed him and the room impartially through her lorgnette.

"Thank you," she said briefly, and seated herself in another chair with her back to the window, resuming her research work on the office.

"I am indebted to your ladyship for calling, but it was your niece—" began Reynolds heavily.

The woman withdrew her gaze from the mantelpiece and turned it on him. "It will be simpler if you address me as Lady Warnham," she interrupted. "I presume you are Inspector Reynolds." Her tone was peremptory.

The detective bowed, momentarily nonplussed by the inadequacy of his social knowledge.

"My niece, Lady Avice Garth, is ill. She insisted that I should keep her appointment with you and explain."

The detective smiled inwardly. These aristocrats imagined they could bluff the law, did they? Ill, indeed!

"Lady Avice seemed in perfect health last night in Paris when I saw her," he remarked blandly.

"And this Leslie Delmond was probably in perfect health on Sunday afternoon, yet he was dead by midnight," retorted Lady Warnham unexpectedly.

"There is no reason to imagine that Lady Avice will meet with such an untimely end," Reynolds observed, cynically.

"Indeed!" his visitor remarked coldly. "Perhaps this note will stimulate your imagination, Inspector."

Reynolds took the envelope she offered him, determined not to be beguiled by any plea of fatigue as a cause for postponing an interview.

Opening it he saw the inclosure was a medical certificate. Persuaded their tame doctor to come in on the job, he murmured to himself.

But his eyes widened as he read the few lines certifying that Lady Avice Garth was suffering from shock and loss of blood owing to a bullet wound in the left shoulder.

"A bullet wound!" he exclaimed. "What does this mean, your—Lady Warnham?"

"Probably just what it says," his visitor remarked indifferently. "I am not a medical man, but should say it also means considerable pain and fever for at least several days."

The inspector swallowed his temper and longed to give vent to a few ungentlemanly words not usually employed when conversing with a countess. Exasperating old woman, sitting there at insolent ease as if she had the whip hand over him. In his own office too!

Controlling his feelings with difficulty, he said quietly, "Please tell me how and when this happened, Lady Warnham."

"At five minutes to ten, just over an hour ago. My niece's friend, Laureen, called to see her at nine thirty, asking Avice to go with her to look over some flat she had been offered."

"Excuse me a moment," Reynolds interrupted. "What time was it, Jenkins, when Miss Laureen rang me up?"

"About ten thirty, sir," replied Jenkins from the far corner of the room.

"Thank you. Please continue, Lady Warnham."

"My niece said she could not do so as she had an appointment with you at eleven o'clock. After a short conversation Laureen went. She was driving herself in her new two-seater car and my niece went down to look at it. They stood by the car for a moment. Then Laureen got in, pressed the self-starter and drove off."

"Where were you at the time, Lady Warnham?"

"Reading the *Times* in the dining-room, on the ground floor. With my back to the window, as I am now," the lady remarked pointedly. "I heard a bang but thought it was the back-fire of the engine. Then a minute later Avice staggered in, holding her shoulder. She looked ghastly. I thought she was going to faint."

"Were you alone? I mean, were there any servants in the hall or dining-room?" the inspector asked.

"Nobody was in the hall, but as my niece came into the dining-room the parlor-maid came to clear away the breakfast. She saw the blood pouring from my niece's shoulder and, of course, screamed."

Inspector Reynolds frowned.

"And you mean to say that Miss Laureen calmly motored away knowing her friend had been shot?" he questioned sternly.

"Nonsense, my good man, I mean nothing of the kind. Laureen motored calmly away not dreaming what had happened. If she heard anything, she probably thought, as I did, that it was an engine back-firing."

"How long after Miss Laureen's departure was the shot fired?"

"I should say at the second she started."

The inspector weighed the matter a moment. No, it was quite evident Laureen had not known her friend had been shot when she telephoned to him so light-heartedly at ten thirty. Then a point struck him. That shot, might it not equally well have been intended for Laureen? If so, who fired it?

"Did you see any one in Curzon Street near your house?" he asked.

"I have already told you, Inspector, that I was reading the newspaper with my back to the window and knew nothing of the incident until my niece entered the room and the idiotic maid screamed."

"Of course you immediately sent for the police."

"Of course I immediately sent for the *doctor*," Lady Warnham corrected caustically.

"The police also should have been informed," he told her.

"Well, I'm informing them now. There was no time before. My niece was my first concern. Directly the doctor had arrived and dressed her wound—a clean flesh wound, the bullet having passed straight through—Lady Avice insisted that you should be sent for. She said you would not believe in the accident unless you actually saw the wound."

The detective reddened.

"I didn't know my previous behavior had been so inhuman, Lady Warnham."

The lady raised her eyebrows.

"One doesn't expect humanity from a detective," she responded with blunt indifference. "*Ce n'est pas son metier*. Also, my niece hasn't forgotten that she evaded her appointment with you in Paris yesterday morning."

"She also promised to see me last night in London and then left a message saying she would call this morning," he offered in extenuation of his apparent disbelief.

Lady Warnham gave him an amiable smile.

"Ah well, we mustn't be too severe on the erratic younger generation, Inspector. The war bred a new type, you know."

The friendly "we" was as balm to the detective after the rankling "my good man" of a few moments before. But it did not blind him to the fallacy of the lady's diplomatic words.

"Perhaps you would like to call at 'Warnham House,' Inspector. The doctor may give you permission to see my niece, even if you may not question her to-day."

"I shall most certainly call there this morning," Reynolds assured her gravely.

He turned to Jenkins and gave him some rapid instructions. His visitor rose, gathering her cloak round her. The detective raised his hand detaining her. "One moment, please, Lady Warnham. There is something I should like to ask you."

The lady's face expressed bored surprise as she resumed her seat.

"I have told you all I know of this shooting affair, Inspector. This morning I have an important engagement."

"Madam," Reynolds said seriously, "there can be no more important engagement than the one you are now keeping. I am concerned with a deeper matter than the unfortunate accident to Lady Avice Garth."

He paused, well aware it would add tension to his next question, hoping to rouse comment from Lady Warnham.

"I am waiting," she remarked imperturbably, lifting her lorgnette and regarding him as though he were a new species of insect under a microscope.

But this time she aroused no irritation in the inspector. The moment he had worked for had arrived, and he used it dramatically.

Leaning across his desk he spoke slowly. "Lady Warnham, what was the object of your visit to Leslie Delmond or Jackson in his hotel on Friday afternoon, June twenty-eighth, two days before he was murdered?"

His visitor lowered her glasses calmly, but her fingers tightened on the handle.

"Are you suggesting *I* killed the man?" she demanded.

The detective waved aside her remark with a gesture of impatience.

"I am suggesting nothing, madam. I am asking a question."

He watched her closely but could detect no sign of fear. Her vague gaze wandered past him as though she were deciding how much or little she should reveal.

"If I hesitate, Inspector, it is because one does not willingly wash soiled linen in public," she explained. "Especially when it involves the honor of a member of one's own family."

"I'm afraid the law does not consider niceties of that kind," the C. I. D. man said in a warning tone.

The lady raised her head proudly. "There is yet another law that my family has obeyed for centuries, Inspector. Its members even endured torture in the observance of it—but they held their tongues." She was silent for a second. Then she said clearly, "I have said this to prove to you that I am not to be frightened into speech. I am old now, but alive to the duty I owe to those of my own blood."

"Even though you protect a criminal by your silence, Lady Warnham?" His voice was toneless but in his heart was a deep respect for this courageous old woman who faced him now.

"Thank God I am not called upon to decide on so serious a matter as that, Inspector," she replied fervently. "No, my problem is purely a matter of family honor and nothing more. Please let me think a moment."

She leaned her head on her thin, finely-veined hand while Reynolds regarded her compassionately. Deeply attached to his own mother—she was about the same age as Lady Warnham, he reflected—how would *he* feel if some man were roughly urging her to speak against some member of her family. But thrusting sentiment aside, he reminded himself that possibly on Lady Warnham's frankness rested the detection of a murder.

"Two years ago last February I went to Nice, Inspector," she began suddenly. "My niece, Lady Avice Garth, was then living with her father, who is my brother."

"The Earl of Brentshire," put in the detective.

"Yes. My brother had been gambling as usual, but with worse than the usual results. I am a childless widow and very fond of Avice. She was leading an unhappy existence; a very undignified one too, for, thanks to her father, they were in debt everywhere. At great personal inconvenience I paid what they owed, stipulating that my niece should be allowed in future to live with me. My brother agreed. He still spends his winters there and gambles wildly, I believe, though where he gets the money is a mystery I've never solved."

Inspector Reynolds thought he could guess, remembering the many company prospectuses on which the Earl of Brentshire's name figured as enticing bait.

"And you met Delmond that winter in Nice," he suggested.

Lady Warnham nodded.

"He was acting in some film and a scene was taken on the terrace of my hotel. The guests were invited to figure in the scene, seated at little tables, and some of them did so. My niece among them. She was very excited about it and became so attracted to Laureen—who was the heroine of this film, that we drove out to the studios and visited the place next day, on Laureen's invitation."

"Was Mrs. de Groot, an American lady, by any chance staying in your hotel?"

His visitor's expression altered slightly.

"She was. A floridly dressed, be-jeweled woman, very wealthy but good-natured. She apparently had few or no friends and my niece with her warm impulsiveness promptly adopted Mrs. de Groot and insisted on taking her in our party everywhere. I was against it at first, but I must admit that Mary de Groot has sterling qualities, even if—" She broke off a trifle confused.

"Even if she became infatuated with Delmond," supplemented Reynolds with a reassuring smile.

Lady Warnham looked relieved.

"Oh, you know about that affair. Yes, Mrs. de Groot was of our party. That is how she met Delmond. After that he spent all his spare time with her while Laureen and my niece became great friends and have remained so ever since."

"You raised no objection to their friendship?" asked the detective.

"Certainly not," the lady replied firmly. "Apart from the fact that Laureen is as charming as she looks, I had no right to interfere. One of the lessons age has to learn is not to antagonize youth by applying ancient rules to these modern times. I love my niece and wish to keep her affection and friendship. Therefore I leave her absolutely free."

"Possibly too free," thought the inspector, remembering that midnight escapade in Paris.

"Were Laureen and Delmond very friendly?" he asked.

"Never," declared the countess emphatically.

"She despised and disliked the man for taking Mary de Groot's money and gifts and laughing about her behind her back. He and Laureen quarreled bitterly about it."

"Maybe Laureen was jealous?" the detective surmised.

Lady Warnham scorned the idea.

"Jealous? Of what? She was the star, while he played a small part. The film director told me that Laureen detested Delmond the first day she was introduced to him. He attempted to kiss her in public and she ridiculed him—also in public. After that, it was war to the knife. She tried very hard to save Mrs. de Groot from a vain, unworthy man."

So Laureen had detested Delmond from the first day! Yet only last Sunday night she said he had been her lover and they had quarreled. Why had she lied? Whom was she protecting? For that her statement was untrue the detective was fully convinced.

"And now I come to the part I dislike, Inspector. My jewels are valuable; a few of them are heirlooms, the rest I have the right to dispose of." Her lips twitched. "And I have exercised that right through force of circumstances in regard to a part of them.

"One day my brother came to me at my hotel in Nice in great trouble," she continued. "Financial, of course! He had gambled and lost and borrowed to such an extent that he owed several hundreds of pounds. He implored me to sell some jewels to help him. I refused and he actually struggled with me to obtain my keys! We were on the hotel terrace and Delmond and Mrs. de Groot came along. Delmond pretended not to have seen or heard anything and Mrs. de Groot introduced him to my brother. To my astonishment my brother and Delmond became friendly and were often together after that."

A tinge of shame crept over the old lady's pale cheeks. "About a fortnight later I discovered accidentally that all my brother's debts had been paid. Discovered—" She stopped and faced the detective steadily.

"I am afraid, Inspector," she went on, "in spite of all you can do to me, that this is where my story must end abruptly. I have no right to tell you more," she said with dignity.

"Since others are involved," finished Reynolds to himself. He changed the subject deftly. "Lady Warnham, where is Tony?" he asked swiftly.

The old lady appeared puzzled or disturbed. He could not decide which.

"Tony!" she repeated blankly.

"Yes. One of Lady Avice's brothers—the youngest, I believe—is called Anthony. Abbreviated, that would be Tony, wouldn't it?"

"Lady Avice's youngest brother was generally known as 'Stinker.'" The old lady's eyes twinkled with amusement. "I never heard him called anything so refined as 'Tony.' I have no idea where he is at the moment. 'Stinker' was painting, or trying to, in Paris when last I heard of him. We are not a particularly communicative family so far as letter writing goes, though we have rather a weakness for loyalty," she added with gentle sarcasm.

Reynolds switched the former subject back adroitly.

"Forgive me, Lady Warnham, for again dragging up this painful question. Your story lacked completion, you see. Can you not explain to me why you called on Delmond two days before he was murdered?"

Lady Warnham rose and drew herself up, eyes tragic with grief. "Inspector Reynolds, you think of Delmond as a murdered film artist to be avenged by the law. I knew him to be a blackmailer." Her voice faltered and she put her hand on the table to support herself. "At this moment I can tell you no more."

XXII. TIGHTENING THE NET

IN Laureen's flat, to which Inspector Reynolds went immediately the Countess of Warnham had left him, there was utter chaos. The photographers and a policeman awaited him.

He addressed the constable sharply. "You were in charge here?"

"Yes, sir. I locked up at six last night after looking round as I've done each evening by your instructions. Everything was in order then."

"What time did you get here this morning?"

"With the photographers, sir, about ten thirty."

Reynolds walked from room to room, and thought a tornado might have produced much the same effect. Surely this could not have been done by a sane person. Was it the result of madness, malice or panic? The answer to that might help considerably, he realized.

The dining-room doors had been locked the evening before. Now the one leading into the hall was open, the lock roughly forced.

Before the big leather chair in which Delmond had been found dead the inspector paused, with pursed lips. For the first time he noticed the space between the seat and the arm, and thought how easy it would have been for something to have slipped from Delmond's hand or pocket and lain concealed. Had the searcher of last night found what he wanted there? Reynolds was inclined to believe not. He slid his hand along the lining but there was nothing there now.

"Lock the place up again, and have it watched. The burglar may come back, but I doubt it."

In Curzon Street, almost opposite the Countess of Warnham's house, he took out a cigarette and asked a man for a match. It was the same constable who had trailed Laureen unsuccessfully three days before.

"Well?" demanded Reynolds abruptly.

"Nobody round here heard the shot or noticed any one loitering before it happened. The bullet struck the wall by Warnham House visitors' bell. You can see the mark. I picked up the bullet, sir. No visitors to the house since I came."

Reynolds slipped the leaden ball in his pocket.

"All right. Hang round," he said.

As the inspector crossed the road a small car driven by Laureen pulled up at Warnham House and its occupant jumped out hurriedly. The actress was about to ring the bell when she saw Reynolds beside her.

"Of course you've heard about Lady Avice?" she said. "I've just rushed back to see how she is."

The inspector eyed her keenly. "When did you learn about the accident, Miss Laureen?" he asked pointedly.

She frowned as she pressed the button. "Ten minutes ago. Lady Warnham telephoned to my hotel and my maid rang me up at the new flat I was looking at. I came here immediately."

The butler opened the door and admitted them at once.

"How is Lady Avice, Mason?" Laureen asked anxiously.

"I hear there is no danger, miss, but her ladyship has lost a lot of blood and must be kept quiet, the doctor says." He cast a frigid eye at the C. I. D. man.

"This is an inspector from Scotland Yard. Lady Warnham expects him," Laureen explained.

"I should like to see the butler alone a moment," Reynolds told her.

Turning to the man, he asked him where he was when the accident occurred.

"In my pantry at the back of the house, sir."

"Any of the other servants see or hear anything?"

The butler shook his head. "I questioned them, but only the parlor-maid knew anything about it. And all she saw was Lady Avice stagger into the dining-room."

"Who closed the front door behind Lady Avice as she came in from the street?"

"The parlor-maid says she shut it. That was only a few seconds before she entered the dining-room," he added.

A dead end there, decided the inspector, though he patiently questioned the staff one by one.

None had heard the shot or been near the front of the house at the time.

"The doctor has just called again, sir," said the butler. "He says he will see you when he comes down from her ladyship's room, if you wish. If you will wait here I will bring him to you."

An elderly man was presently shown into the dining-room where Reynolds was standing at the window, visualizing the shooting affair.

"You signed the medical certificate I received this morning, Doctor?" asked Reynolds.

The doctor assented curtly. "I did; at Lady

Avice's express wish. She seemed more distressed at being unable to keep her appointment with you than by the unfortunate cause."

Reynolds sensed the sting in his words. "How is she now?" he asked.

"In no danger, but in considerable pain and very weak," the doctor announced.

The C. I. D. man held something out on his hand. "Here is the bullet," he said.

The medical man took it to the light and regarded it with interest. "A little lower and the wound would have been serious," he declared, returning the thing to Reynolds. "I suppose you wish to know when you can see Lady Avice?"

"It would help me considerably, Doctor."

"Well, you may see her now, and nothing more. I greatly disapprove, but again it is her particular wish. Perhaps to-morrow afternoon she can talk to you a little, but on no account must she be agitated," he said severely.

"I understand perfectly. Why does she wish me to see her now if I may not speak?" Reynolds asked in a puzzled voice.

The doctor laughed. "Don't ask me to explain the mental processes of a woman. I'm far too busy. Please come with me. Miss Laureen is sitting with Lady Avice. I allowed her to go in on the understanding that she does not permit her friend to speak."

Hat in hand, Reynolds followed the doctor up the wide shallow staircase to a room on the first floor, feeling perhaps more awkward than he had for years.

He stood in the darkened room gazing at the pale

face of the girl who lay propped against pillows. She raised one hand in greeting and smiled faintly.

The detective saw her lips move, and Laureen bent quickly over her friend.

"Lady Avice wishes me to say she is so sorry, but this time it is not her fault, Inspector," Laureen repeated.

"Please believe how deeply I regret that you should be suffering like this, Lady Avice," Reynolds said in a low voice. "Thank you for allowing me to come in."

There was a queer sensation in his throat as he went downstairs. There was grit and fineness in that girl, and with all his heart he wished she had not been mixed up in this business.

"Don't be anxious," he assured the doctor as they stood in the hall. "I shall not do anything to worry your patient to-morrow. If you wish I'll leave it until a day later."

But apparently the medical man was satisfied with Reynolds's discretion.

"Oh, you can have half an hour with her tomorrow if she's had a good night," he conceded. "I don't want to hinder you in your duty. Good day."

Laureen came downstairs as Reynolds was leaving. "I'll give you a lift, Inspector, if you care to risk your neck with me."

"Thank you," he accepted. "Your life is as precious as mine. I'll chance it, Miss Laureen. Just one moment and I'll join you."

He turned aside to speak to the butler.

"Did Lady Avice come here alone yesterday on her return from Paris?" he asked.

"Yes, sir."

"What time?"

The butler reflected. "About four o'clock," he answered.

"Did any gentleman call on her either last evening or this morning?"

"Mr. Spencer called just before dinner, but as her ladyship was out he did not enter the house. He is calling later, I believe."

There was cold reserve in the man's voice, although he replied unhesitatingly. His mistress had given him instructions to answer the detective's questions, but Reynolds realized that the man resented it when Lady Avice was ill and defenseless. Ah well, he thought, his was a ruthless, indelicate job.

Outside, Laureen sat in her car waiting for him. He went out to her.

"I want you to put the car, as nearly as you can remember, in the exact position it was in this morning when you were talking to Lady Avice," Reynolds requested.

The girl measured the distance with her eye and then reversed for about a yard.

"Just here," she said. "I left it where it could be seen from the dining-room. Avice stood there," she pointed to a spot immediately in front of the bell marked "Visitors."

Across the road was a narrow alley running between two houses, where it was obvious that any one could have remained fairly well concealed.

"From the position you were in the bullet might easily have hit you instead, Miss Laureen," he remarked as he got into her car.

"Why, of course," she said, staring at him in

astonishment. "It was *meant* for me," and bit her lip quickly as she pressed the self-starter. "Where shall I drop you, Inspector? I'm going back to my hotel."

"Anywhere near there will do for me," he answered vaguely. "Meant for you, eh!" he thought to himself. "That was a slip, young lady."

"Have you any enemy that you know of?" the C. I. D. man asked quietly, admiring the sure way she guided the car through the busy traffic.

"Dozens, I should think," she replied lightly, her eyes dancing with fun. "But I can't believe they would willingly risk their necks for the pleasure of shooting me."

"Yet you thought that shot was meant for you," persisted Reynolds.

"Well, who could possibly have wanted to hurt Avice?" she fenced. "Whereas I—maybe I've an unknown foe more venturesome than those I know of."

"Among those enemies, known or unknown, do you think there is a man who lacks a thumb?" Reynolds watched her intently and was certain that she started.

"Is it a conundrum?" she demanded. "If so, I can't tell you the answer. My unknown enemy may even lack a nose or ears, Inspector." She pulled into the curb by her hotel. "Here we are, but here I shall not be for many days, thanks to your permission to get my furniture and belongings."

Reynolds got out of the car and stood with his hand resting on the wind screen, a position that gave him a good angle from which to watch her face.

"That reminds me," he said. "I've news for you. Your flat was broken into last night."

"What? With a real live policeman of your own choice on guard!" she mocked.

"He does not stay there all night," the detective told her.

"Well, unless they wanted my clothing or the chairs and tables there wasn't much to interest them. My jewelry is in the hotel."

"Nothing apparently was taken. The intruder seems to have been searching for something and in the process to have gone berserker. He slashed open the padding of chairs and cushions, tore down the pictures and ripped up the carpets."

A look of relief, almost of triumph, crossed her face. "There was nothing there—I mean," she added hurriedly, "nothing of value."

"Have you a matinee this afternoon, Miss Laureen?"

The girl shook her head.

"Not on Thursdays. Matinees are Wednesdays and Saturdays."

"I may need to ring you up," Reynolds explained.

"I shall be at Mr. Spencer's studio all this afternoon. He's doing a portrait of me. You might tell that little pet of yours who is on guard. He lost me twice yesterday and I saw him trotting round like a stray rabbit. I felt sorry for him. Good-by. I'm going to the garage."

She slipped in the gear and slid off, her eyes twinkling. Inspector Reynolds amused her with his stolidity. But he had asked questions that she dared not answer just now. Yet she found something likeable in him, and her heart had warmed with quick sympathy when Bertha showed her the photograph of her quondam lover which Reynolds had not forgotten to send.

"A nice man with a nasty job, Bertha," she had replied, when Bertha had said the inspector was very kind.

The C. I. D. man walked slowly back to Scotland Yard deep in thought and fully aware that Laureen had avoided a reply.

There were so many things to sift out in this case. His chief difficulty lay in deciding which to work at first. Every hour that passed now was that much to the good for the murderer.

Rarely had he come across so, apparently, simple a murder case involving three people that had opened out into one that enmeshed at least a dozen. In his office he found Lansberg and Dr. Tempest waiting to see him.

The doctor greeted him hurriedly. "I can wait, Inspector. Your brother's doing nicely. I'll tell you all details when you've seen Mr. Lansberg."

"Thank you, Doctor. Will you have a hurried luncheon with me?"

The doctor assented. "I'll wait downstairs," he added. "Good-by, Lansberg."

"Can you dine with me to-night, Doctor? Eight o'clock at the club?" Lansberg asked.

Dr. Tempest smiled. "That will make two free meals in one day," he remarked. "Thanks very much, Lansberg. I'll be there."

Lansberg turned to the detective as Dr. Tempest went out. "Dr. Tempest has just told me of this murderous attack on your brother, Inspector. I'm very sorry to hear of it. It was a senseless, cruel act."

The detective sat down at his desk and began slowly to fill his pipe.

"That's very kind of you, Mr. Lansberg," he replied. "I suppose the attack appeared to be senseless, but no more so than the one made on Lady Avice Garth this morning." He seemed to be only occupied with pressing in the tobacco but for one second his swift glance shot to Lansberg's face.

It expressed utter surprise and consternation.

"An attack on Lady Avice!" Lansberg repeated.

Suspense was always a favorite card with Reynolds. He lighted a match and drew several leisurely puffs at his pipe to make sure it was well alight before he answered.

"Yes. She was shot outside Warnham House this morning. Happily only a flesh wound in the shoulder."

Lansberg uttered an exclamation. "She might have been killed," he said indignantly.

"Easily," agreed Reynolds. "Or her companion. They were both within the same range. It's possibly a parallel case with that of my brother."

"I don't understand."

The inspector watched a curl of smoke fade upward. Then he brought his gaze back to the man opposite him.

"It's quite simple," he replied. "The man who struck down my brother mistook him for me. The man who shot Lady Avice," he paused, "was possibly—I only say *possibly*—aiming at her companion."

"And that was?"

"Laureen!" The inspector replied ominously, keenly alive to the pallor that swept at once over Lansberg's face and to the fine fingers clenched tightly.

Now was the time to follow up that blow and Reynolds knew it. Leaning across his desk, he said firmly:

"Mr. Lansberg, there is not only mystery in this murder case, there is undoubtedly grave danger surrounding others. If you value Miss Laureen's life you will be frank and help me all you can—before it is too late."

The lines of Lansberg's face seemed graven with suffering as he sat there, staring blindly at the detective.

"I promise to help you," he said with difficulty. He passed a hand across his face as if he were striving to clear away the memory of what he had heard. Laureen's life in danger! Yes, he would have to speak—but not now. He must have time to think.

"There was something you wanted to see me about," reminded the detective.

The dazed look faded from Lansberg's eyes. "Yes, of course. The shock of your news made me forget. On Tuesday afternoon I motored to Crowborough for golf, with Miss Laureen and my secretary."

"I am aware of that," said Reynolds succinctly.

"On returning to my apartment at four thirty I found some one had got in during my servant's absence and managed to open my safe. Miss Laureen was with me."

"And maybe that's why you're reporting this," thought the detective shrewdly. "Indeed," he replied aloud. "Was anything missing?"

Lansberg shook his head.

"Nothing of value, although the safe contained some valuable things. It seemed purely a voyage of discovery."

The inspector forebore from asking if any article of no intrinsic value had been taken.

"You are sure you locked the safe before going out?" he questioned mildly.

The color was gradually coming back to Lansberg's face now, as he replied in a troubled tone. "I could have sworn I did, only memory plays strange tricks at times. Because of that I might even not have troubled to report this to you but for an extraordinary occurrence."

The detective glanced up curiously. "What's that?"

"My servant Neron—you saw him the previous day—went out that evening and has not returned. He is absolutely faithful and devoted to my interests. I'm afraid something may have happened to him."

The detective regarded his visitor speculatively.

"I remember the man perfectly. He certainly behaved as if you were a minor deity, Mr. Lansberg. But you say he went out on Tuesday evening. This is Thursday morning," he reminded. "Why this delay on your part?"

Lansberg's expression stiffened a little at the implied reproach. "There was no particular reason for informing Scotland Yard at once," he remarked frigidly. "But becoming uneasy yesterday afternoon I telephoned to you and learned you were away. I rang again later last night and heard you had returned but would not be in the office until this morning."

"That's quite correct," agreed Reynolds. "I was informed you had telephoned twice. The news of the attack on my brother sent me home earlier than usual."

"Naturally. Well, this morning I had important

business to transact and came here as soon as I could."

The inspector knocked out his pipe and put it in his pocket. "You've no idea in your mind, Mr. Lansberg, to account for your servant's absence?"

"None. Unless he has met with an accident. Perhaps you could get into touch with the hospitals for me.

"I could—if necessary," Reynolds replied meditatively. "You've no reason to suspect foul play?"

Lansberg made a faint gesture. "To my knowledge he had neither friends nor foes in London."

"Nor reason to suspect his flight?" Reynolds's voice had a clearer, harder tone now.

"Flight!" Lansberg echoed looking puzzled.

"Flight," repeated the detective. "Self-preservation is the first law."

"I don't understand you, Inspector."

"No?" queried Reynolds mildly. He drew a box from a drawer beside him and laid it on the table. "Perhaps this will explain."

He whipped off the lid and exhibited a long curved knife within.

"This knife, Mr. Lansberg, was taken"—he paused a second—"from my brother's shoulder. I think it may account for your servant's absence."

XXIII. BEHIND THE STAGE

LANSBERG looked at the ugly weapon, its curving blade dulled with ominous spots. His face was like a mask, the color again driven from it by the sheer horror this thing had conjured up.

"Mr. Lansberg, this damnable concealment of fact and evasion of frankness has to come to an end," the detective thundered, banging his fist on the desk. "It has already caused suffering to two innocent people. My brother at least is entirely guiltless of complicity. Of Lady Avice Garth's part in this conspiracy of silence I have yet to judge. Her worst crime is shielding some one else, I think."

The ghost of a smile flickered across Lansberg's face, giving it an extraordinary sweetness.

"You may be quite sure of that, Inspector. I know her to be a loyal, courageous and honorable woman. As for my own case, maybe you will not think so harshly of me by this time to-morrow, if I may ask for so much grace to decide my course of action. One hesitates to involve others, you see."

Reynolds was taken aback by Lansberg's obvious sincerity. Before he could speak, Lansberg continued:

"I am neither contemplating flight nor suicide," he remarked with a whimsical twist of his mouth. "And I am quite sure you will be satisfied—when I *do* speak."

"Delays complicate our duties more than the lay mind understands," said Reynolds. He was not unwilling to grant Lansberg the time he asked for because there were many points that urgently needed his attention that afternoon. And also there was the memory that those in authority over him had urged the utmost delicacy in dealing with Mr. Lansberg.

"Very well," he agreed. "Shall we say noon tomorrow in this office?"

Lansberg bowed. "At noon to-morrow," he promised.

On the desk near him was a photograph. Lansberg's eyes fell on it unconsciously as he rose, then his forehead wrinkled in perplexity and he bent over it a moment.

"Leslie Delmond," explained the inspector. "It was taken at Nice two and a half years ago, I believe. I've had it copied for the newspapers."

"Yes," murmured Lansberg, almost as if he hadn't heard. "May I look at it through your glass?"

Reynolds pushed the lens across and watched intently. Lansberg had said he had never met the dead man. Why this sudden interest?

"You did not know him?" the detective questioned.

Lansberg raised his head abstractedly.

"No," he replied. "But he resembles a woman who twice came to me in queer circumstances; once about a couple of years ago, and once more recently. The likeness is so extraordinary that she might be his twin sister," he added as he laid the picture back on the desk.

"Will you tell me about it?" The inspector tried to speak idly and cloak his curiosity.

Lansberg hesitated. "It can have nothing to do

with this case and the woman asked me to tell no one." He smiled. "A promise to a mysterious unknown—it sounds quite romantic."

"You don't know her name and address?"

"Neither. She was thickly veiled each time but her features were unmistakable. After all, as the incident is finished, maybe there is no harm in telling you the rough outline. She asked me the first time to lock something up for her as her husband might steal it. And recently she called to claim it. That's all."

"I see," Reynolds nodded, his eyes bent on his writing pad. "Had she a husky contralto voice by any chance?"

"The very reverse," stated Lansberg definitely. "It was clear, very clear, and rather high." He rose. "I must be off or Tempest will be tired of waiting for you. I'll see you to-morrow, Inspector."

A high, clear voice, reflected Reynolds as he stumped solidly downstairs. Oh, undoubtedly he'd got a very nice little clue that suggested many possibilities.

He was rather distrait over luncheon. Dr. Tempest studied him thoughtfully. "You need not worry about your brother, Inspector. You can see him when you like. Your wife was there this morning. He's enjoying poor health, he says, thanks to a pretty nurse who happens to be looking after him. This morning he informed me he didn't mind how long he was ill."

The inspector roared with laughter. "Bill's at his old games then. He's a rascal; flirts desperately with every good-looking girl he meets."

The doctor's thin face brightened with

amusement. "I can promise you he's losing no time now. Insists on kissing the hand that feeds him, as he puts it. He'll pull through all right."

"I'm deeply grateful to you," Reynolds said sincerely.

Dr. Tempest brushed aside the remark. "Your brother says he has no idea who struck him. He saw and heard nothing. Just felt a terrible pain and went down unconscious."

Reynolds's face was grim.

"I've a pretty good idea, though." He peered at his companion closely. "I say, Doctor, you're eating nothing and look like a ghost. What's wrong?"

"Working a bit too hard possibly."

"And probably up all night with Bill. I shall always feel you saved his life."

"Nonsense," said Tempest bruskly. "Well, I must be off. I've a lot to do."

The inspector was in his office a little later when the telephone bell rang. His wife's voice answered him. "I've seen Bill," she said. "He's getting on well. By the way, the matron told me that Dr. Tempest insisted on blood transfusion at once last night, and he unselfishly offered to be the donor. Couldn't get any one else at that hour. Wasn't it splendid of him? I thought he looked very ill this morning."

So that was why Tempest seemed so wan and tired, thought Reynolds as he put back the receiver. Indeed he owed him a debt of gratitude. A pang of remorse touched the detective as he remembered how he and Dr. Tempest had crossed swords more than once. He had thought the doctor was inclined to be nervous and weak, though clever at his job. Now he realized there was a fine, quiet courage underlying those aloof, gentle manners.

"I've determined to find out something about that Valerie Baird, Jenkins," he said. "Ring up the hospitals again and at the same time ask if a man answering to the description of Lansberg's servant has been brought in. Hang it all, it's ridiculous to think of two people disappearing, both mixed up in this Delmond case."

Reynolds walked up Whitehall in a troubled frame of mind. The murder had been committed on Sunday night. This was Thursday afternoon and he was as far off laying his hands on the culprit as he had ever been.

True, he had discovered many important details, and proved that several people, in a more or less indirect way, were linked up with the affair. Dozens of little irritating clues leading to no real issue. Motive was the main thing to search for, but he could not trace a sufficient reason why any of these people should risk their own lives to put Leslie Delmond out of the way.

Always the detective liked to see a background to the leading actors in a murder drama. It helped him tremendously. Now in the cases of the Countess of Warnham and her niece, of Dick Spencer, even of Mrs. de Groot, it was easy to see more than the bare picture. Their environment stood out around them clearly. But with Laureen, Lansberg, and the valet, he had nothing but the barest silhouette. Of their previous life and surroundings he knew practically nothing.

And three others who undoubtedly played a big part in the affair, Valerie, Tony and the man with the missing thumb, had never really materialized.

They were merely shadows. And who was the woman who had intrusted something to Lansberg's care years ago and had claimed it recently? Was she implicated in this case? *Was* it a woman?

There was a big theatrical agency near, the manager of which he knew well. Presently Reynolds was in that manager's office, refusing a large cigar.

"Can you tell me anything about this man?" he asked, showing him Delmond's photograph.

The manager grinned. "I know he was murdered in Laureen's flat last Sunday and that he'd been doing film work off and on—chiefly off—for the past few years. You probably know all that too, Inspector."

"I meant before that," Reynolds explained patiently. "Film actors often start on the stage."

The manager picked up a desk telephone and talked rapidly for a few minutes. Presently he turned to the detective. "Am afraid I can't help you much. My man says Delmond was doing a turn on the halls for a bit several years ago, but was a failure so he turned to film work. That's all he can tell and he'd know if any one did."

Reynolds got up, a little disappointed. "Thanks very much. You've done your best. Oh, by the way, do you happen to know what Delmond's turn consisted of?"

The manager picked up the instrument again and asked the question.

"Female impersonator," he announced.

The detective wondered whether it was Delmond, dressed as a woman, who had twice called on Lansberg. A high, clear voice! Yes, and that telephone operator said it was a high, clear voice that had answered Spencer's telephone call at nine fifty last Sunday night, and that same voice had called Bertha at eight thirty and sent her out of the flat on a false errand. Suppose *that* was Delmond too! Not too bad a jump so far as guesses went.

Outside the theater, where each night Laureen's name blazed on huge electric signs, he slowed his pace and at the main entrance mixed with the crowd waiting at the box-office.

In a moment, keeping a wary eye on the commissionaire in uniform on the front steps, he slipped out of the queue. Glancing at the photographs on the walls, gradually he edged his way to the darkest end of the lobby where swinging doors led into the theater itself.

Watching his opportunity he tried the door. It was not locked, and going in, he found himself in the corridors leading right and left to the stalls. The same corridors along which he had raced last Monday night searching for the man with the mutilated hand. How easy it was for any one to enter that way and even get to the little iron door in the wall by the stage box, which opened on to the stone staircase by the dressing-rooms.

He retraced his steps to the foyer, attracting no attention from the eager clients at the box-office.

The commissionaire was still looking up and down the street.

Well, Reynolds decided, that showed how easily one could get to and from the dressing-rooms, unseen from the front entrance.

He walked out of the theater and up the alley by the side. Minnis, the stage-door keeper, sat on a high stool studying a racing paper. He raised his eyes as

Reynolds appeared and scanned him from head to toe.

Minnis always swore he could tell what a man wanted in half a minute. Out-of-work actors, hangers-on after the chorus girls, more elegantly attired men wanting Laureen, authors with manuscripts of plays they wanted read—Minnis knew them by heart and could classify them before they opened their mouths.

But the detective puzzled him. There was no category into which he quite fitted. Minnis had another good look: he hated to be baffled.

He saw a stolidly built man of about forty with rather a heavy face and dull eyes. His clothes were neat and well-cut without a touch of flashiness. He carried neither flowers for chorus girls nor a parcel of manuscript. By his assured bearing he was not a betting tout. There was no tinge of nervousness in his manner, no hint that he wanted to curry favor with Minnis, as most of them did.

"What d'you want?" he demanded of the stranger, with a faint touch of aggressiveness. "Whoever you wish to see, they aren't here. There isn't a matinee to-day."

Reynolds glanced round the tiny cupboard of an office as he leaned negligently against the door frame.

"I know there's nobody here. That's why I came," he observed mildly. His sole interest apparently was in the signed portraits, chiefly of actresses, with effusive dedications to their dear Minnis scrawled in large handwriting, decorating the walls.

The detective strolled inside now and gazed at one photograph, which appeared to be chiefly an exhibition of arms and legs, with an intentness his wife might have misunderstood.

Minnis stood up indignant at the intrusion. "Well, you've got no business on these premises," he said with authority.

The detective swung round and transferred his gaze—no longer dull, Minnis noted—to the door-keeper.

"On the contrary, I have quite a lot of business here and every right to be doing it," he contradicted as he handed a card to the man.

Minnis read it, his indignation fading into nervous civility. He had been warned to expect this visit and told how to behave.

"I beg your pardon, sir, but how was I to know? We've got to be pretty strict with strangers."

"That's all right," agreed the detective. "I just want to have a look round the place undisturbed. And don't mention my visit to any one. Understand?"

If there was one weak spot in Inspector Reynolds it was a love of the dramatic. To lead witnesses unsuspectingly "up the garden," and then thrust suddenly upon them the knowledge of who he was, and see them collapse, was sheer joy to him who had sometimes long intervals of dreary routine work with no glimmer of interest to brighten it. He glowed now to see the instant respect in the man's attitude.

"Certainly, sir. There's nobody up there but Joe. He does the odd jobs when the place is quiet."

Half-way up the darkish staircase the detective noticed the iron door leading through into the theater. Along the corridor there was a sound of cheery whistling.

Following the direction of it the inspector came

on a shirt-sleeved workman on a step-ladder, painting a door. He laid down his brush as Reynolds approached.

"Good afternoon, sir," the man said politely.

"Good afternoon," the detective responded in his pleasantest tones. "I'm an inspector from Scotland Yard. I just want to have a glance round the rooms."

Joe looked a trifle apprehensive. Strangers going through the dressing-rooms! Still, that was up to Minnis. If he allowed this detective here, it must be all right.

"Hope there's nothing wrong, sir," he ventured. Had one of those giddy chorus-girls been up to something? The Delmond murder case never entered his thoughts.

"Nothing," murmured Reynolds easily. "You might tell me the owners of the dressing-rooms, Joe, and then I needn't hinder you any more."

Joe obediently indicated the various rooms, and the detective wandered in and out of each one, methodically working up one side of the corridor, remaining only a minute or so in each.

Presently he came to the empty room where Joe was at work on the door.

"I've been doing a bit of papering and painting here, sir," remarked Joe.

"You've made quite a good job of it too," the inspector said approvingly.

Joe surveyed his work from the doorway with some pride. "Not too bad," he pronounced. Nice friendly chap this detective; not at all the pouncing type with hard eyes he'd read of in novels. "The only nuisance is I never can get time to finish a thing, sir. Keep getting called off to do other jobs."

"Papering's difficult," said the inspector. "I once tried to do my attic and it took me nearly two days. Must have taken you some time to hang this paper. It's a largish room. Three or four days, I'll warrant, in odd hours."

Joe scratched his chin.

"No, not so long as that. Let me see. I started Saturday, worked as far as the mantelpiece and finished the rest Monday afternoon. *And* I painted the baseboard too," he added. "But I was able to get on without hindrance."

Reynolds made a mental note. So Joe was here then! "That makes a difference, of course," he replied. "Let me see, Miss Laureen was in her dressing-room on Monday afternoon resting. I expect she finds it's the only quiet place."

"Yes, I saw her, sir. She very rarely comes in if it's not a matinee day. I was working in this room and didn't know she was here then until she called me to get her some cigarettes."

"Well, that was a hindrance you didn't mind, I expect," laughed the inspector.

"Not a bit, sir," agreed Joe fervently, "and anyhow it didn't take me more than ten minutes. Our Miss Laureen's a wonder. The house is packed at every show."

"Yes, she's an extremely clever young woman. Good afternoon," Reynolds said, and left Joe to go on with his job.

He sauntered through two more dressing-rooms before he turned into that of Laureen. A hurried search assured him there was no place to hide anything here. He reverted to the other matter.

It took him less than two minutes to locate a

long dark brown coat hanging in a big wardrobe. He carried it to the window, examined the sleeve and smelled it carefully.

Yes, undoubtedly it had had a large stain on it. In two spots he could even detect a trace of red paint which had resisted the amateur efforts to clean it off. He was replacing it in the wardrobe when a hostile voice made him start.

"What d'you think you're doing there?"

He turned round sharply and confronted a hatchet-faced woman who had just entered the dressing-room.

Without a second's hesitation he attacked swiftly.

"I'm a Scotland Yard inspector. Who cleaned that red paint from this sleeve?" he demanded.

The woman's belligerent tone changed at once.

"I did, sir. I'm Miss Laureen's dresser. Of course if I knew I was intruding I wouldn't have come in. I just thought as I was passing I could do some mending for her."

Her eyes flickered around the room restlessly as the inspector scrutinized her face. He was not concerned with her loquacious and cringing explanation. Somewhere he had seen this woman before.

Suddenly she put her hand up to straighten her hat: he noticed the little finger was bent and stiff. In a second he remembered.

"Got a new job, Lily, eh? We've not seen your face for quite a long while. How's George behaving himself?"

The woman started—then shifted from one foot to the other.

"I've not seen him for ages," she lied boldly. "It was always him that got me into trouble, Mr. Reynolds. I'm running straight now, so please don't let them know anything here or I'll lose my place."

"I'm not sure you've any right to be here at all. But let me catch you either stealing or *receiving*," emphasized the detective, "other people's property again and you'll get a longer stretch than you'll like."

"Yes, sir, I'll remember," Lily promised glibly. "Did you want to know anything about Miss Laureen?"

Reynolds did, badly.

"Not about Miss Laureen exactly," he parried. "But I'd like to know something about her visitors."

Lily at once poured out a stream of useless details about the people who called on her mistress.

"Did a young lady—a Miss Valerie Baird—ever call on Miss Laureen?" he asked to stem the flood.

"No, sir. But," she looked over her shoulder and came a little nearer, "a note from some one who signed herself 'Val' came last Saturday evening."

Lily lowered her voice to a confidential whisper and went on: "Minnis brought it up before the interval and I gave it to Miss Laureen when she came off the stage. It seemed funny to me that she tucked it into her dress and actually went on the stage with it during the second act. As if she was afraid to leave it about."

"Which didn't matter at all, considering you had already read the note before you gave it to her," stated the detective sternly.

The woman colored. Then her face assumed a sly expression. "Well, and wasn't it a good thing I did, sir," she argued, "or else I shouldn't have been able to tell you what it was about."

Reynolds rubbed his chin.

"She tried to burn it down here," the woman went on. "We couldn't find any matches and just then the call-boy came and she slipped it into her dress so I shouldn't read it."

"It will save my time if you tell me the contents. No embroidery, mind. I can easily check up the truth of your statement with Miss Laureen," he warned her with uplifted finger. "I want to find this Valerie Baird."

Lily fumbled in her bag and produced a crumpled sheet of paper.

"I copied it as it seemed so queer," she admitted with a shrewd glance at the inspector's face. "Jolly long time it took me too. But I'm glad I did if it's of use to you, Mr. Reynolds."

Any satisfaction she hoped to get proved disappointing. For the inspector cast a quick glance at it, tucked it into his pocket and strode out of the room, his pulse beating a tattoo of excitement.

XXIV. THE FACE AT THE WINDOW

JUST one little cigarette, Dick," pleaded Laureen from her seat on the dais in the studio that afternoon.

Spencer dabbed some paint on with his thumb and carefully wiped it off again.

"You've done that three times," she teased.

"Can't I have a cigarette?"

"Certainly not," he remarked sternly. "You had one half an hour ago. How can I work? You alter the muscles of your face and neck when you smoke. Heaven knows," he groaned, "it's difficult enough to make you keep still for five minutes."

"Think how boring it is for me to sit here gazing beautifully at nothing."

Dick Spencer ran his fingers through his hair.

"You've got my face to look at," he announced complacently.

Laureen cocked her head on one side and screwed up her nose. "I've seen it. That's what I'm complaining about." She flung up her arms and stretched. "It's no good, Dick. I can't sit still another minute. You're not painting well to-day and you know it. Call it a day and let's make tea and talk."

Dick flung down his palette resignedly.

"Which means I'll make the tea and you'll talk," he retorted.

He filled the kettle and set it on a gas ring.

Flinging himself on the big divan on which she had seated herself, he rested his head against her shoulder.

She picked up a cushion, thereby uncovering a pair of pajamas.

"What's the matter with your bedroom?" she demanded teasingly. "Have you suddenly become so completely artistic that you must sleep in your studio?"

Dick flushed scarlet as he tossed the garments behind the divan.

"Yes—no. Look here, Laureen," he said earnestly, "I'm worried to death about this beastly murder case. Darling, can't you think it over? Let's be married and clear out on a honeymoon."

She looked at his worried face kindly.

"Dear old Dick, one can't run away from the law of England just because you're foolish enough to want to marry me. Indeed that suet-faced inspector would think I'd murdered Delmond and shot Avice into the bargain if I attempted any stunts like that."

"Well, didn't you?" he jested idly, playing with the scarf she wore.

She got up swiftly, shaking him away, her face flaming. "How dare you say that?" she demanded in a low voice.

Dick was by her side in a second, imploring her to forget his clumsy attempt at humor.

"I'm a tactless ass," he groaned. "As if your nerves had not been strained to cracking point already with this tragedy without my teasing you."

Laureen thrust back a thick wave of her hair and pressed her hands to temples that throbbed suddenly.

"Don't worry, Dick. It was foolish of me to mind what you said. I'm tired out with my theater work and the tension of that affair at my flat. And this morning," she shuddered, "on top of all came Avice's accident. I've a queer feeling that shot was meant for me. Maybe next time will be my turn."

Dick caught her hands anxiously. He had never seen Laureen in this mood before.

"My dear, do be careful," he said. "Inspector Reynolds's brother was knifed on Tuesday night, but of course the blow was intended for our lynx-eyed detective."

The girl's eyes widened fearfully.

"I didn't see anything in the newspapers about it," she confessed. "Where did this happen, Dick?"

"In Inspector Reynolds's front garden. Reynolds was away," he smiled as he recalled their meeting in Paris, "and some one who had a grudge against the inspector evidently mistook his brother for him. Rough on the brother, eh? He's getting on all right, I hear."

Laureen caught her breath. If only she could be alone a moment to think undisturbed.

"The kettle's boiling, Dick," she announced.

Spencer obediently vanished to make the tea.

Laureen leaned back against the cushions, staring miserably across the room at the big windows. They nearly covered one half of the wall, one window opening on to a balcony from which a small iron staircase led to the garden.

Her brain reeled with the news of the attack on Reynolds's brother. Was that too mixed up with the Delmond affair? If so, where was it all going to end? Whose turn would it be next?

She felt wearily that she did not care if she were to be the next victim, so long as this lonely terror locked up in her mind could be ended.

Oh, if only she could confide in some one! Almost she had spoken to Lansberg. But now, with a new panic, she feared he also was involved, if not actually guilty.

Dick Spencer as an adviser she rejected from her thoughts. For one thing he was too much in love with her to give unprejudiced advice, and also she could not add a sense of obligation when her feelings for him were merely those of friendship.

Suddenly her eyes dilated as she saw the shadow of a man creep across one end of the window. Before the shadow could materialize she instinctively dived beneath the cushions piled beside her. Leaving a tiny opening between them she crouched, watching.

A man's white face was pressed to the glass. He was trying to peer into the studio. Dark unkempt hair tumbled over his brows, a thin nervous hand shaded his burning eyes.

"Tea's ready," shouted Dick cheerfully from the kitchen. "And I've made some toast."

At the first sound of Spencer's voice the man quickly slid away. Listening intently, Laureen could hear his feet faintly stumbling down the iron staircase.

Trembling, she flung aside the cushions and tried to stand up.

Dick heard a cry and rushed in to find her lying unconscious on the floor. He lifted her on the couch and bent over her anxiously.

"What a fool I am!" she murmured as she opened her gray eyes and gazed round the room. "I've only done that once before in my life, Dick."

"And I've been making you sit in that tiresome

position," he reproached himself. "As if all the other worry and strain were not enough to have exhausted you. Let me get you some brandy, darling. Don't move," he begged.

She declined the offer.

"I'm all right now."

"Can you drink a cup of tea?"

"Two, maybe three," she assured him. "You pour it out and don't look like an old hen fussing over her chicken."

She raised herself and made an effort to draw his attention from her fainting attack.

"You'll not act to-night if I have to get Lansberg himself to stop you, Laureen."

"Maybe I shan't," she agreed. But her decision was not based on physical weakness. Was it wiser not to appear to-night?

The tea revived her and a little color drifted back to her pale cheeks. "Please don't interfere in any way, Dick," she urged. "*I* must decide whether I go to the theater or not. I'll go to my hotel and rest now if you'll get me a taxi."

He flung open the French windows as she pulled on her hat. Laureen looked over his shoulder. The balcony and garden were deserted. She noticed that a door in the far end of the garden wall was an inch or two open.

"Where does that lead?" she asked.

"Into a back lane that goes from our street through to the next," Spencer told her.

She surveyed it thoughtfully.

"Makes it easy for burglars, Dick."

"Wonderfully. Only, my sweet one, burglars don't haunt artists' studios—they're nearly all painter folks round here, you see. Come along. I'm going to take you back."

She paused a moment before her portrait standing on the easel.

"Why, it's nearly finished!" she exclaimed. "Dick Spencer, you've brought me here under false pretenses. You didn't need a sitting at all."

"All true artists need dozens of sittings to get the final nuances, whatever that means. Don't deprive me of the only chance I get of seeing you, Laureen," he pleaded.

In spite of her wish he rang up Lansberg after leaving her.

"Laureen's not fit to go on to-night," he said over the wire. "After her sitting this afternoon in my studio she fainted. She told me not to interfere but I felt you'd persuade her better than I."

Lansberg expressed consternation.

"Thanks, old chap," he said. "You did quite right. I'll go to the theater at once and tell the manager to warn the understudy. Of course Laureen mustn't dream of acting to-night."

Dick Spencer grinned sardonically as he came out of the call-box.

"That's being decent, if not noble," he reflected. "She and Lansberg are getting keen about each other, and here am I, the rejected suitor, lending a helping hand. This is where I untie my knot for the day."

He trudged along the hot pavements to his club feeling rather forlorn and despondent. Even inside its doors his gloom did not pass off. Desperately he hated all the publicity that had centered round Laureen since the murder. Every other man he came across developed a sudden desire to be chatty with Spencer, and sooner or later would ask for the latest news of the murder case, knowing he was a friend of Laureen's.

He wandered into the reading-room but it was even worse in that hall of silence. Every newspaper he picked up had some screaming headlines about Laureen, audaciously recounting supposed interviews with her, reprinting photographs of her at different stages of her career. And all of them fiercely demanded news of Valerie Baird.

Flinging them down in disgust he determined to call at Warnham House to ask after Avice.

He arrived hot and irritable. On the steps he met the Countess of Warnham, about to enter. She cast a comprehensive glance over Dick's angry face and with an inward smile divined the symptoms.

"Come in and have a cocktail with me," she invited. Tactfully adding "And don't mention murder cases or this dastardly attack on Avice to-day or I shall become really violent."

Dick Spencer relaxed. He and Lady Warnham were very good friends. A sympathetic amusing old woman, worth nearly all the young ones put together, he decided. Always excepting Laureen and Avice.

All of which Lady Warnham knew perfectly— including the two exceptions.

"Avice is doing very well," she informed him over an artistically mixed "Soul's Ruin." "Slip up and see her for a minute, but don't let her talk. That inspector person has a rendezvous with her to-morrow afternoon and she'll need all her strength for that."

In a few minutes Dick returned. "She's asleep. I didn't disturb her."

Lady Warnham nodded approvingly. "Good child. Stay and have dinner and cheer me up a little."

It was nearly ten o'clock when Dick returned to his flat in a far more peaceful state of mind. He unlocked his door, whistling a tune from Laureen's revue, switched on the light and strolled inside the big studio. For a moment he stood, blinking, dazed, wondering if he had carelessly wandered into the wrong flat.

The entire place was in the wildest disorder: chairs flung over, draperies torn, canvases trodden on. For once, it would seem, burglars had availed themselves of that convenient back lane!

It didn't greatly disturb him. He was insured and anyhow had no valuables. Except that one picture of Laureen. Suppose—

With one quick stride he reached the big easel and stood back aghast. The canvas had been slashed in all directions, with particular savage gashes on the face and golden hair he loved so well.

Spencer was not quite the good-humored fool Reynolds imagined him to be. There was something cruelly malicious in the way Laureen's pictured face had been cut. An unmistakable menace lay there. With shaking hands he picked up the telephone and demanded Scotland Yard.

"I want Inspector Reynolds at once," he said. "Give me his private number if he's not there. It's urgent."

In a moment he recognized a quiet voice replying, and for the first time was thankful to hear it.

"Inspector Reynolds speaking. What's the trouble, Mr. Spencer?"

Breathlessly Spencer explained what he had just discovered, adding that Laureen was probably not at the theater that night.

"I know she's not," replied the detective. "Meet me at her hotel as soon as you can. I want to make sure she's all right. If so, I'll come along with you and see the damage at the studio."

Laureen had reached her hotel at about five thirty and found Bertha anxiously studying a telegram she had just received.

"One of my friends at Clapham is ill, miss, and they've wired to know if I can go down and stay the night," she explained.

"Of course," assented Laureen at once. "Go by all means, Bertha. You've scarcely been outside this hotel since we came. I may not act to-night. If not, I shall go to bed and shan't need you at all."

"Oh, I can't leave you if you're not well, miss," the maid demurred.

"Nonsense. Off you go at once," insisted Laureen. "I'm going to bed, anyhow, for a while."

An hour later, as she was half dozing, the theater manager rang up and told her everything was arranged for her understudy to appear that evening.

"The slips for the programs are being printed. The girl's rehearsing now, delighted to have her chance," he added, mindful of Lansberg's firm instructions—"At all costs I will not allow Miss Laureen to appear to-night." And Lansberg, the manager knew, was not a man to be trifled with.

Laureen laid her head back on the pillow with a sigh of relief. Nothing to do but sleep until morning. Soon she fell into a troubled dream.

She roused with a start to see a tiny flicker of light in the room. It went out as she moved but she could hear some one breathing.

Her heart beating wildly, she instinctively put her hand to the bell over her head and succeeded in ringing it, but as she withdrew her hand she gave a smothered scream, for a pillow was pressed tightly over her mouth and a heavy hand groped for her throat.

There was a sudden banging at the door, a voice shouting "Laureen" and then the pillow was dropped.

She screamed again, and heard a terrific crash. The next moment the lights were switched on and Dick Spencer and Inspector Reynolds stood beside her.

Reynolds stayed only one second to assure himself she was unhurt before he rushed to the open window and leaned out. There was no sound from the courtyard below.

"Which way did he go?" demanded Reynolds hurriedly.

Laureen shook her head. "I don't know. I saw no one but felt something smothering me."

The detective looked at a drawer turned upside-down on the floor and a dressing case beside it.

"Quick, tell me—whose room is that in there? Your maid's?" The door was slightly open.

"My sitting-room. Bertha's room is beyond that. She's away for the night," Laureen gasped.

"Stay with her," the inspector commanded

Spencer, and rapidly searched the two communicating rooms, whose doors also opened on the outside corridor. Neither room bore signs of disturbance.

He raced downstairs and startled the night porter.

"Seen any one go out?"

"Only the man who went up to see Miss Laureen half an hour ago," the porter replied. "He said she was expecting him."

"Which way did he go? Quick, it's important."

"He got into a bus that was just passing, going toward Charing Cross."

"His hands—did you see them?"

"Going in he had on yellow chamois gloves. I was on the curb when he ran out and as he caught hold of the bus rail his hand looked as if—"

But before he could finish the sentence, the inspector was on his way.

XXV. PIERCING THE VEIL

DICK SPENCER bent over Laureen anxiously when Reynolds dashed into the adjoining rooms on his search.

"Are you sure that brute didn't hurt you?" He gently touched the inflamed marks on her neck where those cruel fingers had gripped her.

Laureen scarcely heeded his question.

"Dick, I—I want to see Mr. Lansberg at once. Have you any idea where he is? The theater?" she suggested.

Spencer grinned. Love's young dream must be very real for Laureen to wish to see Lansberg five minutes after she'd had a narrow escape from being murdered! Well, he'd be a father to them both, he decided, and bury his own feelings.

"For once the fool of the family can help you, lady," he replied. "Lansberg is dining at his club to-night with Dr. Tempest as his guest. They're probably still there talking solemnly in that mausoleum. Shall I ring up and ask?"

"Yes. Tell him what's happened and ask him to come immediately. Use the telephone in the next room."

Directly she heard his voice asking for the number she slipped out of bed and drew a loose dressing-gown round her. Taking a towel, she rubbed the rail at the foot of the bed, the door and drawer handles and any woodwork that might have been touched.

Replacing the towel exactly as it was—she was beginning to appreciate the inspector's powers of observation—she walked rather unsteadily into the sitting-room just as Reynolds returned from his inquiries in the hall below.

"No luck," he said in response to Spencer's lifted eyebrows.

"What's the time, Dick?" Laureen asked. She had curled herself up in a deep arm-chair, one hand cupping her chin so that her throat was hidden.

"Twenty past ten," and under his breath Spencer added, "Lansberg's on his way, so cheer up."

She smiled her thanks as Reynolds glanced quickly up from a note he was writing.

"Been telephoning, Mr. Spencer?" the detective asked amiably.

Spencer checked a facetious remark and nodded.

"H'm," Reynolds shot a keen glance at the young man and then turned to Laureen.

"Please tell me all you know about this assault," he said bluntly.

The girl flushed at his tone. "There is very little to tell. I was asleep and awoke frightened by a slight noise. There was, I fancy, a pencil of light in the room. I rang my bell in terror, probably only half awake, thinking I was being smothered by something. I saw no one. And the next minute you and Mr. Spencer had burst open my door. That is all. How did you get here?"

"A bell rang as we came in the hall downstairs," Reynolds explained. "The porter said it was from your room. As we reached the door you screamed. Not knowing the sitting-room door was unlocked, we broke yours open. *Who was your assailant?*" he snapped.

"How can I tell when I didn't see him?" Laureen retorted.

"Has anything been stolen?"

"Not so far as I can see. Certainly my jewels and money are safe. I have just looked."

"The person who searched your room and attacked you was not after money or jewelry, Miss Laureen. Had you any valuable papers or documents?"

Her gray eyes widened and her breathing was uneven.

"No," she replied. "Why do you ask?"

"Because," the detective said deliberately, "the man who searched here to-night is undoubtedly the man who played such havoc in your flat. The same man," his voice dropped to a tenser tone, "who entered Mr. Spencer's studio this evening and having searched wildly and fruitlessly there, slashed your picture to ribbons. *What does he want?*" the C. I. D. official demanded imperatively.

Spencer moved restlessly, tried to speak, but the detective silenced him.

"I can allow no interruption, Mr. Spencer. There has been too much concealment already, with disastrous results. I mean to know the truth now. Answer my question, Miss Laureen. What is this man searching for?"

Laureen gazed at him helplessly, her dry lips incapable of making audible sound. Spencer hurriedly gave her a glass of water.

As she took it from him her hand dropped from her chin. In one stride the detective had reached her and peered at those telltale marks livid now on her white throat.

"So you would even shelter the man who tried to strangle you," Reynolds said sternly. "This man is desperate, remember. Think! He tore your furniture to pieces in his desire to find something. This morning your friend, Lady Avice Garth, was wounded by a shot undoubtedly intended for you, as you accidentally admitted to me. This evening the man ransacked Mr. Spencer's studio, after you had been there this afternoon and possibly hidden what he wants, he must have thought. Again he was baffled, so to-night he comes here and would undoubtedly have murdered you if we had not been in time. The slashed picture gave me the clue that you were in real danger."

The girl raised her eyes and met the detective's glance steadily.

"He must be mad," she answered clearly. "How can I possibly know what he wants? Perhaps now that he has searched every possible place for this imaginary treasure he will give me a little peace."

"Have you deposited anything in your bank?"

"No," she said nervously. "I had no time, even if I'd thought of it."

"Then there remains only one more hiding place, Miss Laureen." The inspector's face was grim and relentless.

She raised her eyebrows in surprise.

"Where?"

"The dressing-rooms at the theater."

Her cheeks were ghastly, her whole body seemed suddenly rigid.

"That may be his next search," Reynolds went on. "Miss Laureen, for the last time, where have you hidden the thing this man is looking for? And what is it?" As he spoke Reynolds saw in a flash many of the separate links fit together, scarcely heeding the girl's murmured reply, "I don't know what you mean."

He had something more than her denials now. This thing—was it not the packet posted in the hall letter-box to Valerie Baird, later collected by Laureen in disguise, and then probably hidden somewhere in the theater?

Working further back, might that packet not have been taken by Laureen from the dead man's pocket last Sunday night? Had the dead man, dressed as a woman, received it from Lansberg earlier? In other words, had Delmond, in woman's clothes, confided that packet to Lansberg for safety years before?

Ah, it was piecing itself together now! And this man with the missing thumb, he had made two attacks on Lansberg in Paris, attacks Lansberg could not account for. Was not this packet the cause?

And again Reynolds came back to the question of its contents.

"For the last time, Miss Laureen, what was in that packet?" He was angry with frustration. He would *make* this woman speak.

"And for the last time, Inspector Reynolds, I again tell you—the truth—I do not know."

Her voice was despairing but definite.

"Where have you hidden it? I insist upon your reply," he demanded loudly, longing to shake her.

From the doorway behind him came in stern, icy tones from Lansberg: "What is the meaning of this inquisition, Inspector Reynolds? Do you realize Miss

Laureen is ill and nearly distracted?"

Lansberg walked across the room and took the girl's trembling hands in his. She leaned her head against his arm, the tears running weakly down her cheeks.

"Oh, Ivan," she whispered. "Thank you for coming. I—I can't bear any more."

"It's all right, my child," Lansberg murmured protectingly. "Don't be alarmed." He bent over her a moment, an expression of infinite sadness in his eyes. "By to-morrow, or in a day or two at most, I swear to you that things will have straightened themselves out. I think I understand what you've been trying to do."

He stood up, holding her hands in one of his, an arm round her shoulder.

"Now, Inspector," he said frigidly, "that your ill-timed examination has brought Miss Laureen to the verge of collapse after all she had suffered previously, I suggest you put any vital questions to me or defer them until to-morrow when I have promised to be at your disposal. By the way, I should prefer that interview to be at my apartment at two thirty instead of at the Yard."

Reynolds assented reluctantly.

"I have asked Miss Laureen to say what is in the packet and where it is," the detective stated. "She says she cannot tell me."

Laureen nodded, her eyes half closed.

"That is true, Ivan. Please make him believe it," she implored piteously.

"You have had your answer, Inspector. I think you can go no further in this matter to-night," said Lansberg.

The detective bit his lip. Then he smiled frankly. He knew when he was beaten and was willing to admit it.

"Very well, Mr. Lansberg," he agreed. "Will you tell me one thing, please, that may help me very much? When did this woman who resembled Delmond call at your apartment to reclaim that packet from your care?"

"A week ago," Lansberg replied. "No, this is Thursday. She called last Friday evening just as I was going out to dine."

"Thank you," Reynolds acknowledged with relief. That fitted in perfectly with his theory. "I think I'd better leave you now. I'm sorry to have distressed you, Miss Laureen," he said.

She freed one hand from Lansberg's grasp and extended it to the detective.

"Don't think too badly of me, Inspector," she said in a tremulous voice.

"I don't," replied that man gruffly. "Good night."

He turned back as a thought struck him. "Has your servant returned, Mr. Lansberg?"

Lansberg shook his head.

"No," he replied. "Let me hear at once if you get any news of him."

Reynolds walked back to the Yard surprised at many things, himself included. Was there a soft patch in him that needed hardening? Or was that the only decent bit of humanity left in his nature, he wondered?

His heart was lighter than it had been for days as he tramped along the street. So many odd bits had fitted in this crazy puzzle to-night.

To-morrow evening he was to have a conference

with his chiefs. He had been dreading it, knowing they would require a clear statement of the situation and would not be lulled by a collection of odd clues involving many people and pointing to no one in particular.

To-morrow morning he would be able to talk to Lady Avice and drag out the story of the mysterious Tony. In the afternoon he was to have an interview with Lansberg, and in between he determined somehow to ask Laureen a few vital questions. That she knew of this man with the missing thumb he was fairly sure. And that she knew even more of the elusive Valerie Baird he was positive, the proof being in his pocket-book at the moment.

Late as it was Jenkins was waiting for him in his office. "I've telephoned all the main hospitals," he informed his chief. "There are about five accident cases not quite clear on identity. One, a girl, was knocked down last Monday morning and brought there in a private car. She's still unconscious."

Reynolds noted down the address. "I'll go round there early to-morrow morning," he promised. "It's probably nothing to do with our case, though."

At his ear the telephone bell rang shrilly. He picked up the receiver, listened a moment, asked a few questions and banged it back on the hook.

"Get a taxi, quick," he ordered Jenkins. "You come too."

Jenkins, slightly bewildered, obeyed and got in the car with his preoccupied chief.

In silence they rattled across a bridge over the river and along gloomy streets until they came to a wharf.

Telling the cabman to wait, the inspector got out

with Jenkins, and the two men picked their way through bales and kegs to a large shed.

A policeman flashed his lantern on them inquiringly, but at a few words from Reynolds unlocked the shed door, led them inside, and produced an electric lamp.

On a rough table lay something covered with a tarpaulin.

The policeman raised it and Reynolds looked at the still form.

"They got him out of the river an hour ago, sir," the constable explained.

Jenkins stared at the features of the man lying there. "Do you know who it is, sir?" he asked.

Reynolds nodded. "Lansberg's missing servant. The man who stabbed my brother. I expect you'll find his fingerprints tally with those on the knife."

XXVI. VALERIE

ON that journey from Victoria to Dover, Valerie had ample time to read and reread the whole history of Leslie Delmond's murder. The newspapers of earlier date that she had brought from the hospital linked it all up clearly. Yes, undoubtedly suspicion rested heavily on her and she had no means of proving her innocence.

Who would believe her story of how she passed last Sunday night? And if she could prove it, would not the very publicity tell that other man she so feared where she could be found?

After church last Sunday night she had walked past Laureen's flat and he had seen and followed her. She had run wildly, trying to dodge him. Afraid to go back to her room, lest he was following and even that refuge would be taken from her, she had gone by bus to Richmond Park and slept fitfully hidden in a bank of fern.

Who would believe that story? What witnesses had she?

Next morning she had determined to see Laureen, to warn her, but in crossing the road near her friend's flat a car had knocked her down.

No, she decided, there only was one way. She must hide until this hue and cry had died down and Leslie Delmond's murderer was discovered.

Folding the newspapers mechanically, her glance fell on the "agony" column. One notice stood out, for her, in letters of fire. Tears blinded her eyes as she read the appeal:

> *Remember Tuileries Gardens, May 20, 1927.*
> *Implore you to write or telephone my number in*
> *London directory. Am in terrible anxiety about*
> *you. D.*

He remembered then and cared still, this man she loved! Two years of sorrow had divided them, but now that she was alone and in terror he had sent this assurance of his love to comfort her.

Hurriedly she took paper and envelope from her case and wrote:

> *My beloved,*
> *I have just read the Times personal column. You*
> *can never know what comfort your message has*
> *brought. Try to believe in me. I cannot extricate*
> *myself from these complications. I can only hide.*
> *As soon as possible I will let you know where I*
> *am. I dare not explain more clearly. Always yours.*

She did not even sign an initial to this letter. Addressing it, she dropped the envelope into the post-box at Dover station.

As she did so, a well-dressed woman, also posting letters, looked at her curiously, but the thick veil hid her features fairly well, and she was sure the woman had not definitely recognized her.

Suddenly she felt faintness creeping over her and realized that only excitement had buoyed her up since her escape from the hospital. Whatever happened, for the moment she could go no further without rest. Checking her luggage she went to a small hotel near the station and asked for a room.

"I've had a long journey and need sleep before going on," she told the proprietor.

The man assured her she should not be disturbed. "A nice cup of tea when you wake up and you'll be all right, ma'am. The sea's a bit choppy to-day. There's plenty of trains to London."

She sank down on the bed and drew the cover over her thankfully. Anyhow she was safe here for a few hours. The hotel proprietor evidently mistook her for a weary passenger *from* France.

It was late afternoon when Valeria awoke and rang for tea. After drinking it she felt much more able to plan out clearly what she must do. Her idea had been to bury herself in Paris in some quarter where tourists and English-speaking visitors did not come. Thanks to ten years spent in a Belgian convent school she could always pass as a Frenchwoman.

It might be safe there, but it would certainly be terribly lonely, and she dreaded solitude now unspeakably.

Then the memory returned of the woman she had encountered at the post-box on Dover platform that morning. What was Mrs. de Groot doing there? Probably going to London. In a flash it came to her that Mary de Groot was going to Avice and Laureen because she knew they were in trouble. It was like Mary, the girl reflected. The American woman was brimming over with kindness and generosity.

Yes, that was it, Valerie decided. Mary de Groot was going to stand by her friends and prove her affection, while she—Valerie—was stealing away to hide, regardless of everything except her own safety.

Laureen must be unhappy and anxious, fighting bravely—this much was obvious to her—to keep Valerie's secret. So far she had succeeded wonderfully.

But suppose by this very secrecy Laureen herself should be suspected, perhaps arrested! Her career would be ruined, even if she cleared herself: mud always stuck.

Besides, worse than that in Valerie's mind was the knowledge that she had abandoned Laureen, leaving her defenseless to the attacks of a man who had always hated her, and who would now certainly try to do her harm in some way. Maybe even bodily injury.

Valerie recoiled from the thought of what might happen if she carried out her plan to run away and to hide. She must go back to London at once. No matter what the result might be, that was her plain duty.

First of all, she must see Laureen and warn her of the danger. Suppose after this delay she could not get to her in time! Oh, how unutterably selfish had been this flight!

She rang for a time-table and looked up the trains. The next one arrived in London at eight thirty-five. Laureen would be in the theater then.

"I must go straight there and see her in her dressing-room," she made up her mind. "After that I don't care what they do to me."

Leaving her other luggage in the cloak-room and taking only a suitcase, she entered a compartment, drawing her thick veil carefully over her face. She must run no risk of being discovered before she had seen Laureen.

Disgust at her previous cowardice grew upon her, with every passing mile. How could she have thought of deserting Laureen in such a crisis? Knowing her loyalty, Valerie was well aware that nothing would induce Laureen to protect herself by breaking faith.

There was that note, Valerie remembered, in which she had desperately revealed her fears to Laureen. That, if nothing else, would make Laureen do her utmost to protect her.

The slow train fretted her but at last it arrived almost half an hour late.

In the taxi Valerie wondered how she should get to the dressing-room. That stage-door keeper, with whom she had left her note last Saturday, had looked very stern and forbidding. He would probably refuse to admit her unless she gave her name. And if she did that, she might be arrested before she could speak to Laureen!

Dismissing the taxi she took her bag and walked up the alley. Minnis was in his office talking loudly to two or three men.

Like a shadow she slipped through the doorway and went noiselessly up the stairs.

"Which is Miss Laureen's dressing-room?" she asked as authoritatively as she could of a workman in the corridor. The man indicated an open door and with a beating heart Valerie stepped inside.

Early that morning in London, Inspector Reynolds had telephoned to Lansberg. "I'm afraid your man has been found, sir. He was taken out of the river last night. Will you come along to the Yard now and go with me to identify the body?"

A little later Lansberg stood looking down at the still face of the man he had known as a faithful servant.

Reynolds handed him a note, still damp. "This was tied in his handkerchief," he said. "Can you translate it? It's in a language I don't understand."

Lansberg smoothed out the paper and with difficulty deciphered the smudged words. He read aloud:

> *"To my master. Farewell. I have sinned greatly. Forgive thy servant. I make this reparation."*

"Poor Neron!" Lansberg murmured. "It's hard to imagine his committing any sin that could require this penalty."

"He probably thought he had killed me?" said Reynolds, watching Lansberg's face.

"I don't understand, Inspector."

"Yet it's easy if one traces cause and effect, Mr. Lansberg. My brother was stabbed last Tuesday, undoubtedly in mistake for me. The knife found in his shoulder was taken from your safe. You remember finding it open last Tuesday afternoon when you returned from Crowborough with Miss Laureen."

Lansberg assented with a puzzled frown.

"Something else had been taken from your flat— from your servant's room—before that. Something," the detective went on deliberately, "that your servant had hidden fearing it might incriminate you. He naturally imagined I had searched your flat."

"But you were in Paris. Spencer told me so."

"Your man didn't know that. He recalled my

questioning of the day before and saw my name and private address on your desk." Reynolds raised his hand. "We know the result."

"Your reasoning is logical, Inspector. It appalls me." He pressed his forehead. "If there is nothing more you need me for, I will go now. I have much to do before we meet this afternoon."

As Lansberg's tall figure vanished Reynolds for one second wondered if he would ever see the man again. But reflection reassured him. Lansberg was being carefully trailed and, short of suicide, could not escape.

At Scotland Yard, Jenkins was waiting for Reynolds with news.

"No need to go to the hospital about that girl, sir. They have just rung up to say she vanished during the night."

"Vanished!" exclaimed his chief. "How could she? You told me she'd been unconscious since the accident."

"The hospital is overcrowded at the moment and apparently this girl's case has not been closely examined. It's all very mysterious."

"Mysterious," snapped the inspector. "It's incredible. Unconscious people don't get up and walk. We should have had her watched. Give me the telephone."

After five minutes of extremely irate questioning the inspector thumped the receiver back on the hook and scowled at his assistant.

"I'll bet a dollar this girl was Valerie Baird. We can try her old address in Bloomsbury. But I'm sure she won't go back there. She was knocked down about twenty yards from Laureen's flat last Monday morning, between eleven and twelve." He swore softly. "I was actually in the flat at the time. Think of it! But for that accident this girl would have walked right into our arms."

"You have proof of that, sir?" queried Jenkins eagerly.

"I've a copy of a note she wrote to Laureen saying she'd call. Here, read it." He passed over the copy given him by Laureen's dresser.

Jenkins read it with great interest.

"Did you notice that bit: 'I've been in England some weeks'?" He put his finger to the phrase as he passed the note back.

"Well, what of it?" demanded the inspector impatiently.

"As so much of this affair has centered in Paris, sir, perhaps Valerie might have come from Paris to England. And if so—"

Reynolds nodded quickly. "Yes, I've got the rest. She might try to go back. We must watch for that. Let me see, she probably aimed for that nine o'clock boat train. Is it Victoria or Charing Cross it starts from? Don't waste any time. And tell the men to use their brains for once."

Jenkins was hurrying from the room when the telephone bell rang.

"You answer," the inspector told Jenkins. "I must get off to my appointment with Lady Avice Garth. Ring me at Warnham House if necessary."

He was half-way down the stairs when Jenkins ran after him, breathless. "It's from Cripps, who's trailing Miss Laureen. He says you told him to ring you if she went to the theater."

"I did. What's the message?"

"Cripps says that Miss Laureen has just gone in by the stage-door of the theater, sir. He telephoned at once."

The inspector took the remaining steps in one leap and jumping in a taxi gave the address of the theater.

"Drive like blazes," he ordered.

XXVII. LADY AVICE EXPLAINS

WHEN Reynolds arrived at the theater huge placards were already displayed announcing that Laureen would positively appear that day at both performances.

"If not otherwise engaged," Reynolds reflected grimly. He was determined to speed up events to-day whatever happened, his softer mood of the night before gone in his irritation because Valerie had again slipped through his fingers.

He hurried along the alley to the stage-door, brushed past Minnis and ran lightly up the stairs.

The door of Laureen's dressing-room was open, but she was not there. Reynolds was not surprised. He had been sure she would visit the other dressing-rooms and now she had acted more quickly than he had expected.

He tiptoed silently along the stone corridor, stopping every now and then to listen.

Outside the empty room that had been newly papered, he paused. The door was shut but he could detect faint sounds from within.

With the utmost caution his fingers closed on the door handle and began to twist it. It turned without a squeak, and by delicate pressure he found the door was not locked.

Suddenly he flung it open and entered.

Laureen was on her knees near the mantelpiece. She gave a startled cry as she saw who it was and struggled to her feet.

"An early visit, Inspector," she remarked.

"A surprise visit," emphasized Reynolds mildly, strolling toward her. "An ingenious hiding place, Miss Laureen. Don't let me interrupt you."

He bent down and examined a long slit in the wallpaper parallel to the baseboard.

She rested one arm on the mantelpiece to support her shaking limbs, but made no reply.

The inspector opened his pocket knife and slipped the blade into the aperture between the board and the wall.

"Ah, here we are, I think. I was so afraid I should be too late to see this part of the drama." He stuck the blade into something soft and with a little difficulty worked into sight a thick envelop.

He turned it over curiously. It had been through the post but was unopened!

"You have not opened it since—" he stated.

"Of course not," replied Laureen. "I had no right to do so."

"But you know what is inside. You addressed it to Miss Valerie Baird."

"I have my shoes on but I'm not walking," was her swift retort. Her composure was coming back rapidly. There was almost relief in her face.

Inspector Reynolds weighed the packet in his hand reflectively. This girl was either the most consummate actress he had ever encountered, or else she had been shielding some one else desperately and was rather thankful the matter had at last been forced out of her hands.

"Then you still insist on saying you do not know the contents of this packet, Miss Laureen?"

She sighed.

"I don't wish to say anything. I do not know what is in that packet, but I *suspect* there is something there that would injure some one I love very dearly," she replied simply. "There is also a document in it that belongs to a third person. I can't understand why it should be there at all. I have not read it, but I saw the name on it. And neither you nor I have any right to touch *that*, Inspector," she added firmly.

"I take it that you had no time to examine these papers and sort them out to their different owners," the detective remarked.

"That is so," she readily agreed.

"Only the few minutes when Mr. Lansberg was searching your flat last Sunday night."

Her breath came quickly but she made no reply.

"You slipped into the dining-room," he went on slowly, "found Leslie Delmond there dead in the arm-chair and took these papers from his pocket."

"They were not in his pocket," she replied. "His hand was tucked down between the chair arm and the seat. I lifted his hand and found the packet in the lining of the chair. He must have slipped it there when he was dying." She shuddered at the memory.

"Then you went into your bedroom and glanced through the packet before you sealed it in this envelop. Or was it sealed before?"

"I did as you said. The packet was not sealed. I hurriedly looked through it and discovered a paper belonging to—somebody else," Laureen murmured.

"Fearing you and the flat might be searched that night, you addressed and stamped the envelope and, on the pretext of whistling for the policeman, ran down and dropped it in the hall-box. Carter took it from there and posted it next morning," he went on.

"Yes." She was watching him with fascinated eyes as he told the story of her movements.

"The next afternoon you came here ostensibly to rest, disguised yourself as an old lady and called at Valerie Baird's address in Bloomsbury. The red paint from the wet railings has now been cleaned off the brown coat you wear in a sketch each night."

This time Laureen gave a gasp of astonishment.

"That is all perfectly true, Inspector," she admitted, with a touch of admiration in her voice.

His lips twisted in a faint smile. "Not quite such a dull old fool as you imagined, eh, miss!" he thought.

"You then went to the hotel to which you had sent this letter, booked a room in order to get a number and called for this packet at the letter bureau."

"I did. Inspector, you're a wizard."

The inspector waived aside the compliment and went on.

"You returned here, sent Joe for some cigarettes and hid the packet where I have just found it."

"Please don't open it yet," she pleaded earnestly. "I'm sure we have no right until I've spoken to—"

"The owner of the document?" put in Reynolds.

"Yes."

Reynolds took a letter from his pocket and opened it.

"Listen, Miss Laureen, and check me up if at any point in this note it differs from the one you received on Saturday night in your dressing-room. There is neither date nor address on my copy." He read aloud slowly:

"Laureen darling,

I've been in England some weeks, but have not dared to see you and on the telephone I'm always told you're out or engaged because I dare not give my name.

L. D. is in London searching for me, and you know who is after him! If they meet it will be terrible. I believe L. is watching you too, to see if we're meeting and find out my address.

One night I was at the stage-door waiting to see you come out. He was there, saw me in the crowd and ran after me. He threatens to get me ten years if I won't do what he wishes. He has those papers. *Oh, if only I could get hold of them! I don't know where he's staying but be careful. My life is one long terror now. I'm afraid of L. D. but far more afraid of—you know who. I'd die rather than see him again.*

I'm staying at 30 Carisbroke Road, Bloomsbury, but don't write there. I don't trust the landlady.

Will call at your flat on Monday morning if I'm sure L. D. is not watching there. I wouldn't bring you into this mess for anything, darling, after all your kindness to me. Have sold a few sketches soam not needing money.

Your devoted Val"

"I think it is absolutely identical with the one I received, but I burned—"

Reynolds smiled casually.

"Yes, you burned the original in the ashtray last Sunday night," he replied. "Your dresser is an old acquaintance of mine. She opened and copied this before giving it to you on Saturday night. She supplied me with this. Beware of her: she's a wily old creature with a streaky past."

Laureen looked at him calmly.

"Probably you know where I went after dinner on Sunday night also," she suggested.

The detective's eyes twinkled.

"I think so," he answered. "You left your friends in the restaurant, strolled out in your pink velvet cloak. Later you reversed it, pulled a small black hat on and called at Valerie Baird's address. After that you walked toward Regent Street and drove to Mr. Spencer's studio." He glanced at his watch. "I have an appointment."

"The packet?" she questioned earnestly.

"I can make no promises," he told her. He felt certain there was a document there belonging to Lansberg. He must consult his chiefs on the matter. He buttoned the packet carefully into an inner pocket.

All that he had reeled off to Laureen had sounded very glib and impressive, but actually he feared that the things which really counted in this case had yet to be discovered. Suddenly he recalled another point on which Laureen might be able to help him.

"Do you ever remember hearing Leslie Delmond speak in a falsetto voice?" he asked.

She seemed a little surprised at what was apparently a trivial question.

"Often," she replied without hesitation. "It was a favorite trick of his."

"Where did you hear him do it?"

Her eyes opened in wonder.

"Why, in Nice, when we were acting in the film. He used to do it for fun, perhaps also to attract attention. I told you I had not seen him since."

"Thank you, Miss Laureen," he replied. "That's all for the present, I think."

At Warnham House he found the countess awaiting him. She met him graciously.

"My niece is much better and quite ready to see you, Inspector."

He was taken up to the darkened room in which he had been on the previous day. Lady Avice was lying on a couch, and after an inquiry concerning her health the inspector sat down facing her, his back to the shaded alcove window.

Buried in a big easy-chair, only his long legs showing, was a man who did not move at the inspector's entrance, and Reynolds made no comment on his presence. But Lady Avice did.

"I have asked Mr. Spencer to be present at our interview, but to take no part in it until I ask him to do so."

Reynolds agreed amiably. Half London could be there as far as he was concerned, as long as he heard Lady Avice's explanation.

"First of all, where were you and Lady Warnham on the night of the murder, Lady Avice?" Reynolds asked.

"We dined here and played chess until it was time for me to go to Mr. Spencer's studio. Then my aunt went to bed and I went to the party. The servants will probably be able to corroborate that."

"Who sent the telegram you received early on Tuesday morning immediately before you rushed off to Paris?"

The girl bit her lip to hide a smile.

"My dressmaker, canceling an appointment. I threw it into my drawer, so mercifully it was saved. Here it is."

"Thank you," said Reynolds, glancing at the telegram and observing that date and hour tallied. "Please give me your account of things in your own way."

"My aunt, Lady Warnham, did not complete her story for two reasons, Inspector," Lady Avice began. "She tried to protect my father's name and, indirectly, mine."

"I gathered that," the detective replied.

"My aunt has already told you that a little more than two years ago she came to my rescue in Nice, of our meeting with Mrs. de Groot, and later with Laureen and Delmond. She, however, did not tell you that Mr. Spencer was with us part of the time, and that he and my father gambled a lot together."

"No, she did not mention Mr. Spencer," said Reynolds. "Before we go any further, Lady Avice, I have an important question to ask you. Was Tony, your brother, I believe, with you also?" He watched her keenly.

Lady Avice's lips twitched.

"No," she said gravely, "Stinker was not there." Then in her cool voice she continued:

"You know of Mary de Groot's infatuation for Delmond. Well, a big fancy-dress ball was to be held in Nice and we decided to go together in various costumes.

"A week before the ball Mr. Spencer came to my aunt and Mrs. de Groot and casually said they ought to have their jewelry cleaned for the great occasion and that he had heard of a wonderful jeweler who would do it beautifully.

"My aunt and Mary de Groot thought it an excellent plan. Mr. Spencer took their jewels—very valuable in both cases—and four or five days later brought them back, glistening marvelously.

"You understand, Inspector, *Mr. Spencer alone took them and brought them back and was entirely responsible for them.*"

The inspector nodded. "It is quite clear."

"A few days after the ball," went on the girl, "we discovered that my father's debts had been mysteriously paid. But we suspected nothing."

"Naturally, Lady Avice."

"After the film was finished Laureen went to America, and Delmond to Paris, I think. Mrs. de Groot and Mr. Spencer came to London with my aunt and myself. We were trying to cure Mary of her infatuation, you see."

"A difficult task," asserted Reynolds.

"A hopeless one," the girl sighed, "for soon Mrs. de Groot went back to Paris to find Delmond. Occasionally I went over to see her, and once she told me she wanted to marry Delmond but he always made some excuse and that she was sure there was another woman."

"There seem to have been several," commented the detective dryly.

"I must tell you that my aunt very rarely wore her jewels—those she had in Nice, I mean. At times, when we were hard up, she would sell a brooch or a ring, but the more valuable articles were kept at the bank.

"About fifteen months ago I had an agitated

letter from Mrs. de Groot, asking me to have my aunt's jewels examined at once but giving no reason. We took them that day to a well-known expert and to our distress found that every alternate stone in a big diamond necklace was an imitation. And the same trick had been performed on the other articles."

"Where was Mr. Spencer at the time?" questioned Reynolds.

"In Paris. I crossed that night and saw him with Mrs. de Groot. At first she tried to protest that her jewels were all right. It was a magnificent gesture on her part to save the honor of my family. In the end she owned that her jewelry had been faked like my aunt's."

"But why should she try to protect Mr. Spencer?"

The girl flushed.

"Because she knew it was he who had given my father the money to pay his debts. And he had given it *after* those jewels had been received back by us in Nice from the cleaner. Remember, Mr. Spencer had been gambling, had lost heavily and was not a rich man."

"Leslie Delmond was at the back of the whole thing, I gather," Reynolds put in. "What was Mr. Spencer's explanation?"

Lady Avice nodded.

"He said Delmond had suggested that the jewels should be taken to the cleaner's, and later on had given Mr. Spencer the money to pay my father's debts, saying it was a gift from Mrs. de Groot, but to be anonymous.

"She was furious to hear this; declared that Spencer was trying to drag Delmond in to save himself, and that she would rather lose all she possessed than allow him to malign Delmond. There was a dreadful scene."

"I can imagine it," murmured the detective. "Meanwhile Mr. Spencer was incriminated unless he had proof against Delmond."

"He had no such proof. Indeed, he was nearly mad with rage, and vowed he'd get those jewels back if he had to wring Delmond's neck to do it."

"Where was Delmond at this time?"

"He had left Mrs. de Groot just before this, and *even then* she believed in him. Mr. Spencer stayed on in Paris to search for Delmond, and at last he traced him."

She hesitated a second. "I remained in Paris too. Just over a year ago Mr. Spencer came to me in great excitement. He had found Delmond, who had owned up after being threatened. Delmond told him where the stolen gems had been pawned and promised Spencer the money the next day."

She paused and glanced toward the figure in the window.

"I didn't like the story at all. Mr. Spencer was very credulous and impulsive, and knowing Delmond, I feared a trick. But Mr. Spencer wouldn't listen to me. Next day he fetched the money and the pawn-tickets."

Again she hesitated.

"A friend insisted on going with him to the pawnshop. He and this friend were arrested on the spot. The bank-notes were all forged. To put it briefly, he was sentenced to one year's imprisonment and his companion to nine months."

She caught her lip as if the memory were painful, but finished firmly: "Mr. Spencer was released a few weeks ago."

The inspector frowned. Spencer, he knew, was in love with Laureen. "But, forgive me, Lady Avice, you ought to have told me all this before."

Lady Avice shook her head and smiled. "I think not, Inspector. You see, when I heard of the murder I feared naturally that Mr. Spencer had committed it."

"Then surely you should have been frank with me earlier. The law demands that," Reynolds asserted.

"The law also makes an exception to that rule, Inspector."

"I'm afraid I don't understand you. Neither do I understand where the mysterious Tony comes in."

Lady Avice laughed softly and beckoned to the man in the window. He rose instantly and came to her side, looking full at the detective.

Reynolds stared blankly. He had never seen this fellow's face before!

The girl twined her soft fingers round the man's hand. "The law concedes that a wife need not give evidence against her husband," she said clearly. "Inspector Reynolds, this is my husband, Tony Spencer. Dick Spencer's twin brother, whom I secretly married in Paris a little more than a year ago—almost against his will too."

XXVIII. THE LINGERING SHADOW

AUTOMATICALLY Inspector Reynolds took the hand that Tony held out, looking into clear brown eyes which still held a hint of suffering. He could see the strong resemblance now to the artist brother, and began to fathom the reason for Lady Avice's wild rush to Paris. She had feared then that her husband had murdered his enemy. That much was clear.

Lady Avice's voice broke in on his thoughts. "Now you will understand why Delmond blackmailed my aunt, Inspector. He found out I was married to Tony Spencer and threatened to expose the fact that my husband had gone to prison for passing false bank-notes. Delmond wrote me giving his address and demanding money. My aunt courageously went to see him and said he could do his worst. And I wrote him:

"If you write or attempt to see either my aunt or myself again, I shall immediately go to Scotland Yard and tell the whole story.

"That must be the note you found. I never wrote to him before or since. But I telephoned to him twice. The last time was on Sunday afternoon—the day he was murdered."

"Thank you. That clears that up, Lady Avice. And it explains why he was desperate after your message and went to Laureen's flat."

Reynolds was still churning over his surprise

about Tony when he heard Laureen's voice in the doorway.

"May I come in?" she asked.

Reynolds assented, still a little bewildered. What new knot would be unraveled now?

Suddenly he turned to Tony. "Where were you, Mr. Spencer, on the night of the murder, Sunday, June thirtieth?"

"Roaming about London, extremely drunk and angry, up to six o'clock looking for Delmond," the young man replied frankly. "Accidentally I met my brother who begged me to come back to his studio and go to bed. I refused and broke away from him. Ten minutes after, in the Berkeley, I met three men I know who were motoring to Dover. They made me go with them and I crossed on the night boat to Paris. I can give you their names and addresses, of course."

Tony paused. "I—I wanted to see my wife, but I was too ashamed of myself then," he went on. "I'd written to her, when I came out of prison, saying I must get that horror off my mind a bit first."

With a glance at the detective, which demanded permission for the interruption, Laureen bent down and kissed her friend.

"Mary de Groot's downstairs, Avice," she said. "She crossed yesterday from Paris but felt so tired that she stayed the night in Dover. This morning on Dover station whom do you think she saw posting a letter?"

"I can't guess," smiled Avice.

"Valerie," said Laureen emphatically, casting a mischievous look at the detective.

Reynolds's lips parted in surprise.

"Valerie!" he repeated in amazement.

"Why not?" asked Laureen lightly. "She has to be somewhere if she's alive, so why not Dover station?"

"She only left the hospital early this morning," the detective almost stammered.

Laureen caught his arm anxiously.

"Hospital? What do you mean? Please tell me quickly."

"I have every reason to believe that Valerie Baird was knocked down and stunned by a car last Monday morning. It happened in Berkeley Street, quite close to your flat."

"I heard the crash and Mr. Lansberg went to the window," cried Laureen. "Oh, to think my poor Valerie was so close and I never knew it. Was she badly hurt?"

"It was thought that she was still unconscious up to ten o'clock last night," Reynolds observed drily. "But during the night she was well enough to get up, dress, and get out of the building unnoticed."

"Don't they have nurses there?" indignantly demanded Laureen. "Poor girl, she was probably delirious at the time."

"Well, for a delirious person she seems to be remarkably capable, Miss Laureen. Posting letters on Dover platform appears very normal."

"Possibly to you," commented Laureen bitterly. "But where is she now?"

"That is what I should very much like to know. May I use your telephone, Lady Warnham?"

Hurriedly he rang up Jenkins and told him to telephone the Dover officials to find and detain the girl. "Hold the line a minute," he added.

"Mrs. de Groot," he said, entering the dining-room and surprising that lady considerably, "how was Valerie Baird dressed when you saw her this morning?"

"In black with a heavy veil," she replied.

He thanked her, gave Jenkins the description and returned to the American woman.

"When Lady Avice arrived at your hotel in Paris last Tuesday did you know Mr. Tony Spencer was her husband?"

"I sure did, Inspector," replied Mary de Groot, lapsing for once into her vernacular.

"Did you telegraph for her to come?"

"I did not. On the contrary she cabled me. Also she cabled my maid telling her to hide the English newspapers so that I should not get a shock."

"About this affair of the jewels being cleaned at Nice. How did Tony Spencer hear of this jeweler?"

A red flush swept over the woman's face and neck.

"Leslie Delmond gave him the address but told Tony not to mention his name in the matter for fear the ladies might imagine he was getting a commission out of the job. Of course Tony promised and, like the good-natured, honorable fool he is, kept the promise."

"Have you any idea who his companion was in the false bank-note arrest, Mrs. de Groot?"

She stared at the detective as if she doubted his sanity.

"Sakes alive! Have I any idea? I should say so."

Reynolds restrained a smile with difficulty. He was getting plain truth from this daughter of God's own country, and the novelty was refreshing.

"There has been so much concealment in this

case, Mrs. de Groot, everybody trying to protect somebody else, that my way has been made very difficult. I shall be grateful if you will be frank and tell me what you know," he said tactfully.

The lady extended her bejeweled fingers.

"Well now, isn't that what I've come from Paris for? Judging by the newspapers you're all in an unholy mess through this damfool secrecy. The truth has to come out sooner or later. What do you want to know?"

The inspector repeated his question. "Who was arrested with Tony Spencer?" he asked.

"Valerie, of course."

"Valerie Baird," exclaimed the astonished detective.

"Fiddlesticks!" snapped the American. "Valerie's maiden name was Baird, but it isn't now, worse luck for her."

"What is it?' asked Reynolds, his pulse thumping with eagerness.

"Valerie Delmond. She is Leslie Delmond's widow."

The detective gazed at her, speechless. Never once had he dreamed of this. It explained a thousand things.

"They were married in Nice," Mrs. de Groot went on, pluckily reciting these painful reminiscences, "before I ever knew Delmond. She was a marvelous black and white artist and also did—what do you call it?—they draw with acid on metal."

"Etching," suggested the inspector, recovering a little from this series of surprises.

"Yes, etching, I never can remember that word. I didn't know her in Nice. None of the Warnham party met her, neither did any of us know Delmond was married." She sighed. "Might have saved me from making such a prize idiot of myself."

"But why did none of you meet her as Mrs. Delmond?"

"Because Delmond was at the studio most of the day and she never went near the place. She's a very shy, refined girl, who hates publicity. Poor child, she's having enough of it now, one way and another. And then, Delmond got more fun out of life posing as a bachelor."

"When did you learn of Delmond's marriage?" Reynolds questioned.

"Only when Valerie and Tony were arrested. Leslie had taken good care I shouldn't know before. He vanished at once. He could disguise himself remarkably, so it was easy for him. You see, Leslie Delmond was clever but a coward. When I first found out about the jewels being faked and wrote to Avice, she came to Paris and insisted on marrying Tony first of all, to prove her faith in him. He on his side made her promise to keep the marriage secret until he'd cleared his name. Have you got that straight?"

Reynolds smiled his assent.

"Right, on we go again," snapped Mrs. de Groot briskly. "Tony promptly swore he'd wring Delmond's neck if necessary to get those jewels back. I got angry then—I still loved that scamp, you see. Well, Tony found Delmond and thrashed him, threatening to kill him if the jewels or the money were not given back."

"But some of the money had been spent in paying the Earl of Brentshire's debts, I was told," put in the detective.

"Oh, you do know that much, do you, Inspector? His debts were about thirty thousand francs and Leslie Delmond, working in league with that Nice jeweler, must have cleared at least six hundred thousand francs on the faking of that jewelry. I can't do your crazy English arithmetic, but you can easily see that paying Lord Brentshire's debts didn't make much of a dent in their haul."

Reynolds worked out a calculation on a scrap of paper.

"They got nearly five thousand pounds and paid the Earl of Brentshire about two hundred and forty. And you didn't prosecute Delmond or Tony Spencer?"

"How could I when I cared for Delmond, and Tony was the husband of my best friend. No, I may be a vain and silly woman, but I'm at least half-way human. Besides Delmond had left me. I didn't know where he was, and Tony had only been a tool."

"Yes, I understand," Reynolds replied sympathetically. There was something very likeable in this frank woman. "Please explain to me about the bank-notes. I know nothing about that."

"You don't mean to say so, Inspector," and Mrs. de Groot laughed heartily. "But it's not your fault when they've all conspired to conceal things. I talked to Lady Warnham on the telephone from Dover last night and said I was coming to town to-day and that I meant to open my mouth."

Reynolds's lips twitched. "What did Lady Warnham reply?"

"She said, 'Come along and talk as much as you like. I can't and Avice won't, and soon we'll all be in jail together if this goes on.' She's a wise old lady, I'll tell you, Inspector. What was it you asked?"

"About the bank-notes," prompted Reynolds.

"Oh, yes. Well, Tony frightened Delmond, and at last Delmond said the jewels were pawned, but in a few days he'd give Tony the money to redeem them. It was a lie to begin with, for most of the jewels had been sold, not pawned. He told Tony to call in three days at an address he gave him, when the money and pawn-tickets would be handed to him. Delmond added that he might have to go off on a film job at a moment's notice."

"Very nicely arranged," put in Reynolds. "Delmond could slide out of view easily."

"Tony went to the address and found a girl he'd never seen before. It was Valerie, Delmond's wife, but Tony didn't know and she didn't tell him who she was. She gave him the packet but insisted she must go to the pawnshop with him—she seemed frightened, Tony said. They were both arrested there for having false money.

"Tony sent for me. He told me the story and made me swear not to let Avice know if he was convicted, but to get her back to England. Family honor and all that bunk. I tried everywhere to find Delmond, but it was no use."

"Tony Spencer got a year and the girl nine months," said the inspector.

"Yes. I met Valerie when she came out and made her stay with me. About a month ago she left me to go to London. I believe she'd met Delmond, or some man, and was worried about Laureen."

"Why should she be? Were they such close friends as all that?" asked Reynolds with interest.

"Friends! Why, listen—" She looked up and saw Laureen standing in the doorway. "I say, Laureen, you all have sewed up the facts of this case so tight that what this poor man doesn't know will never hurt him. Think of it! He's just asked me if you and Valerie were friends." Mrs. de Groot laughed heartily at the thought.

Laureen smiled rather pathetically as she walked into the room and stood before the inspector.

"Valerie is my sister; a very dearly loved sister, Inspector," she said.

"You told me you were an only child. You told Mr. Lansberg that also," the detective exploded in irritated tones.

Laureen shook her finger to and fro. "These were my exact words: 'My father and mother believed in a small but good family and I'm it,' " she repeated. "Valerie is my stepsister."

"Yes, those were your exact words. But they deceived me."

"I'm afraid I meant them to," she replied frankly. "You see my father died when I was a few months old and my mother married again very soon. Valerie was born when I was two and a half. We grew up together, went to the same school in Belgium and were only parted when my mother died. Then Valerie went to live with my stepfather, who had always disliked me, and I went on the stage. She came to stay with me at Nice, met Delmond and they were married very soon, greatly against my wish."

"Where were you when she was arrested?"

"In America. I knew nothing of it until my return, when Mrs. de Groot wrote and told me. She said Valerie didn't want to see me yet, fearing Delmond was watching me to find her. It seems incredible but Leslie Delmond loved Valerie, though he was so cruel to her and made her do things that put her in his power."

"Such as what?" Reynolds asked quickly.

The girl pressed her head with a nervous gesture. "Please, Inspector, don't make me say, here. I'm afraid you will know when you open that packet. You can't imagine the torture I'm suffering because of that."

Inspector Reynolds studied her for a moment. "Very well, Miss Laureen. I shouldn't worry too much if I were you. The man is dead," he said in gruff sympathy.

"But his malice is alive," she replied. "Think, if by my words I torture poor Valerie who has already suffered so much!"

"By the way, Miss Laureen, was Mr. Lansberg in Nice that winter?"

"For a day or two only. He was financing the film. One day I heard his yacht was in the harbor and that afternoon I was introduced to him by the manager. We exchanged a few words and I did not see him again until this revue started."

Reynolds turned to Mrs. de Groot.

"You know him, of course."

She raised her hands in surprise. "I know him?" she exclaimed. "Why Mr. Lansberg's a personage. No, I've never met him."

"May I go, please, Inspector?" Laureen asked.

"Certainly," he agreed.

At the door she paused, fidgeting restlessly with the handle. Then she said in a half-frightened whisper:

"Inspector, could you possibly come to the theater to-night? It's stupid of me, but I feel as if something—something horrible may happen."

"Nothing *shall* happen if I can prevent it, Miss Laureen," he assured her. "I will most certainly be there."

"Thank you. I'll have a box reserved for you," she promised.

XXIX. A CONFESSION

LANSBERG rose from his desk to greet Reynolds as he entered the room that afternoon.

"Sit down, Inspector," he invited courteously. "I have quite a lot to tell you. Dr. Tempest insists on being present." His eyes twinkled. "He and I had a long talk after dinner last night and I think he wishes to protect my interests. I'm expecting him at any moment. Are there any preliminary questions you'd like to ask me?"

"Several," said the detective curtly. He was not going to be swerved from his purpose by this man's calm dignity, nor allow him to be unduly backed up by Dr. Tempest. The doctor was a good chap—didn't he owe his brother's life to the surgeon's prompt and generous action?—but inclined to be fussy over one's methods.

Boiled down, all he had learned this morning brought him no nearer the actual criminal. It merely eliminated certain suspicious characters and explained how and why they had been entangled in the case.

"How and where did you first meet Miss Laureen?" he asked.

"In Nice, when she was acting in the film I was financing. I called at the studios one afternoon, was introduced to her and didn't see her again until this year."

H'm, that agreed with what Laureen had said. Reynolds loved checking up statements.

"Did you meet a Mrs. de Groot then?"

Lansberg smiled. "No, I've not met her yet, but I have heard a lot about her from Lady Avice."

"Did you meet Delmond in Nice?"

"I have never met Delmond," Lansberg asserted.

"Lady Warnham and Lady Avice Garth?" Reynolds queried.

"I've met them many times, of course, in London. Never on the Riviera, which I dislike and rarely visit."

"Do you know Valerie?" Reynolds asked, with emphasis.

Lansberg's eyebrows lifted slightly. "No, Inspector, I do not. But I've read of your search for her in the newspapers this week."

"Tony Spencer. Do you know him?"

"No. But I remember hearing some one say that Dick Spencer had a twin brother whom one never saw nowadays."

"Thank you, Mr. Lansberg. Those points are settled."

The door was opened at that moment and Dr. Tempest came in. Reynolds looked at him anxiously and decided he seemed a shade better than at luncheon yesterday.

"First of all, Inspector," Lansberg said, rising and going toward his safe, "there is something here of which I fancy you have already heard. You had better learn its history now." He smiled humorously over his shoulder as he manipulated the lock and swung the heavy door open. He beckoned Reynolds to his side and pointed to the magnificent collection of jewels glistening on the shelves.

"These are the crown jewels of what was once a

tiny kingdom in the Balkans. My eldest brother was
the ruling prince. He died and his family was wiped
out in the revolution that followed. It is now a
republic.

"That," he pointed to the jewels, "is all that is left
me of our former rank. I saved them from the wreck.
It is quite a healthy, sane republic. Indeed, the
president and I are the best of friends. I am
godfather to his small son, for whom I am now
taking up my old hobby of collecting butterflies. I
send him cases of them from time to time."

"You dropped your title, sir?" questioned
Reynolds rather deferentially.

"Long ago, and, as I told you, became a
naturalized Englishman. But my interest in my old
country is strong and I am now negotiating a treaty
on its behalf with our government. This information
is, of course, for you only and not for the newspapers.
Two high officials from the republic were here on
Tuesday to see me privately. I motored to a house
near Tunbridge Well and met them, leaving Miss
Laureen at the golf house for an hour. As you were
probably told."

"That is so, sir," Reynolds replied. Most heartily
he wished Lansberg had no connection with this
murder case. Yet what about that gashed shirt and
vest? And the knife in the safe which was later used
to stab his brother? Why was Neron alarmed if his
master had nothing to do with it?

And what was inside that packet he was half
afraid to open? He decided to plunge boldly.

"Could there be any document of yours in the
envelope the mysterious woman brought you to take
care of and reclaimed recently?" the detective asked.

"How could there be?" Lansberg replied. "It was brought to me sealed and was returned intact, of course."

Reynolds took it from his inner pocket.

"Is that the same one, Mr. Lansberg?"

Lansberg inspected it closely and handed it back to the detective.

"It appears to be of the same size and weight. But the one I guarded was in a plain envelop. This is addressed to Valerie Baird."

Reynolds tore off the outer cover, revealing a plain white envelop, slit open along its length.

"Yes, that looks like it. Only it's been opened since it left my possession."

The first paper the inspector took out was boldly headed "Lansberg." This must have been what Laureen glanced at and, being startled, replaced it, having no time to investigate.

"It seems to be a description of these jewels and your habits and characteristics." Reynolds thought for a minute. "I've a feeling this was tucked in by accident, a few days ago. Probably Delmond was in with a gang of crooks and, having been here disguised as a woman, he wrote out a description of what he'd seen when you opened your safe to get the packet."

"That's exhibit number one," remarked Lansberg. "Those jewels had better be sent to the bank strong-room, eh, Tempest?"

The inspector was deeply engrossed with a thin sheet of metal he had taken from the mysterious packet. It was finely and delicately etched. An engraved plate of a foreign bank-note! Folded round it was a brief letter to Delmond.

Dear Leslie,
Here is what you asked me to do but I'm not sure
it's right even if only for fun to win a bet as you
say. I can't send you any money this week but will
next, if I can.
Yours,
Valerie

So here was the history of Valerie's fears! Delmond had got this and had told her afterward it would get her ten years' imprisonment if found. The poor child had been terrified knowing he had it. No wonder she was afraid, no wonder Laureen had concealed the packet.

Looking further he discovered Tony Spencer's and Avice Garth's marriage certificate, and folded in it Avice's note to Delmond. One or two old letters from Mrs. de Groot were there, but these he only glanced at. There was also a tiny clipping from a French newspaper dealing with the prosecution of Tony and Valerie.

The papers of recent date had evidently been slipped in the envelope after the owner had received it back from Lansberg. Probably to ensure all the valuable articles being kept together.

Reynolds put the packet away safely after showing Lansberg and Dr. Tempest the etching and Valerie's note.

Lansberg drew himself up stiffly, almost as though he were standing at attention. "And now, Inspector," he said slowly and emphatically, "we come to a more serious matter. Dr. Tempest has heard my story and absolutely disagrees with the action I have decided on. He insists on being present at this interview and I in turn insist that he shall be silent until I have spoken."

Dr. Tempest's eyes had something akin to agony in them as he gazed mutely at Lansberg.

"I have agreed under protest," he murmured.

Lansberg faced the detective. "Then, Inspector," he said calmly, "I wish to give myself up for the murder of Leslie Delmond."

The detective forced himself to appear as emotionless as the man who stood before him uttering those amazing words.

"You know I collect butterflies," Lansberg went on, "and realize that I have probably used chloroform to kill them. I have no proof and cannot expect you to believe that I had only a tiny phial of it in my possession last Sunday night. You have a list of my movements—with reservations. I dressed here, dined at my club and having ample time, thought I would walk part of the way to Mr. Spencer's studio."

"Yes, that is correct," Reynolds agreed.

A flicker of sadness crossed Lansberg's face. "For several months I have been deeply attracted to Miss Laureen, and last Sunday night I was looking forward to meeting her at that party. As I neared Beresford Street I suddenly decided to call and see if I might escort her. I walked up the stairs, scanning the doors to see which was her flat."

"You saw nobody loitering near the flats outside?" questioned Reynolds.

"No. I rang her bell, indeed rang twice, because I heard a woman's voice answering the telephone."

"Did you recognize it?" asked Reynolds quickly.

"Impossible through the door," replied Lansberg.

"Then I rang a third time. A man—it was Delmond but I didn't know it then—opened the door and asked my business in so curious a fashion that I determined to go inside. He was obviously startled, and was furious at my visit. His first words staggered me. He shouted, 'So you've followed me, have you, you swine!' He sprang at me with a knife and slashed my clothes without hurting me. Then he seemed to go mad and I knew he meant murder. All the time he was shouting about Laureen. He had locked the dining-room door on the inside and was barring the other, brandishing the knife."

Lansberg paused a moment.

"Near me on a low table was a large bottle marked 'Chloroform,' with a handkerchief beside it. Suddenly the fear gripped me that he had attacked Laureen—that he had even already killed her. Unexpectedly my chance came. Delmond dropped a packet he was holding—I now believe it to be the one you have. He stooped down to gather up the papers, as if he had forgotten my presence. I got hold of the chloroform bottle, wrenched out the cork, swamped the handkerchief and sprang on the man's back, pressing the handkerchief over his face. He was quiet so quickly that I thought he was shamming. But as I pulled the wet cloth from his mouth he fell down, limp. I dragged him to the big chair and left him, expecting he would come round almost immediately."

"How long did you hold the handkerchief over his mouth?" questioned the detective.

"A thousand times I've asked myself that, these past days. I was too angry to think clearly. One minute he was struggling and the next still, it seemed to me. Nearly frantic with fear for Laureen I searched the flat. She was not there nor any one else. I gave one more look at Delmond and I will swear that he was breathing heavily when I went away.

"I left the chloroform bottle there, but brought away the knife and also this which I picked up." He took a tiny stone seal from the table and passed it to Reynolds.

"Then, to calm myself a little, I walked to my apartment, locked the knife in my safe, and went on to Victoria where Laureen's maid saw me get on a bus."

"You did not change your shirt at your flat?" the detective asked keenly.

Lansberg shook his head. "I didn't think of it. Only one thing was in my mind, that at all costs I must manage to see Laureen home in case that man was still there. That he was dead never occurred to me.

"When we entered one could smell chloroform, but she thought it was benzine Bertha might have used. I was longing to look in the dining-room but did not want to rouse her fears unduly, as you will easily understand."

"Do you remember closing the door of the flat after you, Mr. Lansberg?"

"That is what I cannot remember. Sometimes I think I must have left it unfastened in my agitation."

"Why didn't you call in the police?"

Lansberg raised his hand with that rare gesture of his. "And draw lurid attention to the woman I cared for!" he exclaimed. "It was quite obvious that Delmond, from his wild remarks, had known

Laureen. Do you think I wished to drag some past episode into publicity?"

"You never thought of burglary as his object?" questioned Reynolds.

"Burglars don't behave in that fashion, I imagine. One had not much time for analysis but his visit seemed to be one of malice, not robbery, Inspector."

"How much chloroform was left in the bottle?" the inspector asked.

"I re-corked it after I had dragged the man to the chair and—to me—it seemed that scarcely any had gone. The bottle must have held a pint, and as nearly as I can remember it looked almost full."

"When you went into that room again at one in the morning and discovered Delmond there dead, was that bottle of chloroform still there?"

"No," said Lansberg positively. "I hunted around for it, but it was gone. And I'm certain Miss Laureen could not have taken it," he added eagerly.

Dr. Tempest opened a bag he had brought and lifted out half a dozen bottles of various sizes.

"What size was the bottle containing chloroform, Lansberg," he asked seriously.

Instantly Lansberg selected one and held it out. "I think that size exactly."

The doctor nodded toward Reynolds.

"That," he said, "is a surgery bottle. No chemist would dream of supplying such a quantity except to a medical man. You see my point, Inspector? The quantity Mr. Lansberg would get for killing his butterflies would be given him in this size." He touched a tiny bottle.

"Those small phials might have been emptied

into the large one," argued the detective.

Dr. Tempest swept the idea aside. "But," he said, "Mr. Lansberg had never *seen* Delmond and knew nothing against him. My contention is that although every word Mr. Lansberg has uttered may be true, he *did* not kill Delmond. As to Delmond's rapid unconsciousness—at the post-mortem we found practically no food in the stomach, proving the man had not eaten for several hours and so would need less chloroform."

"That's a most important item, doctor. But possibly Mr. Lansberg poured more chloroform than he thought on the handkerchief."

The doctor lifted a carafe of water and carefully filled and corked the large bottle. Taking a handkerchief out of the bag he said:

"Mr. Lansberg, will you please reconstruct your actions of last Sunday night? Tip the bottle as many times as you think you did then and for the same length of time, and then press the handkerchief to my face."

He threw some papers on the floor a little distance from the desk, and stooped down. "I think," he went on, "this was Delmond's attitude, wasn't it? Please act as you did then."

The inspector watched with keen interest as Lansberg grasped the bottle, pulled out the cork, and tipped it three times on to the handkerchief. Making a quick stride he sprang on the doctor's stooping form and held the handkerchief to Tempest's mouth while the inspector counted the seconds.

Then Lansberg withdrew the handkerchief and laid it on the paper.

"I can't be positive," he said, "but it seemed about

that length of time."

Reynolds nodded and regarded the bottle. Only a very little of the water had been used in Lansberg's demonstration.

Dr. Tempest rose to his feet.

"Absolutely impossible," he declared, "to have killed Delmond in that short time, Inspector, as I said before. And, *in any case*, remember Mr. Lansberg acted in self-defense. The whole thing lacks motive. Why should a man of Mr. Lansberg's wealth and position wish to murder an unknown film actor?"

"Why did you offer to give yourself up, Mr. Lansberg?" asked Reynolds.

"Because," replied he clearly, "the situation these past few days has been intolerable. I have been spied upon from morning until night, my rooms were entered by a trick last Tuesday afternoon and searched, and my safe was opened presumably by one of your men, Inspector. Miss Laureen's safety has been threatened and her health is at stake if this condition lasts. At first I kept silent believing some one else must have entered that flat, finished what I began, and afterward removed the chloroform bottle. But now I can bear no more. Frankness is infinitely better than this suspense, especially when it is damaging the reputation and strength of the girl I care for. That is my answer."

There was a fineness and sincerity in Lansberg's words that Reynolds did not miss. Added to that, he reflected, was the convincing statement of Dr. Tempest. Who was this other person who entered the flat after Lansberg had gone? A thought struck the detective.

"Could your servant, Neron, not have followed you and killed Delmond?" he asked.

"Impossible," said Lansberg emphatically. "I dined at my club after leaving here. Why should my servant have prowled about watching me? He would not have dared to do so. He had never seen Miss Laureen and did not know her address. No, Neron was afraid after your visit, and I told him roughly the outline of the case, explaining who you were. Don't blame him for a crime he certainly did not commit."

Reynolds summed up the points in his mind. Undoubtedly Delmond had answered Dick Spencer's telephone call in a woman's voice to prevent any suspicion arising of a strange man being there. Then Lansberg had rung the flat bell and Delmond, seeing him, imagined his disguise—as the woman receiving that packet—had been discovered, and he had been followed. He attacked Lansberg in sudden fury. Lansberg went out of the flat and some unknown person entered, and after murdering the unconscious Delmond took away the chloroform bottle.

Who was his assailant? Could it have been Valerie? Everybody else implicated in the case was accounted for on that night.

Then suddenly he remembered there was one other. Where was the man with the missing thumb whose fingerprints had been found on the dining table?

"Mr. Lansberg," Reynolds said firmly, "I have not sufficient evidence to prove that Leslie Delmond died by your hand."

XXX, A SHOT IN THE THEATER

night, accompanied by Dr. Tempest whom he had invited.

"Laureen's in a highly nervous condition and if she collapses to-night, Doctor, you'd be mighty useful, knowing the cause as you do."

Throughout the first part of the revue, the detective's attention was occupied chiefly by the audience. From the box which Laureen had reserved, he scanned her closely when she first came on. She received a tremendous ovation and her vivacity seemed normal rather than forced.

When the curtain was rung down for the interval Reynolds strolled round the corridors, observing the people.

"Boxes full?" he asked the attendant.

"Two of the parties haven't come yet," was the answer. "That often happens. Especially with young gentlemen who've seen the show several times. They come in after the intermission usually."

Leaving the stage as the curtain fell, Laureen had pushed open the door of her dressing-room. There she saw a girl in black, heard an eager cry of "Laureen, my darling!" and felt arms enfold her.

"I can't believe it's you, Valerie! Oh, my dearest, how ill you look!" She drew her to the couch, holding on to her tightly. "Take off your hat and coat and tell me all about it. I needn't change for ten minutes. I'll send my dresser away."

Rapidly Valerie poured out the history of the past weeks, ending with her encounter of Mrs. de Groot at Dover.

"So you see I had to come back, Laureen. What will they do to me?" she asked pitifully.

Laureen hugged her sister protectingly.

"Nothing, my angel, except over my dead body. Sit there while I dress. I'm so afraid you'll vanish again. Think, darling," she said, stripping off her frock quickly and pulling on the garments needed for the next scene, "it will be like old times to-night. You shall sleep in my bed and we'll talk and talk. Oh, I'm so happy! And you soon will be, too, for at last you are free to marry the man you care for. Does he know you're here?"

"No," she replied firmly. "I won't meet him until this horrible affair has been cleared up. How could I allow his name to be clouded? I'll wait until Leslie Delmond's murderer is discovered."

As she had finished Inspector Reynolds tapped on the door and entered at Laureen's invitation.

"All right, Miss Laureen?" he questioned.

"Thank you, yes, Inspector. I was just a nervous fool, I suppose. Oh," she laughed suddenly, "shut your eyes. I've a surprise for you."

The detective obeyed, amused at the spectacle of a Scotland Yard officer, intent on a murder case, being led with closed eyes across a revue actress's dressing-room!

"You can look now," Laureen allowed. "Guess who that is!"

Standing before him was a frail slender girl with soft fair hair. Her violet eyes gazed at him sadly but with no hint of fear. He didn't need Laureen's introduction to tell him her name, for she was undoubtedly the original of the snapshot in Delmond's attaché case.

"This is the inspector engaged on the case, Valerie," Laureen explained. "He probably hates me. I've been a mass of prevarication for your sake— until to-day."

"Don't hate Laureen, Inspector," pleaded Valerie. "Hate me if you like. I deserve it for my cowardice in running away. But my sister's the most wonderful being in the world to me."

"I don't hate either of you," said Reynolds. And meant it as he took Valerie's thin fingers in his own big hand.

"Probably you want to ask me hundreds of questions, Inspector. I promise to answer them truthfully," Valerie offered.

"I can only think of one urgent one at the moment. Other people have told me so much that I can trace all your movements, excepting this. Where were you on the night of the murder?"

"After church," Valerie replied, "I was walking in Beresford Street near Laureen's flat before going to my rooms when I saw a man whom I knew. Terrified I ran away and spent the night hidden in the bracken in Richmond Park. I've no proof to give you," she added helplessly. "Next morning, after some breakfast at Charing Cross station, I started to go to Laureen but was knocked down by a motor-car.

Reynolds was about to ask the name of the man who had frightened her when the call boy knocked for Laureen.

"Come, Val, quick. I'm not going to let you out of my sight. You can have a chair in the wings. It's against the rules, but the stage-manager will forgive me this once. Do come up here when the act's over, Inspector," she begged.

The second half was nearly finished when Laureen, her scene ended, darted over to Valerie who was sitting between the wings.

"Val, don't be frightened, dear. *He* is here, in a box immediately over Inspector Reynolds. What am I to do? I'm sure he means murder."

Valerie rose quickly.

"Take me round the other side where I can see him. He won't hurt me, Laureen."

With beating heart Valerie stood in the shadow looking up at the white face and blazing eyes of the man she feared. He was not looking at her. All his gaze was concentrated on Laureen, who was again on the stage for the finale.

Suddenly Valerie saw him raise his arm. Without hesitation she ran across the stage in full view of the audience, and putting herself in front of her sister, looked directly at him.

The man gave a hoarse cry, stared a moment and then slowly turned the glistening thing in his hand toward his own breast. There was a sharp report, and then the curtain descended rapidly.

Upstairs on the floor of the box Reynolds and Dr. Tempest bent over the man lying there.

"Dead?" questioned Reynolds.

"No, but he can't live many minutes."

An attendant brought brandy and the doctor swiftly administered it.

"It may help him to speak," he whispered to Reynolds.

The door opened quietly and Laureen and her

sister crept in. Valerie bent over the man while Laureen stayed in the background.

The man's eyelids flickered and then as they opened he saw the face of the girl. "Valerie!" he murmured. "Valerie, you're safe now! I can die in peace. I did it all for you, my beloved girl."

"Quick, ask him if he was in your sister's flat and saw Delmond last Sunday night," urged the detective.

The girl asked the question gently.

"Yes, yes, I was there. I couldn't find those papers. No matter now. Delmond's dead and you're free. You have had all the suffering—Laureen all the money and pleasure. Your turn now, Valerie!"

He muttered inaudibly for a minute and then Reynolds drew the girl away.

"He's gone," said the detective softly. "Who was he?"

"My father," replied Valerie simply. "He had fits of madness at times. He worshiped me but was bitterly jealous of Laureen and her success, for my sake. He was a brilliant artist until that accident to his hand." She was trembling violently.

"Take her back to the dressing-room, Doctor," said Reynolds. "She'll faint in a minute. I shall be here some time."

As the door of the box closed behind them the inspector stooped over the dead man. Yes, undoubtedly this was the same type of pistol as that used in the attack on Lady Avice.

Suddenly he drew back. The pistol was near the dead man's left hand! Reynolds paused a moment, then pulled the right hand into view and gazed at it. Here, he reflected, his task obviously ended. The last link was complete. For this hand lacked a thumb!

THE END